SCRAPBOOK
of
SECRETS

SCRAPBOOK
of
SECRETS

Mollie Cox Bryan

𝓚

KENSINGTON PUBLISHING CORP.

http://www.kensingtonbooks.com

KENSINGTON BOOKS are published by

Kensington Publishing Corp.
119 West 40th Street
New York, NY 10018

ISBN-13: 978-0-7582-6631-6
ISBN-10: 0-7582-6631-6

First Mass Market Printing: February 2012

10 9 8 7 6 5 4 3 2 1

Printed in the United States of America

Dedicated to my daughters, Emma Aine and Tess Mathilde, and my nieces, Carly Richanne, Abbey Lee, and Andi Rebecca. May you always know the pleasure, comfort, and strength of good friends.

Acknowledgments

When my children were toddlers, a group of scrap-booking women reached out to me. Though our lives are not in the same place now—our children and professional lives going in differing directions—I still think of them and the time we shared with great fondness. So I'd like to thank them here, first, as they were the inspiration for this series of books. They are: Jennifer Ledford, Debbie Powdrell, Paige Edwards, Mary Thomas, Susan Horn, and Denise Thornton.

As these women can attest, I've been thinking about this story for a long time. So when National Novel Writing Month came along in 2009, I decided to write it down and take the challenge of writing a fifty-thousand-word novel in thirty days. Another group of individuals—my NaNoWriMo partners—spurred me on when I thought I could not write one more word. Thanks to Kate Antea, Steve Whitaker, and Mary Sproles Martin.

Speaking of spurring me on, I'd like to thank Sharon Bowers, my agent, for her steadfast belief in my fiction writing. And thanks to my culinary agent, Angela Miller, who pointed me in Sharon's direction.

Much gratitude to editor Martin Biro and the Kensington team for taking a chance on me. I'm so proud to be a part of Kensington.

Thanks also goes to friends who read the manuscript at various stages: Jennifer Feller, India Drummond, and Leeyanne Moore. I'd also shout out to friends who supported me in other ways—whether it was watching my girls so I could get some work done, or just being there to deal with my writerly angst. Gratitude goes to Marijean Jaggers , Christy Majors, Karen Pickering, Kristie Cross, Chrissy Lantz, Cortney Skinner, Matthew and Deena

Warner, Brooke Sollis, Kelley Wood, Robin Bryan, Kevin Reid Shirley, Monica Bhide, and Paula D'Allessandris.

Special thanks to a group of generous and supportive writers who have advised and encouraged me along the way: Emilie Richards, Clare O'Donohue, JoAnna Campbell Slan, Meredith Cole, Therese Walsh, Elizabeth Massie, Alison Hart, Inman Majors, and Marie Bostwick.

Last but not least, I'd like to thank my family—my mom, dad, and sister, Becky, who have had to put up with my stories since the day I could talk; my daughters, Emma and Tess, who still think I'm the coolest mom in town, even though I spend way too much time in front of the computer; and Eric, my husband of twenty years and the love of my life.

Thanks to you all.

Chapter 1

For Vera, all of the day's madness began when she saw the knife handle poking out of her mother's neck. Her mother didn't seem to know it. In fact, she was surprised that the blade was inside her. "How did that happen?" she demanded to know from her daughter.

Vera just looked at her calmly. "Well, now, Mother, we need to call someone, an ambulance . . . a doctor. . . . I don't know. Should we pull it out, or what?"

If Vera only had a nickel for every time her mother gave her that look. A look of unbelieving pity, as if to say, *Sometimes I can't believe the stupidity of my grown daughter*. Having a brilliant mother was not easy— ever—especially not as an adult. As a child, Vera assumed all grown-ups were as smart as her mother, and it was easy to acquiesce to her in all of her grown-up, brilliant, scientific knowledge. At the age of eighty, Beatrice showed no signs of slowness in her mind or any forgetfulness. Nothing. Vera almost looked forward to the day she could help her mother remember something or even tell her something that she didn't know.

As she sat in the X-ray waiting area, looking out the window over a construction site, with a huge dilapidated barn in the distance, she marveled once again at her mother's strength and tenacity. Evidently, she was stabbed during her travels through the town this Saturday morning. She didn't feel a thing—and with three grocery bags in her hands, Beatrice walked four blocks home, the same path she'd traveled for fifty years. "Four different grocery stores have been there and have gone out of business," Beatrice would say. "Yet, I'm still here, walking the same street, the same path. I refuse to die."

Beatrice would not allow her daughter—or anyone— to pick up groceries for her or take her shopping. She said that as long as she could keep getting herself to the grocery store, she knew she was fine. Food is life. "It's the ancient food-foraging impulse in me. I feel it even stronger, the older I get. I want to take care of myself."

How could a woman who still fended for herself every day—cooking, gardening, canning, cleaning, and writing—not feel a knife jab into her neck?

"Vera?" said a man in medical garb who stood in front of her.

"Yes," she said, standing up.

"I'm Dr. Hansen. We've just X-rayed your mom and looked over the film," he said, smiling, revealing two deep dimples and a beautiful set of teeth. He held the film in his hands. "Would you like to see them?"

She followed him over to the wall, where he clicked on a light and clipped on the X-ray to it.

"As you can see, the knife is pretty deep." He pointed to the blade. His nails and hands were the cleanest Vera had ever seen on a man. An overall well-manicured appearance.

"Y-yes," she stammered. That was a knife in her mother's neck. A knife. Long and sharp. Menacing.

"Here's the thing, rather than give you a bunch of medical mumbo jumbo, I'm just going to put this in lay terms."

She despised his patronizing tone. He wasn't even born yet when her father was practicing medicine out of their home. She knew about the human body. She was a dancer; her father was a physician. Her mother might be old, but she was no slouch.

"The reason your mom didn't feel this is because it's lodged in an area where there are few nerve endings, which is a blessing because she is not really in any pain," he said, taking a breath. "You just don't see this every day."

"No," Vera said.

"We can pull it out, using local anesthesia, with great risk for potential blood loss and so on. If she flinches or moves while we're removing it, the damage could be severe. We can also operate to remove it, put her under, which I think is the safest thing."

Vera looked at him for some guidance or answer. *Damn it, Bill is out of town.* "Have you talked to her about it?"

"Well, yes. . . ."

"And?"

"She doesn't want surgery. She wants us to pull it out."

"So what's the problem? It's her body. I can't make decisions like that for her."

"Your mom is eighty years old and we're not sure she's thinking clearly. And the danger—"

"Doctor," Vera said, trying not to roar. She felt an odd tightening in her guts. She stood up straighter. "My mother's mind is perfectly fine. It's her neck that seems to be the problem right now, and the fact that a knife is sticking out of it."

He looked away. "Vera, I know this might be hard for you. A lot of times we don't see the truth when it comes to our aging parents."

"What exactly are you talking about? I am very close

with my mom and would know if something was wrong. I don't understand."

"Well, she's been talking to herself, for one thing."

Vera laughed. "No, she's not. She's talking to my dad. He died about twenty years ago. She talks to him all the time."

He looked at her as if she had lost *her* mind. "Do *you* think that's normal?"

"For her, it is."

Vera's mind wandered as the doctor was called away. He said he'd be back. She looked at the crisp blue hospital walls, with beautiful landscape paintings, all strategically placed. One was above the leather sofa so you could lie or sit in style to await the news about your loved ones and gaze into the peaceful garden gazebo landscape; one was above the chair; the hallways were lined with them. Vera saw herself walking down the hall and looking at the same prints twenty years ago. Tranquil settings of barns and flowers did not help the pain. She was only twenty-one then, and she thought she'd soon be back in New York City. As soon as her father healed, got home, and was on the road to being himself, she'd hop on the train to continue her dancing career. She had no idea she'd never see her father again—nor would she ever dance professionally again.

The last time Vera was here was with her father. The hospital had just opened, and he was impressed with the technology and the vibrant pulse of new medicine. The research arm intrigued him. Some older doctors were jaded and looked at the new hospital with suspicion, but not her father. Ironic that he died here, under the new establishment's care.

She sighed a deep and heavy sigh.

"Vera!" It was Sheila running up the hall, wiry brown hair needing combing. She was dressed in a mismatched sweat suit. "Oh, girl! What on earth is going on? I've been hearing rumors. Is your mama okay? Lord!"

For the first time that day, Vera smiled. "Sit down, Sheila. You're a mess."

Sheila took a quick look at herself and laughed. "You know, I just threw anything on. Is your mother—"

"She's fine," said Vera. "She's trying to tell the doctors what to do."

"Really?" Sheila sat up a little straighter, looking very serious. "I can hardly believe *that*," she said, and a laugh escaped. Then she grabbed her belly and howled in a fit of laughter.

Vera felt tears coming to her eyes through her own chortles. "You haven't heard the best part," she managed to say, trying to calm herself down as a nurse passed by, glancing at them. "Mama was stabbed and she never felt a thing."

"What?" Sheila stopped laughing for a minute. "Are you serious?" Her face reddened and laugher escaped. "Oh, girl, only Beatrice. Only Beatrice."

Vera's mother had just been stabbed, and she and her best friend were laughing about it, like schoolgirls unable to control their nervous giggles. A part of Vera felt like she was betraying her mother. However, she knew if Beatrice had been in this room, she'd be laughing, too.

When the women calmed down, Sheila brought up Maggie Rae, which was the other startling news of the day. "Did you hear the news?"

Vera sighed. "Yes, I heard about it. I saw the ambulances and police at her house and went over to see what was happening. You know, I blame myself. I knew something was wrong. I just didn't know what to do about it, or maybe I just tried to talk myself out of it."

Vera thought about the tiny young mother, always with her children clinging to her, and with a baby on her hip— or in a stroller. She was pretty in a simple way—never made-up, always pulled her long black hair into a pony-tail and wore glasses most of the time. Though once or twice, Vera had seen her wearing contacts, which really opened up her face. Even though Maggie Rae rarely made eye contact, she always held herself erect and moved with a graceful confidence and sway in her hips.

"Now, Vera," said Sheila, "you hardly knew that woman. Who really knew her? She kept to herself."

"She brought Grace in for dance lessons once a week," Vera told her. "I know her as well as any of the rest of them. Except she was awfully quiet. And so small. Like a bird. Every time I saw her, it looked like she had gotten even thinner."

"Hmm-hmm, I know. It's odd. She was one of my best customers, but she never came to a crop," said Sheila, who sold scrapbooking supplies for a living. "I invited her. She never came, so I just . . . stopped. You know, you can only push so far. "

They sat in their own silence, with the hospital noise all around them, each knowing her own sadness and her own triumphs and joys, but neither knowing what it was like to be pushed quite that far. To be pushed far enough to put a gun to one's heart while the children were peace-fully sleeping upstairs. What kind of darkness led Maggie Rae Dasher to that moment? And what do people ever really know about the neighbors and townsfolk who live among them?

"Did she leave a note or anything?" Vera wondered out loud.

Sheila shrugged.

A nurse dressed all in blue passed them; a mother carrying a baby in a carrier and holding the hand of a toddler limped along; someone was coughing and another person laughed. A man in a wheelchair wheeled by them, while another gentleman hobbled with a cane.

Phones were ringing. Announcements were being made, doctors were paged.

"Damn," said Sheila. "This place sucks."

"Wonder where the doctor is?" Vera looked around. "I'm going over to that desk to see what's going on. I should at least be able to see Mama."

As Vera walked around the nurses' station to try to find some help, she thought she could hear her mother's voice.

"What?" the voice said. "Listen, you twit, you'll do it because I said you will. Stop treating me like I am five. I am eighty, of sound mind and body, except for this friggin' knife hanging out of my neck. And oh, by the way, I am a doctor of physics myself. So don't tell me—"

"Mama," Vera interrupted as she walked into the room. Sitting up in bed, her mother looked so small, which belied the sound of her voice and the redness of her face. "Calm down, sweetie."

She folded her arms over her chest. "Son of a bitch!" She cocked her head and looked behind Vera. "What's the scrapbook queen doing here? Am I dying or something?"

"Hey," Sheila said. "You've got a knife sticking out of the back of your neck. Don't get too cocky, old woman."

"Huh!" Beatrice said, and smiled. "Glad to see you, too. Now, Vera, what are we going to do about this mess?"

"I told the doctor that it's your body. You do what you want, Mama."

"Yes, but," she said, after taking a sip of water, leaning forward on the pillows that were propping her in an awkward position, which forced her to sit up so the knife would not hit the bed, "what do you think? What would you do?"

Vera could hardly believe what she was hearing. Her mother was asking for her advice. She couldn't remember if that had happened before. "Honestly, if it were me, I'd want to be put out. I'd be afraid of moving, you know?"

"I don't know about being operated on at my age. . . . You know they killed your daddy. What if they kill me, too? I can't leave yet. I've got too much work to do, and then there's you. I can't leave you without a parent," she said quietly.

Vera knew that's what it would come to—this is where he died, not for his heart problems, but from a staph infection.

"Just do what she asks," Vera said to the young doctor, who was still hovering. "She won't move."

Chapter 2

I saw your local newspaper is hiring. They ran an ad on the Web. They say the "bar is high." Jeez, do you think you could do it? (GRIN)—Yolonda

The bar is as high as my relatively low-slung ass. Even so, I think the job is a night job and I am half dead by then. I know you don't understand, but running around after two little boys all day long is a killer on your nightlife—even a working nightlife.

C'mon. I've worked with you. I know what you can do.

It's different. I promise. Back then, I did get breaks and even slept the whole night through. . . . But guess what, after a year of being here, I am actually starting to get invited to parties. Tupperware. Mary Kay. And oh, yeah, there's the scrapbook party, which I am actually looking forward to.

WHAT? My eco-feminist, radical-poet friend is going to a scrapbook party? The Annie I knew would have rather carved her initials into her skin with a sharp blade than sit through one of those things. (In fact, so would I.)

That's before I found out the truth.

The truth?

Yep. This town is run by scrapbookers. They are the women who run everything—the music and dance schools, the public schools, the churches, government. Everything. And they all have one thing in common. They crop till they drop.

They WHAT?

It's part of the lingo, man. "Crop" is the term they use for parties. It comes from actually cropping photos. They have their own lingo and cool paper. What more could you ask for?

Pause.
Pause.

A stiff drink?

Annie sighed. She didn't know if these women would have drinks at their parties. She really didn't know what to expect.

"Why don't you come to our crop?" Vera said to her at the library a few weeks ago. Vera and her dancers entertained at lunchtime. Annie thought the boys would enjoy it. She honestly didn't know what she would do without the library and its programs.

"What's that?"

"We all sit around and work on our scrapbooks, share stuff, and visit. It's a lot of fun," Vera replied.

"Oh, okay, sounds good," Annie said, thinking she would have to dig out her second son's book, and she was not even sure where it was. Poor Ben, he was such a second child. Annie just could not keep up with his baby book, let alone a scrapbook.

One sleepless night, she awoke from a fit of mother guilt and filled in all of the blanks on Ben's baby book. She had no idea if any of the measurements, dates, and whatnots were actually correct. In fact, she was fairly sure they were not. Ben would never know that. At least it would look like his mother had paid attention to these things. Not like the mother that Annie actually was—harried, tired, struggling, and sometimes bored. Yes, even with her own children. And so she still tried to write—but not in baby books.

When Ben's older brother, Sam, was born, Annie did fill in the blanks on all the baby books—well, for the most part. After Ben was born, those blanks went blank as well. And she was going to be the mother who nursed her kids until they were two and fed them only home-made baby food. And they would never watch television, let alone the inane, insane children's videos.

Right.

When they first moved to Cumberland Creek, Virginia, they thought they would be welcomed with open arms. It was a peaceful, rural place. Rural people were friendly, warm, community-minded, right? What Annie and Mike found was that they mostly were met with indifference, sometimes tempered with suspicion, especially in their peaceful little town of Cumberland Creek, with its beautiful Victorian architecture and quaint shops, luring tourists. Pleasant place to visit—but not to live, if you are an outsider. An outsider seemed to be anyone whose family did not stretch back at least three generations, and who did not belong to the much-vaunted First Presbyterian, First

Baptist, or Episcopal Churches. And in Annie and Mike's case, that was impossible, since they both hailed from Bethesda, Maryland, and were Jewish.

Annie grimaced the first time she was asked the most popular question that new residents were asked, "What church do you attend?" She felt violated. She was used to living in an urban community, where such questions were not asked. She had friends for ten or fifteen years, and she was sure they were Christian, but the topic of religion was never even broached among them. They talked about politics, art, office gossip, and so on. Never religion.

A few months after moving, Annie realized the question was not going to go away. Everybody asked her the same question, and she just told them she was Jewish. Some would stare at her blankly. Others would attempt to pander to her. "Oh, we have Jewish friends, who live in Charlottesville," or "Look, we have a menorah in our home."

Annie and Mike never really considered their Jewish faith much when living in Bethesda, surrounded by other Jews, Jewish delis, several synagogues to choose from, and the cloak of urbanism that called for a religious privacy in which both of them felt comfortable. Not so here. It made them both consider their religion in ways they hadn't before—which, for Annie, turned out to be a good thing. She now found herself feeling more Jewish than ever, especially on the inside, and she heavily relied on that inner world she created.

But now, Mike and Annie faced a dilemma they had not considered when they moved here. The local school system, which was good enough for a public school, still held weekly religion education classes, which were, of course, Christian. Annie was appalled to learn about this program in which children were bused from the school grounds to a local church for "Bible" study. At first, she thought it was a rumor—in this day and age, schools systems could surely not get away with such a thing. But, much to her dismay, it was perfectly legal in the state of Virginia and her local school system still practiced it.

Since they were getting ready to send Sam to first grade the following year, she found herself wishing that they could send him to a private school. She had one year to figure this out, because the program started in first grade. Kindergarten in the fall would not be a problem.

"Of course, we can just opt out," Mike said to her one evening over spaghetti and their sons' squabbles. "Damn good spaghetti sauce. It just seems to be getting better, this batch, I mean."

Annie smiled. She loved to make spaghetti sauce. When she did, it was huge amounts of it. She froze it and they lived off it for months. Her mood and frame of mind played into cooking it. All of those spices, herbs, and tomatoes frothing together sometimes brought her to the edge of delirium. And so, she mentally prepared herself. It was almost like having sex—so much more delicious after waiting much longer than one should.

"Yes, that is what they say," Annie said back to her husband. "But if your child is the one that stays behind while the others are being bused off to church, how is that child going to feel? What are they going to do with him?"

"We're Jews in a very Christian area. Ben and Sam are going to have to learn to deal with this sometime."

"Yeah, but not when they are six years old," Annie said.

"I'm six. I'm six," Sam chimed in, giggling. "I'm six years old."

"Silly boy, you are not six," Annie said to her son, whose face was covered in spaghetti sauce. She just had to laugh.

"I better get going." Mike popped up and was off again, briefcase in hand. At least this time it wasn't his suitcase. His job in pharmaceuticals took him away at least once a week. After four years, it was getting a little easier because Sam could be helpful—if he wanted to be. And he was not as needy, of course, as when he was younger.

Thank God for that.

Now, today, as she watched over her sons playing with puzzles, Annie thought, *This is good. I can handle this. I wonder how long this quiet and cooperation will last.*

Her next thought, *What am I going to wear tonight? What does one wear to a scrapbooking crop?*

"Ow! Mommy, Ben hit me with a puzzle!" Sam ran to her, and then buried his dark curls into her lap.

"I sorry," Ben said, immediately at her side.

"Ben, don't hit your brother," Annie said. "Time-out."

"No!" he said, and growled at her. Literally growled at her.

"Ben, go sit in the chair. Now." She tried to sound authoritative without yelling.

He folded his little arms. *"Hmmpphh."*

"We do not hit," she said, still cradling her oldest son. She watched her younger walk away toward the chair. Could see his heavy diaper. *Oh, great, another diaper change.*

While still holding Sam, she noticed her fingernails, uneven, chipped, and dirty. She at least needed to cut them before her big night of scrapbooking. She sighed.

While she knew it would seem strange to Yolonda, Annie had been working on this night for a long time. She sorted photos and put them in a much-used paper gift bag, which she set on top of the china cabinet so that her boys could not get them. It literally took her weeks to accomplish sorting and separating the pictures. Stolen moments during naps. Or when the boys were playing quietly. Or, God forbid, but yes, watching television. Her "stolen time" strategy worked, and she was prepared for tonight's crop.

At least she would get Ben's book started, she told

herself. That was the goal. She had no idea how she would steal the time to finish it, but she would. Then she planned to go back and bring Sam's up to date. But in the meantime, the boys hungered for lunch; and oh, yeah, she needed to finish folding laundry and put another load in. It was never-ending—the piles of laundry.

She saw herself in the mirror in the hallway—baggy sweats, nightshirt, and no bra—as she moved through her house to her kitchen. She could not remember if she brushed her hair or not, but it needed it. She also probably needed a haircut. Funny, she thought as she ran her fingers through her long, dark hair, she didn't think about her hair until she needed to go out.

She briefly wondered if Mike would get home in time for her to steal away to get a haircut before the big crop. Was she making too much of this? She laughed. Probably, she answered herself.

"Okay, Ben," she said. "Time-out is over. I want you to understand the consequences for hitting your brother. If you do it again, there will be no ice cream tonight."

"Yes, Mama," he said, walking off into a corner in his room. Ben always took his punishment to heart and tried to behave himself.

He's a good kid, she thought, and felt a twinge of guilt for his punishment. Still, she would not tolerate him hitting Sam.

The phone ringing interrupted her thoughts.

Both boys ran for the phone and struggled to answer it—she grabbed the receiver from Ben, with him screaming, "Hullo! Hullo!"

She pointed with her finger for them to go and sit down.

"Hello," Annie said.

"Annie?"

"Yes."

"This is Sheila Rogers. I was just checking to see if you are still coming tonight."

"Oh, yeah, I'll be there," Annie said, distracted by the

level of noise her boys were making. "I'm sorry about the kids."

"Don't worry about that. I have a few of my own," Sheila said, sort of giggling.

"You do, don't you?"

"Some of us just don't know when to stop." Sheila, the mother of four children, sighed. "They keep you busy."

"They sure do," said Annie, wondering where this conversation was going. "So I'll be there. Is there anything special I need to bring?"

"Oh, no, just your pictures and scrapbooks—if you have them. Of course, I'll have some books if you want to buy them. But it's really a no-pressure situation. A crop is for us to make the time for ourselves, do what we enjoy, not really to sell stuff," Sheila said.

"Good," Annie said, hearing a strange beeping noise in the background. "Where are you, Sheila?"

"Vera Matthews mother was brought in to the hospital earlier. I'm just here checking on her. It's taking the doctor forever. I'm sure she'll be fine," she said, with a note of finality in her voice, which made Annie feel like she shouldn't pry.

"Okay. Bye," Annie said.

The boys scurried off into their room. Annie surveyed her house. She was glad that the ladies were not coming here tonight. The floor needed sweeping—bits of some kind of food from last night's dinner were scattered under the table. She just did not have the heart to investigate at this minute. Toys were spread all over the floor, crayons, coloring books, trucks, and dolls. She thought of something her mother always said: *"Clean the kitchen first. A clean kitchen is a clean house."*

She walked toward the sink of dishes and began rinsing them to place in the dishwasher. Sippy cups half filled with spoiled milk, juice, and God only knows what else. She held her breath as she poured the mystery liquid down the sink. She rinsed the sink and squirted it with cleaner, allowing herself to breathe.

Ben ran across the floor behind her. "Mommy, can I have a snack and some juice?"

She glanced at the clock—was it only ten in the morning?

"Yes, sure. It's snack time. You want a cereal bar or yogurt?" she asked. "Go and sit at the table."

Her other son came into the room and sat at the table, too.

They decided on cereal bars and juice. Annie quickly grabbed the bars and took off the wrapping paper.

"Mommy, what's a tornado?" Sam asked.

"I want a blueberry cereal bar," Ben said.

"We only have strawberry," Annie replied.

"Mommy, what's a tornado?"

"No. No. No! I want blueberry!"

"We only have strawberry. A tornado is—"

"Strawberry is good," Sam said.

Ben shrugged. "Okay," he said, and began gobbling his cereal bar.

"Mommy, can we get a dog?" Sam asked.

"No, a cat," Ben said.

"Neither one," Annie said. "We will someday, when you get a little older. But right now, it's all I can do to take care of you two."

And that was the truth, she thought, turning back to her sink. Had she wiped it down? She couldn't remember. So she squirted it again, grabbed a paper towel, and wiped it down, wondering how long her spotless sink would last. She began to wipe the counters off, when she heard a cup fall over. Of course, it was Sam's non-sippy cup. Grape juice went everywhere.

"Mo-om!"

She ran to the table with the roll of paper towels—which, somehow, never managed to make it to the paper towel holder.

If she only knew how many diapers, paper towels, bread, and toilet paper they would have gone through as a family, Annie would have bought stock in those companies before she had children.

Then there was the juice—sticky, nasty stuff. She used to love juice, but now the sight of it sometimes wanted to make her heave. It was the same thing with macaroni and cheese, which her boys would eat every night, if she let them. And sometimes she did. She planned her meals around the stuff, she was ashamed to admit. But it was better that they ate something than nothing at all. She theorized that they would grow out of it eventually.

Annie actually had nightmares about getting stuck to the floor because the juice hadn't been cleaned up. After being stuck—and in the dream, nobody was there to help—she would begin to sink through her hardwood floor, as if it were quicksand.

Her other nightmarish dream was about packing and moving. She would be given a deadline by which she'd need to have everything packed and ready to go. She'd be packing and packing, and would think she was finished; then she would turn around and find more packing to do. She would wake up from the dreams, exhausted.

Her inner life was one that she had not paid much attention to while living in Bethesda. Her brain was filled with writing and production deadlines, lunch dates, poetry readings, shopping dates. But now, she found her dreams to be fascinating and rich. And sometimes the thought pattern that she was focused on during a specific day became her only source of sanity. For a while, her thought patterns acted as a mantra—to stay focused in the moment. If she tried to stay focused on what she was doing, *I'm changing a diaper, I'm changing a diaper,* she would not get as frustrated as say, when she was changing a diaper and allowing herself to think about all of the other things she needed or wanted to do.

Sometimes her dreams led her to writing. And that had never happened before. For a while, she dreamed about an old lover. Filled with such sweetness—and sometimes passion—that she didn't want to wake up. It was easy to figure out why she dreamed of Wes—that was a time in her life that she was completely unencumbered. Now her life seemed so thick with responsibility that if she let it, it would drag her down. Sometimes when she thought of her life now, she felt like a big, fat whale moving through the ocean.

For a while, it bothered her that she was dreaming of Wes. Should she see a psychiatrist? Talk to Rabbi Joe? Was everything okay between her and Mike? Was her psyche trying to tell her something? But then the dreams stopped. So she kept them to herself. In truth, she kept most of her inner life to herself.

Mike was too exhausted most of the time to share any of the details of dreams, thoughts, or prayers with him. She was lucky they communicated enough to try to keep their schedules in sync. She never imagined how difficult communication would get once children arrived on the scene.

Annie's memories of their time together before the children helped her to cling to the hope they would get there again someday. They had met at a book fair—and their conversations were often about literature, politics, and philosophy. Mike's mind was a beacon that lit a fire in her. She always found that something he said sparked the desire in her to learn more. Do more. Be more.

Of course, his body sparked other ideas in her. She could hardly contain herself on her first date. "Never sleep with a man on your first date," she heard from all of her women friends. It was more difficult for her with Mike because she knew she would marry him. It just felt so right that she thought, *What the heck? Maybe I'll jump his bones the first date.*

But it was not even an issue. Nor was it on the second date. Nor when she expressed her frustration.

"I think we should wait. I'm not in any hurry. There is so much more to us than the physical thing," Mike said.

Annie smiled and fell even more in love.

She often thought about the meaning of that in her life. And she thanked the universe that it was true—there was and is so much more than sex between them. Otherwise, they would be in real trouble, now that they had children. Sometimes it was months until they could get together. But when they did, it was always right.

She glanced at her box of gathered photos and looked forward to more organizing and placing the pictures of her boys on scrapbook pages, which she could share with them someday. One neat and orderly facet to her life was appealing to her. God knows the rest was just a mess. No longer was she living in her own world; she now lived in the realm of two messy, active, all-encompassing, energy-sapping little boys. And she embraced that—most of the time.

Just then, Annie's phone rang. It was Sheila, again, canceling the crop that she'd called earlier to confirm. Vera Matthews's mother was being operated on that evening. They would be in touch with her soon about rescheduling.

She turned the teakettle on and sat down in front of her computer. Maybe she could catch a little news before the boys woke up from their naps. She clicked on the local newspaper's website and gasped.

Chapter 3

Vera sank into the hospital room chair; Sheila was in the other. Both listened intently as Beatrice explained to a police officer what had happened. The knife was still in her neck and she was lucid. The nurses were going to prepare her for surgery in about an hour.

Beatrice sipped water from a straw as the nurse held up a cup for her. She swallowed hard.

"I remember it being cold, and, oh, the eggs at the store, most of them were broken," she said. "I thought it was odd. And then I noticed how crowded it was getting."

"Oh, for heaven's sake, Mother, what does this have to do with—"

"Was it unusually crowded?" the officer asked her.

"I think so," Beatrice said, ignoring her daughter. "In fact, Mrs. Hawthorn pushed up against me."

She remembered Betty's deep, manly voice. "Oh, sorry, Bea," Betty Hawthorn had said. "It's so crowded in here. I feel like I'm tripping over myself. I guess it's the funeral."

"What funeral?" Beatrice had asked, almost embarrassed not be in on the latest funeral news. She was often the first person to know. After all, she lived wedged between the only funeral home in town and the largest church in town—First Baptist.

"You haven't heard the news? It's all over the place. That young woman? That Maggie Rae Dasher? They found her dead in the middle of the night. It's awful, just awful," Betty had said as she drifted away.

Well, now, Beatrice had thought, *why don't I know that name? And surely they wouldn't be having her funeral today if she was just found. Betty must be confused.*

Just then, she had felt someone else brush up against her, harder, and turned to see who it was. Was that someone's elbow in her neck? She looked around and hadn't seen a thing. *Well, for heaven's sake.*

"Do you think that could be when you were stabbed?" the officer interrupted Beatrice's recounting.

"It's hard to say, really. I still can't get over not really feeling it."

"I need to make a call to the store to get a look at their security tapes. I'll be back to talk more," he said, and left the room.

The women sat quietly together.

Beatrice thought about being in Wrigley's that day and tried to remember every little thing that could help the officer.

She remembered feeling tired and glad to be only four blocks from the Wrigley's. She'd rather be at home— such as it was. No longer the grandest house in town, her Victorian pink-and-blue home used to be a beacon to the townsfolk. It's where she raised her daughter, where she held PTO, church, and town meetings, and where her husband had practiced medicine for thirty years. It was once the largest place in town. Now, just a few blocks outside of what used to be Cumberland Creek proper, sat mansions on tiny lawns. It was absurd.

She remembered the cashier's hands were adorned with rings on every finger and her nails were painted bright, fiery red. "Thank ya, hon," she said, not even looking at Beatrice, who was still wearing her hat, scarf, and coat, never bothering to take it off. Eh, well, she was used to being ignored, and she didn't even really care to be acknowledged by the brassy young woman. She looked at the woman behind her—she looked vaguely familiar. Beatrice managed a quick smile—just in case she knew her.

The cashier was involved in a heated discussion with the bagger about suicide. "It's a sin," she said. "That's what my daddy always said."

"Well, who cares what your daddy said," said the bagger, whom Beatrice did not recognize. More and more people were moving into Cumberland Creek, and she had no idea who they were—or who their people were.

"My daddy was a preacher," Beatrice overheard the cashier say as Beatrice grabbed her bags and walked off. *Yeah, your daddy was a preacher, all right*, Beatrice thought. *He was also a prick.*

She pushed her still mostly red hair up farther into her black knit hat and thought about the old reverend; he was always cheating on his wife with the youngest woman he could find, and she was always forgiving him some Sunday at church. There would be a spectacle. The parishioners knew they were in for a show when Michael started his sermon with "I stand before you a sinner. I am only a man."

As if half the population didn't know what was going on already. Poor Sarah would stand up, awash in tears and humiliation, and forgive him in front of everyone. Beatrice always wondered if they went home and made passionate love after the emotional spectacle—not that she even wanted to think about that.

Beatrice held on to her bags and coughed a little as she made her way to the door. Poor Sarah. Always so worn-out from her children and from trying to be a good preacher's wife. In his final days, he left her, anyway. Beatrice grinned. It was probably the younger woman who killed him. He couldn't keep up with her.

She had always felt sorry for Sarah; though now the widow seemed happy alone. Her children and grandchildren were always around. Her house was always full.

As Beatrice walked out of the grocery store, she turned left and walked toward her house. These walks were a part of her sanity and helped her keep in decent shape. But they were getting harder to take, especially in the dead of winter. She was glad for the spring, even if it was a cooler than usual one. She looked across the street to the school—under construction—a group of tiny children, faces peeking out of their coats, hats, and scarves, were being led across the street by a group of adults. One child pointed at Beatrice and said something she couldn't quite understand.

"Hmm," Beatrice said. "I wonder if that child saw the knife."

"What child, Mama?"

"I decided she wasn't pointing at me, but maybe she was. On my way home, she kept pointing at me, but she was across the street and I couldn't hear her."

"Where was that?"

"Right past Dolly's, across from the school."

Dolly's Beauty Shop, on its last legs, but still the same women's faces were looking at her through the windows and smiling as she waved. None of them, it seemed, looked hard enough at her to see the knife jabbed into her neck. Women were loyal to Dolly and her beauticians, but last month she announced that she just could not compete with the Hair Cuttery and the new mall beauty shop. She'd be closing in a few weeks. The thought of it made Beatrice's eyes sting with tears. *Old fool, I am an old fool.*

The weight of her bags seemed to be getting heavier. She looked across the street at the church and saw plenty of cars in the parking lot, people going in and out. A good many cars in the neighborhood. Something was definitely going on, but it wasn't a funeral. At least not yet. She stopped in front of her iron gate and looked farther down the road at the sign out front of the Greys' funeral home. No names appeared on the announcement board. She wondered if Betty Hawthorn had been mistaken. She slipped her hand through one of the bag handles and reached up for her newspaper.

"Mother!" said her daughter, opening the door. "Where've you been?"

"What are you doing here?" Beatrice answered Vera.

"I came to check on you," she said.

"Well, Lord, Vera, I just talked to you this morning. I told you I'm fine."

Beatrice could not stand the way Vera preened over her at times, the way she tried to treat her like a child. *How does she think I got to be this old, by being stupid and frail?*

Vera grabbed her bags. "Mom, you don't need to walk to the store, especially on cold days. Such a cold spring. I'd be happy to pick a few things up for you on my way home."

Beatrice ignored her, taking off her coat and her hat.

"Mama, what's that you have stuck on your hat?"

Vera pulled her hat off. "Nothing." She looked incredulously at her daughter, whose brows were knitted.

"Turn around. Let me see what's going on back here."

Bea smiled. It might have been worth it—just to see the look of horror on Vera's face.

"Well," said the officer as he walked back in her room, with heavy steps, the jangling of keys, and the sound of leather squeaking—was it his gun in the holsters against his regulation belt? Or could it be his new, shiny shoes? "The Wrigley's security cameras were on this morning. I am going to head over there and check out the tapes. We'll get your man, Mrs. Matthews."

Chapter 4

After the squeaky police officer left the hospital room, a team of nurses came in. One took Bea's pulse; the others were poking her with an IV needle.

"Guess, I'll be going to sleep now," Beatrice said. "When I wake up, I'll be a new woman—sans knife."

Vera harrumphed. She should have known her mother would agree to the operation when Vera said it was fine not to do so.

"Vera, you better get down to the studio. Don't you have a class to teach this evening?" Beatrice managed to say.

"I put a notice up on the door," Sheila said. "It'll be fine. Don't you worry," she said more to Vera than to Bea. "I'll go get us some coffee."

"Hey," said Bea. "If anything happens to me—"

But Sheila kept walking. "I won't hear of it, you old bat."

But she caught her daughter's eye as Sheila walked out. "You know where all my papers are," she said.

"Yes."

Was that all it had come to? Vera's stomach churned. Her life, her life with her mother, her mother's life? A box of paper in a fireproof safe? Hidden in the basement closet? Was she not going to speak to her of love? Of the past? Of her father?

Her mother's face suddenly softened, the lines almost fading. "I'm an old fool," she said. "And where is your father? I cried about the beauty shop. It's closing. . . . Things have a way of changing before you know it. . . . I do love you, Vera, even if you are getting fat. . . . Ha! My fat little ballerina . . . ," she said, and seemed to fall asleep.

Vera laughed. "I love you, too, Mama."

Vera had made up her mind to stop dieting last year. She decided to become a better role model for her students—and there was just no point in starving herself any longer. She would never be a ballerina. She had been on a diet for more than thirty years—after her dance teacher made a remark about her thighs when Vera was ten years old. *Forget her. I am not starving anymore.*

It was so freeing.

The first thing she ate—really ate with abandon—was her mother's blackberry cobbler. Not a piece of cobbler, but the whole thing.

She sat at her mother's 1950s chrome-and-turquoise Formica kitchen table set—the same table from which she had eaten almost every meal when she was a girl— and ate a piece while it was still fresh out of the oven.

"Do you have any vanilla ice cream, Ma?"

"Huh? Yeah, sure," answered Beatrice, who was visibly taken aback by her daughter's sudden love of blackberry cobbler.

"I have always loved it, Ma," Vera said, as if reading her mind. "I just was always watching my weight. And I figure, well, what's the point?"

Vera then ate a slice covered with vanilla ice cream. Real ice cream—for her mother never bought anything low fat or low carb or low sugar. She almost fainted at the creaminess, the mixture of textures and temperatures in her mouth. The next piece was covered with a dollop of whipped cream, while her mother tried to look busy wiping off a nonexistent crumb from the teal-speckled Formica counter, not wanting to stare at her only child as she seemed to be enjoying a private moment with the cobbler.

As Vera relished each bite—the mixture of the gritty and gelatinous mingled with sweet, juicy berries, covered with a light but substantial crust—her mother gave up her stance and watched intently. Her mouth hung open after Vera's fourth piece.

She handed her the pan. "Here, baby, this is the best way. Have at it," she said, and left Vera alone with the blackberry cobbler. Later she explained that she felt it was the only proper thing to do.

After all, Vera had not touched cobbler, pie, or cake since she was ten years old.

So Vera had put on about twenty pounds. But it was a good gain. She had more breasts and hips and thighs than ever before. And she loved her body. It was hers, and it did everything it was supposed to do, and more. She rewarded it often with good chocolate—preferably fresh and artisanal. She was still a graceful woman and dancer, even with the extra twenty pounds, and she was a happier person.

Vera caught a view of her blond hair in the mirror above the sink in her mother's hospital room. *Maybe it's too blond this time,* she thought. But she loved the way it looked with her bright fuchsia lipstick and blue eyeliner. Maybe next time, she'd go red. She loved her red hair with the blue eyeliner. She never left her home unless completely made-up—and then some.

Sheila could use some color in her hair. Vera tried to

sway her for years to go blond or red, but Sheila wouldn't hear of it.

"I don't have time to keep up with such nonsense," Sheila would say.

"It's all about priorities," Vera often said back. "I want to look good, don't you?"

"Sure. I'm clean. My hair is combed, most of the time. Sometimes I put a little lipstick on. But to have to run back and forth all the time to get my hair colored, you know, to keep up with it? Nah."

Sheila always was that way. Vera remembered all through high school, Sheila never wore a bit of makeup. But then again, she was an athlete and a budding young artist, and just had a different sensibility than Vera had. But they knew each other since before they could walk—their mothers were good friends and neighbors.

When Vera thought of Sheila's mother, her heart sank. If she thought hard enough, she'd sit here and cry. Poor Gerty died a horrible death, racked with cancer, which started in her breasts. She wondered if Sheila had gotten over the anger she felt about that.

"The old fool never had a mammogram in her life!" Sheila had spat through tears. "She refused. So, of course . . . it's too late."

Too late. Beatrice had mouthed those same words to her as she exited Gerty's hospital room, tears forming in pools in her gray eyes. Suddenly Vera saw her mother's age, her deep creases around her eyes and mouth and on her forehead. Most of the time, Beatrice's age hardly showed at all—or at least not that Vera had noticed.

Funny how people's looks changed, sometimes almost momentarily. For an instant, today, Beatrice's face looked almost childlike, and Vera had caught a glimpse of her own mother's vulnerability.

Chapter 5

"Why don't you go out, anyway?" Mike said to Annie as they were clearing away the supper dishes.

Annie leaned against the counter and crossed her arms. "I'm not sure where I'd go."

She thought momentarily of the mall. It would be nice to shop without the kids along—but it would also be nice to shop if she had more than fifty dollars in the bank. Movies? Nah, nothing she wanted to see bad enough to spend the money on.

Just then a crash came from the other room—where both of the boys were. Annie and Mike ran into the room to find the boys were into the box of pictures that she so carefully gathered and labeled. Pictures were scattered across the carpeted floor and the furniture. Ben looked sheepishly at them, while Sam danced around with the box on his head.

Annie's stomach twisted. She worked on gathering and organizing those photos for weeks. "Ben! Sam! Damn it!" she roared, lurching forward and gathering the crumpled pictures, with tears falling from her as if someone had died. She knew she was overreacting. A part of her seemed to be watching herself. She gathered the pictures, sobbing. "I can't believe it," she cried. "Look at this!"

Mike rounded up the boys and took them into their room. Annie saw her hands shaking as she lifted her treasured photos off the worn couch. She took a deep breath. *How did the boys get the box?* She had left it on top of the TV stand. Then she saw the chair behind the stand. As she placed the pictures in the now-disorganized box, she turned to face her husband.

"Hey," he said, with his dark eyebrows lifted, "you need to take a deep breath. You scared the boys half to death."

"I've been working on this for weeks."

"I know, but still, you lost your temper."

Next she was in his arms, sobbing. What was wrong with her? The boys were always into everything. This was really nothing new. What was different? She was disappointed at not getting to go out. Then she read the awful online report about Maggie Rae—a woman she saw around town a few times and had hoped to get to know better. A stay-at-home mom, like she was.

Maggie Rae was always alone with her kids. When Annie first glimpsed Maggie Rae, she wondered if she even had a husband. She was surprised later on to find out she did. It was jarring to read about her, so alone in this town, and driven to kill herself. God, she lived just down the street, and Annie never heard a gun go off, never knew her neighbor was in such emotional turmoil.

What could make a person do it? She looked up at her husband and took another deep breath. "Being a stay-at-home mom is harder than I thought it would be."

Her eyes met his watery brown ones.

He gently stroked her hair. "I know."

"Maybe I should go out for a walk," she said. "Or better yet, I'll go to the hospital to see how Vera's mom is doing. I'll bring flowers."

"That sounds like a good idea," Mike said. "But first—" He placed his lips on hers and held her firmly;

then he cradled her chin in his hands. "Mmm. I love you. That woman, that Maggie, if you ever feel—"

"I'll let you know. I promise. But for now, I need to go and say good-bye to the boys."

She cracked open the door—as she often did, just to watch the boys while they didn't know she was watching—they were both coloring while lying on their stomachs. Ben's elbows formed triangles against the blue carpet. Sam was so intent on staying in the lines; his tangled dark brown hair was in desperate need of a good brushing.

"Boys," she said in a low voice. They both looked up at her and dropped their crayons. She sat on the corner of the toddler bed. "I wanted to tell you both that I'm sorry I yelled."

"Why did you yell?" Sam asked. "We just wanted to look at the pictures."

"Those pictures are very special to me," she said, and paused. "It's like your blankies. You know how it's hard to share them sometimes?"

"It's okay, Mommy," Ben said, and hugged her.

"It's okay," Sam said almost at the same time—and then both boys were in her arms. Warm boys. Her boys. Flesh of my flesh.

"Well, now, I'm going out for a while. Will you be good boys for Daddy?"

They both nodded their heads.

After the gift shop soaked her for thirty dollars for a small flower arrangement, Annie walked over to the information desk to see where Vera and her mom might be.

"Excuse me, please. Where might I find Beatrice Matthews?"

"Now, let's see." The receptionist looked at Annie through thick glasses, and then turned to her computer. "Room one-thirteen."

"Thanks," Annie said.

"Sure thing, hon," she said in a warm voice as she looked back to her computer screen. Annie could hear her fingernails clicking on the keys. Why didn't she cut those nails? How could she stand that?

Saturday night at the hospital: Annie noticed clusters of people around chairs. Some were sitting; some were standing. Others were drinking coffee and soda, eating snack machine potato chips. The very worst food for stress, Annie thought. She saw room numbers on the sign up ahead, with arrows pointing in both directions. She at least could still follow directions, she mused as she walked down the long hallway with barn paintings on either side of her.

Don't these people ever get enough of barn art? As if there aren't plenty of barns to look at in person, they have to have paintings everywhere with barns in them.

Her tennis shoes squeaked on the shiny floor as she turned the corner. Standing five-nine, Annie used to wear pretty little flats with her business suits. Flats that didn't squeak on shiny floors—but these days, she was all about the sneakers and blue jeans. A brief flash of her old closet in D.C. came to her mind—all of the designer flats she had donned were lined up neatly. The Guccis were her favorite.

She thought she heard music as she approached room 113 and knocked lightly on the door. Vera answered.

"Well, hello, Annie. How lovely to see you," she said, with a huge smile on her face.

Annie thought she smelled wine. As the door opened, she could see why. Four women were scattered through the room—each held a glass of wine, and one was pouring more. A huge platter of cheese and dark bread sat on the bedside table; a basket of muffins sat on the other side. One woman was reaching for the biggest blueberry muffin Annie had ever seen—not much smaller than Ben's head.

"Mama is still in surgery," Vera said as she grabbed

Annie's hands. "Let me introduce you. Well, now. You know Sheila."

Vera moved her arm with the grace of a dancer—even now, in the hospital room, looking slightly haggard, she still held herself with such elegance.

"How are you?" Sheila came up to her and took the flowers out of her hand. Annie had never noticed how small and thin Sheila was. "Let's see where we can put this. Oh, there's a little space on the window shelf over there."

Annie was shocked at how many flowers and plants were in the room. She smiled.

"This is Paige. She teaches history over at the high school," Vera said, opening her arm to a slender, shaggy-haired blonde, with huge blue eyes, wearing a green tie-dyed T-shirt, which was a bit too tight and revealed an ample, freckled chest. The name "Paige" somehow didn't suit. Annie had always thought of a "Paige" as having a more classic look. She looked more like a "Willow" or a "Star." Annie shook her cool hand. "Pleased to meet you."

"Likewise," Paige said, turning back to the cheese plate. "Help yourself to some food."

"I will, and thank you," Annie said.

"And this is DeeAnn," Vera said. "Owner of DeeAnn's Bakery in town. Ever been there?"

"Oh, yes," Annie said, politely shaking her hand. "Very good bread."

"Thanks, but you need to try these blueberry muffins. I hired an intern and she just seems to have a way with the muffins. Good God, I can't get enough of them," she said.

She looked like a baker, Annie mused. Large, but not really fat; more muscular, with a little extra on those muscles. Huge hands and her forearms were sort of sculpted. Veins were popping out.

"Mama loves Vivaldi, you see," Vera told her as she

walked over to the boom box sitting on the floor. "We thought it would be nice for her to wake up to it."

For such an event, Annie thought Vera would be a mess, but her blond hair was neatly brushed in its page-boy style and her makeup was flawless—of course, to Annie's taste, it was a bit too much. The dark eyeliner, rouge, and lipstick looked a little like stage makeup.

"Now that you've met the scrapbook club, have a seat," Sheila said, pulling up a chair and looking quite a mess, mousey brown hair barely combed, lipstick carelessly splashed on. "Oh, and have some pie. Do you want chocolate or apple?"

"Chocolate," she replied. "Are we allowed to have wine in here?"

Vera shrugged. "I don't see why not. We didn't ask permission. Why would we?"

Annie sat in the chair and looked around at the group of women. For the first time since she had moved to Cumberland Creek, she felt the possibilities.

Chapter 6

Annie seemed completely unaware of her beauty, Vera mused as she looked at the new arrival enjoying a slice of chocolate pie. Beautiful, naturally curly, chestnut-brown hair, long eyelashes framing hazel eyes—and that skin, so smooth, wrinkle free. Those cheekbones—to die for. She sighed. The woman didn't even wear an ounce of makeup. Vera closed her eyes as she sipped her wine and leaned back in her chair. She glanced over at the painting of morning glories climbing up a barn. No artist captured the brilliance of morning glories. She loved them. They grew all over her backyard and patio.

The purple of the morning glories always surprised Vera. Each morning, while having her coffee on the screened-in patio, it mesmerized her. There were other colors, some pleasant, some foreboding, that she reckoned with every morning. But the splash of purple offered a respite for her eyes, which feasted on the flowers—until her husband came bounding clumsily through the door, always making more noise than any one person ever needed to do for just the simplest of life's maneuvers. Did he have to slam the screen door? Couldn't he pick his feet up when he walked? Every morning, when he was home, it would happen—just yesterday, for example.

"Well, I'm ready to go," he said, bending down to kiss her in the everyday, mechanical, see-ya-later kiss.

"I'll see you in a couple of days," she whispered back, and smiled at him. He looked for it—every morning.

"You're not one to smile easily. The world has to work to get a smile from you," he had said to her once.

Maybe that was true. But she did smile every morning.

It wasn't as if she were unhappy, or so depressed that she wanted to kill herself, and, the way she looked at it, if anybody had a right to be depressed, she did. But that wasn't it. She just felt flat. Nothing excited her anymore. This Maggie Rae death made her wonder how bad a person would actually have to feel to take her own life. Must be pretty damn bad.

Vera placed her wineglass on the hospital table and it clanked. She wondered if this was how it felt to get older. The wisdom she thought would come with age hadn't. Instead, she had gotten, well, ambivalent. She looked out the window as her friends were chattering in the hospital room.

"I'm glad I got my run in this morning," Sheila said. "I probably won't get to tomorrow."

"You'll live," Vera said.

That damn running. Doesn't she have anything better to do? Vera smiled—of course, she did. There was always the house to keep, the kids to feed, and yes, Sheila's business, Creative Scrapbooking, which she ran out of her basement. But Sheila, insisting her run was where she had time for herself, carved it out every morning—right after her youngest was put on the bus to kindergarten.

Choices, thought Vera, *they can make all the difference.* And Sheila was in incredible shape. Vera thought about the choices that she had made in her life and the ones she didn't get to make. *Some things just are and there's nothing you can do to change them.*

She admired people with the clarity of mind that enabled them to make the right choices at the right time. She was always too pensive. By the time she'd make a decision, often things had changed.

She wondered how her life would have been different if, say, she had decided on a real dancing career in New York, instead of opening a dance studio in Cumberland Creek. Her business was one of the most successful in the county. Which really didn't say much.

Vera ushered several generations of dancers through the door of her dance studio. Some of them went on to fame—or near fame. She followed their careers closely. They were almost like her children, since she did not have any of her own. She kept scrapbooks on all of them—and gave them to the dancers usually as a high-school graduation gift.

Now that she was in her forties, her dancing career would have assuredly moved into teaching. But instead, she taught all that time, her own passion for performing poured into her students. And a performance—once a year, at the recital—was something she looked forward to.

Her recitals were efficient masterpieces. One number after the next. Children lined up and ready to go. Plenty of adult supervision. She worked hard to get the right music with the right costumes with the right theme. And she saw to it that the production people were top-notch.

Vera was always complimented about the professional quality of her shows.

"Why didn't you go on Broadway or something?" Sheila wanted to know at the last crop.

Vera shrugged. "There was Bill."

"You mean he didn't want you to do it?"

"Well, he never said so, not in so many words. But the hours that dancers work just don't fit into the hours lawyers work. We'd have never seen each other, for one thing," she replied.

"And that's a bad thing?" one of the women said, and

they all laughed. The subject was changed and Vera was grateful.

It wasn't as if she kept secrets from her dearest friends. Some things were too private to talk about at a crop. After all, crops were primarily for scrapbooking. Oh, yes, the social aspect couldn't be denied. But nothing deep or heavy should be broached.

Vera glanced at the clock and realized her mother had been in surgery for three hours. What was going on?

"You'd think they'd let you know something," Sheila said, her coral lipstick long faded.

"I'm sure they will soon," Paige offered, reaching for a muffin, her bracelets jingling as she did so.

Just then, the door opened and the doctor stepped into the room.

He looked tired, but he was smiling, with pleasant, deep creases framing his smile. "Are you having a party?"

"We just wanted to make it as pleasant for Mama as possible," Vera said, standing.

"Well, I have good news and bad news. Your mom is fine—but the party will have to move into the hallway or go," he said.

Vera sighed as she felt her heart race. She grabbed her chest, and then fell into Sheila's arms. She felt unraveled suddenly, awash in emotion and tears and sweat, sobbing in relief.

"Vera?" the doctor said.

She turned to look at him.

"Have you been drinking?" He looked amused as he took in the scene of empty wine bottles and spent plates sitting around the hospital room.

"Well, of course, she has," Sheila said, as if it were a matter of course.

"Well," he said. "That's a first. I was just going to suggest that you go on home and get some rest. But I don't think that's a good idea."

"I'm not drunk, Doctor," Vera said.

"But you're not sober, either."

"I'll drive her home," Sheila said, swaying a bit.

"No offense, but you're drunker than she is," he chided, but he was obviously amused.

Sheila placed her hands on her hip. "Now, look here—"

"I'll drive them both home," Annie spoke up.

"Finally a voice of reason," said the doctor, looking straight in Annie's eyes, with an obvious spark of interest.

Like most beautiful women, Vera noted, Annie completely ignored the doctor's spark. That endeared Annie to Vera even more.

The women cleaned up the room a bit and, one by one, filed out. Annie, Sheila, and Vera hung out in the hallway until they wheeled a sleeping Beatrice by them.

"You both look tired," Annie said. "Let's go home."

Vera and Sheila stood outside Annie's minivan while she moved books and blankets and God knows what else from the front seat to the back of the van. Sheila climbed in the front and Vera sat in the middle seat, next to a car seat.

As Annie drove by the Dasher house, which was still brightly lit, and had strange cars sitting in the driveway, Vera gasped.

"My Lord," she said.

Annie slowed down. "What is it?" she asked; then she saw the huge pile of boxes piled out at the curb for the trash, which came every Wednesday.

"They are already cleaning her stuff out," Sheila whispered.

"But she just died last night . . . ," Annie said. "And the trash collector doesn't come until Wednesday. So what the heck is going on?"

"Oh Annie, this is Cumberland Creek, not Washington,

D.C. Sometimes you just have to put the trash out. No problem. Go around the block," Vera said. "Please."

Vera and Sheila gaped at the pile of boxes, the streetlights were shining directly on them.

When Annie pulled around again, Sheila whispered, "Stop. I recognize those boxes."

Annie glanced at the well-lit house. "I don't know. I'm not sure if I should."

"Go around one more time and pull the car behind those shrubs over there," Vera said.

"I don't know if this is a good idea," Annie said, suddenly catching on.

"They obviously want to get rid of her stuff," Vera said.

"It's her scrapbook stuff," Sheila said with a note of steel in her voice. "The bastard."

Chapter 7

Beatrice's head ached more than it ever had in her whole life. She struggled to open her eyes. When she did, she just shut them again. The bright light sent jabs of pain through her skull.

She sank into a pleasant dream about making love with her husband. They were in their bedroom, on their own chenille bedspread. As he took her, she saw the sheer curtains blowing in the breeze just over his bare shoulder, and she smelled the lilacs just outside the window. She cherished that moment with him. It felt the same every time; yet, it thrilled her: the thought of the man she loved inside of her like this, being a part of her—that he would want this as much as she. He had desired the same woman, the same love, for all of these years. It was such a comfort to have love like this in one's life—even if it felt so brief. Once a woman had it, it was always hers. His love had comforted Beatrice for most of her life. It was a thing her science could not explain.

She felt his hands on her face, cradling her head. Her pain now was lifting through her dream—as if his hand was healing her. She smiled as she woke up to see her daughter looking out the window. She loved looking at Vera's face as the sun streamed in on it. She looked so much like her father, with that strong, almost square jaw-line and her heavy-lidded blue eyes.

Beatrice cleared her throat. Her tongue still felt heavy.

"Mama?" Vera turned around, came to the bed, and reached for her mom's hand. "How are you feeling?"

"Fine," Beatrice answered, with a little trouble. "I had a headache, but it's gone. My neck is a little sore."

"You did have a knife lodged in it." Vera smiled at her.

"Well, I know that," Beatrice said, finding her tongue, looking around the room. "Look at all the flowers."

"Oh, yes, Mama, almost everybody in town sent you flowers. Isn't that something? Even the new family—the Chamovitzes. By the way, Annie Chamovitz was here last night and gave Sheila and me a ride home," Vera told her.

Bea thought a moment. "Too drunk to drive?"

"That's what the doctor thought, but we were both fine," she said, and smiled. Then she changed the subject. "Bill will be home today."

"Bully for him," Beatrice said, grimacing. Her son-in-law was okay. Vera could have done worse. But damn, he was boring. What on earth did her daughter see in him?

"You know the oddest thing happened last night," Vera said, changing the subject again. She then told her mother the story of the boxes of scrapbooks.

"What was in them?" Beatrice wanted to know.

"We didn't have a chance to look through them. It was late and we just left them in Annie's van. We're going to get together Saturday night and look through them. Isn't that awful? I mean, dead less than twenty-four hours. "

"It does seem odd, like someone couldn't wait to get rid of her—and her memories."

"Those poor children," Vera said after a silence.

A nurse came into the room.

"How are you feeling?" she asked, while checking Bea's IV.

"I've been better, " Beatrice said, felling a sudden wave of weariness. "I think I need another nap."

What is wrong with people? Is there any love left in the world? How could her husband pile up her scrapbooks on the pavement the day after she died? It took Beatrice months to even think about going through her husband's things when he passed away—and, in truth, she still kept a few things. His pipe still sat on the dresser with a chunk of that tobacco that she loved to smell. His camel hair scarf and three silk ties hung on the back of her closet door. Then there were the books, which she would never get rid of—they would have to pull Walt Whitman's *Leaves of Grass* from her cold dead hands— if she was lucky enough to die with the book in her hands, remembering the sound of Ed's voice reading Whitman's words to her:

"'*A woman waits for me—she contains all, nothing is lacking,*'" he would whisper to her in the wee hours of the morning after he had just delivered a baby or performed an emergency appendectomy. He would wake her gently and they would make love until they both were spent. He would lie next to her, snoring and murmuring.

About a year after he had died, he came to her. He sat on the edge of her bed and told her that she needed to get rid of his clothes, that the living needed them. And so the very next day, she boxed up the bulk of it and gave it to Goodwill.

It didn't frighten her to see her husband's ghost—for she always believed in the possibility—one doesn't study physics, then quantum physics, for a whole life, without seeing the possibilities of life after death—and the possibility that there is more to the world than what people think they see and feel. Besides, it gave her hope that she'd join him when the time came. She also felt a great comfort, knowing he was still around. It would help, of course, if he would come to her when she wanted him. Instead, he showed up at the damnedest times.

Once, she was on the toilet. He knew she didn't like him being anywhere around when she was using the bathroom. Gas pains ripped through so badly that she thought she might die—and there he stood next to the sink.

"Don't worry, Bea. It's not your destiny to die in the bathroom on the toilet."

"Well," she told him, *"thank God for that. Now, get the hell out of here, Ed."*

Ah, well, maybe she was crazy. Maybe he was a figment of her imagination. But even if he were, she knew it didn't matter. Imagination was a powerful thing. Sometimes she wondered if half the world wasn't based on it. Where was the line between imagination and so-called reality?

Now, this knife-in-the-neck business concerned her. Who would do such a thing? And what would have happened if it had not been lodged just exactly where it was? She could have died—or worse, been paralyzed, at the mercy of the likes of Vera and Sheila, a pair of midlife fools, if ever there were two. Sheila and her damn scrapbooks; and Vera and her damn dancing school, flitting around town like a diva, made up like a hussy half the time. It never mattered what Bea told her daughter. Vera had always had her own mind—if it could be called that. Her daughter was so different from her that it was hard to believe that she carried her in her womb. Didn't give a lick about the beauty of mathematics and could care less about chemistry, let alone physics. She wanted to dance.

Beatrice smiled. Oh, but to watch her dance. Her daughter inherited her father's long limbs and the grace—Bea just figured it was a gift from the universe. It was like watching an angel move across the stage. She would never understand why Vera insisted on coming back to Cumberland Creek to open the dance school, rather than staying in

New York. But she was sure that Bill was at the root of it. Boring old Bill, who was steady and stood by her daughter, and that was a good thing. But she never saw a spark between him and Vera. Curious.

But she did see an enormous amount of tenderness between them, at times. She always knew that Bill loved Vera, but Vera never behaved like a woman in love, even from the very start. Never even took his last name—Ledford. Was dance the only thing that Vera loved?

Damn, her neck hurt. Suddenly a shot of pain rippled through Bea and woke her from her revelry. Had she been sleeping or just thinking?

She hit the button for the nurse. She could do with a little more morphine. Yes, she could.

Chapter 8

Vera was pleased that she could make her Monday ten o'clock class with the preschoolers. It was one that she cherished. Half of them probably would not make it until they were eight or nine years old—when the real work started. They would get bored or get involved with other things—mostly soccer, one of Bill's great loves.

He helped send a lot of juvenile offenders to soccer teams instead of detention facilities depending on how bad the crime: "A good soccer coach can work wonders."

"Well, so can a good dance teacher," Vera usually retorted. True, he had sent some children her way—one girl in particular, Renee D'Amico, who was a dream student now dancing in *Annie Get Your Gun* on Broadway.

Usually, dance was a good thing in a child's life. Only one dancer, ever, in Vera's twenty-plus years of teaching was lost to anorexia. When someone mentioned Wendy, Vera's heart still sank, and that was fifteen years ago.

Now Vera was more educated about body image and she made sure there were no snide remarks about weight at her studio. Not only that, but she endeavored to have pictures and posters around of dancers with less than "perfect" bodies.

She turned the thermostat on and the lights, sat at her

desk, and saw the red light blinking. "Oh, bother, phone calls to return."

She pushed the button reluctantly. "Ms. Vera? This is Maggie Rae Dasher. My three-year-old daughter also wants to take ballet. I thought we might stop by tomorrow," the voice, so quiet it was almost a whisper, said.

Three years old! Vera wanted to bite her tongue. No three-year-old should begin dancing unless they were truly exceptional. She did have a group of age threes coming in today. The class started out having eight members. Slowly the others drifted off when they realized that ballet was not all tutus and sparkles. But the businesswoman in her thought: *Okay, I'll take your money.* And she did.

"Wait a minute," Vera said out loud, her heart lurching. "Was that Maggie Rae?"

She pushed the button again. "Ms. Vera? This is Maggie Rae Dasher. My three-year-old daughter also wants to take ballet. I thought we might stop by tomorrow,"

It was! She looked at the date on the phone. It was three days ago, the night before that Maggie shot herself. Eight o'clock at night. Vera's heart raced. Why would a woman who was planning to kill herself call and make an appointment for her child to sign up for dance class?

Just then, the phone rang.

"Hello," she answered.

"Hey, Vera, it's Sheila. How are you?"

"I'm fine, I'm sure. And you?"

"Very good. I had a great run this morning."

"Oh, you old fool."

Sheila laughed. "And I stopped by to see your mom."

"And?"

"She was sleeping. The nurse said I just missed you."

"Hmm."

"Are you coming to the crop on Saturday?"

"Yes, I'll be there," Vera said, looking at her pink fingernails. "Who else? The usual crowd?"

"Yes, and Annie."

"She'd like to start a scrapbook for her second son, I think."

"The second-child syndrome?"

Sheila laughed. "I believe so. Oh, guess what I've been doing," she said with a more serious tone.

"I couldn't imagine."

"Picking up Maggie Rae's trash again."

"What?"

"Yes. More boxes of scrapbooks, letters, postcards, and photos."

"Good Lord," Vera said, feeling a sinking in her stomach.

"I need to go. I was getting a head count for next Saturday. Don't dance too hard today, Miss Twinkle Toes."

"Fat chance of that happening," she muttered. "Bye."

In the door walked two of the little girls in her first dance class and their mothers.

"Hi, Miss Vera!" they squealed, delighted to see her and to be in the studio.

"Hello!"

Once again, Vera was swept into her students' world: a place where ballerinas were beautiful fairy princesses, all sparkles and feathers and grins. This was the magic class, the magic age. They believed they could do anything— and she wanted them to think that. If only she could crawl into their fresh little skins, and believe hard enough, maybe, just maybe, she could end up with a child of her own.

A child of her own.

Just then, the door flung open. A harried, small woman peeked her head in the door.

"Ms. Matthews?" the woman said softly.

"That's me," Vera said; then she turned her head. "Girls, let's go sit in a circle."

She turned back to face the woman. "Yes?"

"I—I am sorry. Someone told me you were a redhead. I was a little confused," she said.

"Oh, a redhead? That was last week" Vera said, and laughed.

The woman smiled politely. "I am sorry. It looks like you're busy. I'll stop back." She turned and walked way so quickly that Vera did not get a chance to ask her name. As she glanced out the plate glass window, all she saw was Harv, the mailman, and she could not help but roll her eyes. Everybody knew he read all of the magazines before he delivered them, and some folks thought he even opened letters and resealed them. *Damn Harv,* she thought, *has thirty years with the post office under his belt and can do whatever he wants.* But then again, he and his brother, Leo, had always been like that, ever since she could remember.

Chapter 9

"Hey, Annie, I've been meaning to ask you, what's all that crap in the back of the van?" Mike said, coming out of the shower with a towel wrapped around him.

Annie was lying on the couch, after just putting the boys to bed. Friday night and all she could think about was zoning out in front of the television and sleep. "The boxes?"

"Yes, what the hell?" he said, sitting on the couch next to her.

"Well, let me finish the story before you make any harsh judgments."

"Okay. Jeez, the plot thickens," he said, grinning, water beads clinging to his face.

"The other night when I went out to the hospital, I drove Vera and Sheila home. They were a bit tipsy."

He chuckled. "Now, I bet that was something to see."

"And remember that Maggie Rae had just died early that morning?"

His smile vanished.

"We saw those boxes on the curb—"

"And you took them?" he said as his eyes widened.

"Well, no. . . . I didn't. I just drove the getaway car," she said, grinning.

"Annie!"

"Oh, I know. It was sort of a perfectly madcap and evil thing for us to do," she said, looking away from him and fidgeting with the remote.

"And?"

"It was all sitting there for a reason, Mike. Her husband was cleaning out already. Getting rid of her stuff. She wasn't even dead twenty-four hours. I mean, what kind of an asshole does that?"

Mike leaned back on the couch. "That house is awfully small. Maybe he just couldn't stand looking at all the scrapbook crap. It takes up so much space."

"Yeah, well. It feels to me like he's dancing on her grave."

"Oh, c'mon. He's probably in shock. His wife shot herself. Can you imagine? And who knows what kind of hell she was putting the family through if she was sick enough to shoot herself."

"Have you ever seen this guy?"

"No."

"Me neither. But I've only seen her a few times," she said, getting up from the couch. "I can go for a beer. Do you want one?"

"Sure," Mike said, following her into the kitchen.

Annie pulled out two light beers from the fridge and opened them both.

"So what you're telling me is that I have a dead woman's scrapbooks in my van," Mike said after taking a swig of beer. "And that you stole the stuff from the curb—er, no, you were just the driver of the getaway car."

"It's not stealing if it's trash, Mike."

"Are you sure?"

"Oh, well, pretty sure," she said, grinning at him. Then looking at him furtively, she teased, "You know, if you play your cards right, you could make love to a thief tonight."

She wrapped her arms around him and leaned her

head back. She could smell the soap on him, the fresh smell of the floral shampoo, and his own scent beneath all of it—a subtle saltiness.

"Hmm, well, now. Don't think I've ever done *that* before," he said before kissing her.

"Nice," she breathed.

"Mommy!" came a scream from the boy's room.

"Not so nice . . . ," she whispered.

"You deal with that, and I'll meet you in the bedroom," Mike said, grabbing her beer.

She went into the room to deal with Ben, his brother already asleep.

"Kiss," he said, but she knew the trick. He wanted a kiss; but once she got close enough to him, he'd latch onto her and wouldn't let go. She'd have to rock him to sleep.

"I already kissed you, Ben. How many kisses does one boy need?"

"Lots," he said, and grinned at her.

An hour later, he was asleep in her arms as she sat in the rocking chair. As she carefully placed him back in his bed, he stirred a little. *God, please don't let this child wake up again tonight.*

She left the room and shut the door halfway behind her. Would Mike even be awake? She opened the bedroom door. And there he was, with a huge grin on his face, completely naked. Both beers had been drained.

Afterward, Annie lay in her bed and listened to Mike snore. She wondered if she would ever feel like the sexual person she used to be. Almost every time she used to have sex, it resulted in orgasm. These days, it didn't. She didn't know what the problem was—was it exhaustion? Was it the fact that her boys were sleeping in the next room?

She closed her eyes and thought of the goods in her van. Maybe Mike was right. Maybe the women were making too much of it. Maybe it was too painful for a new widower to look at. Maybe the scrapbooks and all the ephemera just took up too much space in that little house.

But a sinking feeling crept in her stomach. It was the same kind of feeling that she used to have when she was tracking a story. A knowing that there was more to it. Like the time that chef fired his sous chef for no apparent reason and then turned up dead—she followed that story and helped track down one of the biggest cocaine rings in Bethesda. What a story.

She also reported on the dogfights they were having in a rural part of Maryland—she tracked that bunch of criminals through one meeting with a woman at a bar. Something just hadn't seemed quite right to her.

And something wasn't quite right here.

But this was Cumberland Creek—and there was a lot about it that she thought wasn't quite right. But maybe it was just different from what she was used to. Maybe.

The next day, Saturday, Annie awoke with a start when she realized how still it was in the house. Was everything okay? Mike wasn't next to her, and it was way too quiet. She sat up and placed her feet on the floor. Then she heard the television noise that she hated so much. She cracked her bedroom door open and saw her husband and boys watching cartoons together, with empty cereal bowls and sippy cups scattered around the living-room floor. Was that coffee she smelled? She almost hated to open the door, but the coffee beckoned.

"Mommy!" came the screams from her boys as she made her way to the kitchen.

They ran to her and wrapped their arms around her—almost knocking her down.

"Daddy not let us wake you," Sam said, with knitted brows.

"Good Daddy," she said, and smiled. "Oh, I need some coffee. It smells so good."

"Good morning," Mike said, slipping his arms around

her as she poured coffee. He felt warm and strong. His breath played against her neck.

"Good morning," she said, turning around and kissing him.

"I have to go into the office for a few hours, Annie," he told her. "But I promise I'll be back in time for you to go to the crop tonight."

"Okay, well, you better get your shower. I'm on," she said, smiling.

She knew her day would be filled with messes and squabbles, and that she would be dead tired by the time she was able to get to Sheila's, but just the thought of getting together tonight with a group of women gave her a little shred of light.

"Mommy, play trucks?"

"No. Cards."

"Wait, boys, let me have some coffee and something to eat. And if it doesn't rain, we'll go to the park."

"Yay!"

Later they tumbled out of the van and began running before it seemed that their feet had even hit the ground. Annie explained to them what part of the playground they were allowed to play on—"Don't go past the swing sets. Do you understand?"

She sat down on a bench and watched the boys play on the swings. Another woman sat down beside her. She pulled out bags of snacks and drinks, which made Annie feel a little unprepared. She made eye contact with her and smiled, then looked away. Her heart skipped a beat. *Damn, if this woman doesn't look like Maggie Rae.* Annie glanced at the children, who were filing onto the playground. Yes, she thought, they were Maggie Rae's children.

"Excuse me, do I know you?" Annie managed to say.

"No, I'm sorry. I don't think so." The woman smiled.

Her eyes were swollen and puffy. "I'm just in town for the funeral, and things."

"Maggie Rae?"

The woman nodded her head and looked away, toward the children.

"My sister," she said hoarsely. "I'm Tina Sue."

"Oh," Annie said, drawing in a breath. "I didn't know her well, but I am so sorry."

Her boys' laughter filled the air, along with the creaking of the swings. Maggie's three children were each on a swing—none were smiling.

"I thought I'd try to get them out of the house for a while," she whispered, her voice quavering. Her lavender winter coat made a crinkling sound as she reached up to blow her nose. "The baby . . . is sick. I left her with my mom."

Yes, the woman was clearly distraught, and she looked a lot like Maggie Rae. However, she was not as thin as her sister—or as pretty. Her ski jacket looked about twenty years out of style. She looked like a puffy, haggard version of Maggie Rae. Same doelike brown eyes. Her dark hair was pulled back into a loose bun. She was in bright colors—the lavender ski jacket, dusty rose jeans, and her fingernails were even painted a bright pink. Funny, Annie didn't realize until now that every time she'd seen Maggie Rae, the woman had been in black or very dark blue. In contrast, her sister was all color coming at you.

A large, dark man emerged from what Annie assumed was Tina Sue's car. A brooding presence walking up to the bench. Annie glanced at him and smiled. He looked away quickly, sticking his hands in the pocket of his camouflage jacket. This must be her husband. Tina Sue hadn't realized he was standing behind her yet.

"Will they stay with you, then?" Annie asked, immediately sorry that she had. The man looked at her—and she almost gasped as his hand went to Tina Sue's shoulder. The gesture was a silencing one.

Tina Sue looked daggers at her. "Are you kidding? He won't let them go. He won't let them go."

"Oh, well, " Annie said, feeling as if she had stepped into a snare. "Of course not—they are his kids. But I remember Maggie Rae saying he travels a lot for work. Who will take care of them?"

The woman looked at her, but without meeting her eyes. Then she started to say something, but instead looked at the man and shrugged, lifting her hand up as if perplexed. Annie noticed how red Tina Sue's hands were, as if she had been cleaning or gardening hard.

Annie's thoughts were interrupted by Ben's screams. He had fallen off the swing. She ran to get him, and wrapped him in her arms and calmed him down.

When Ben's cries finally subsided, she looked up, and they were all gone. All of them, leaving Annie with another odd feeling as she watched the empty swings still moving.

Chapter 10

After Vera said good night to Beatrice at the hospital, she hurried over to Sheila's home—where all of the other scrapbookers were.

She walked in through the glass sliding door in the basement and saw Annie looking over Sheila's shelves. She was wide-eyed and in awe of it.

Scrapbooks were coded by color and stacked neatly on the metal shelves. Plastic containers held colorful pens, markers, and cutting tools. Other shelves were stacked with paper. Once again, coded by color. Smooth, milky vellum papers were their own category. Handmade paper, like mulberry, was in its own stack. The rest were categorized by color, and within the color by occasion—birthday, wedding, anniversary, and so on. On her desk sat craft drawers filled with embellishments—charms, ribbons, stickers, wire art. Each drawer was labeled. If anybody called Sheila to ask if she stocked a certain scrapbook, marker, paper, or embellishment, she could get her hands on it quickly. Efficiently.

"It's a sickness," Vera said to Annie.

"Oh, hi, Vera. I was just admiring it all," Annie said.

"She knows where everything is, that's for sure," Vera said. "But she was always like that, even as a child. She'd line her Barbie dolls up just so, knew where all of their clothes and accessories were. Me? I lost everything. Still do. I don't know. It must be an extra gene that she has."

"I can't keep track of my own stuff, let alone my boys' stuff," Annie said. "It's overwhelming. And they are always getting into my things, so it makes it even harder."

"I don't allow my children into the basement," Sheila said as she approached them. "C'mon. Look at this."

The women followed her around the corner to a huge table. Paige and DeeAnn sat looking over pictures. The table behind them was piled with baked goods—muffins, bread, and cupcakes.

The pictures were in envelopes, neatly labeled with names and dates, sometimes events: *Grace's Fifth Birthday, Daniel's First Christmas, Bringing Joshua Home.* Annie gasped when she realized what these pictures and envelope were—Maggie Rae's things.

"I think we should each take a child, and one of us could take Maggie Rae. The box over there seems to be her photos—wedding, graduation, postcards, letters, things like that," Sheila said.

"I'll take that one," Annie offered.

"I'll take Grace," Vera said. "She's one of my students."

"I'll take Daniel," Paige volunteered.

Sheila took the youngest daughter, Beth, which left DeeAnn to work on Joshua's scrapbook.

"This will be a great thing for these children to have someday," Sheila said, turning to the stereo. "Classical tonight, ladies?"

"Hell no," DeeAnn said, getting up to head for her bag and pulling out a CD. "Let's hear some Stones."

"Sounds great," Vera said, sitting down in her usual chair at the table. She opened the envelope that held the pictures of Grace dancing. She was a good little dancer, Vera mused. Grace at her first recital smiled up at her from a photo—dressed in a pink tutu and silver sequins.

Her jet-black hair was pulled from her beautiful little face, with a wide grin splayed across it. Such a happy kid. A born performer.

This would give her a chance to work some fabric into a scrapbook. She'd wanted to experiment with this for quite some time, and even already collected some cotton pieces in her scrapbook bag for just such an occasion. Pink-and-black calico. Black velvet. Pink tulle. Pink and black would be her color scheme. Perfect for a ballet scrapbook.

Mick Jagger sang in the background. The sounds of "Brown Sugar" filled the air.

"I'll do a dance scrapbook for Grace," she said almost to herself.

"You may as well," Sheila said. "There are plenty of books—probably more than we need. Maybe that pink one over there?"

Vera reached for the book and dug in her scrapbook tote for her fabric. She placed the black velvet against the soft pink leather and decided to use a brad to make a bow for the cover. She wrapped the bow around her fingers and pinned it to the book. Usually, she did not think about the cover until the book was done—but the black velvet and pink leather just spoke to her. She would place Grace's name in the center of the cover.

"Lovely," Sheila said approvingly.

"You know, Daniel looks so much like her," Paige said, holding up a picture. "It's kind of scary." She took a sip of wine.

"I wish I'd known her better," Vera said. "She just wasn't an easy person to get to know."

"She'd never come to our crops," Sheila said. "I invited her all the time."

"She probably just couldn't get away from the kids," Annie offered. "It's not easy when they are little. And if her husband was gone a lot . . ."

"Yeah," DeeAnn said after a while. "I forget what it was like to have little ones. I have two in college. But that was tough."

"There's plenty of wine and soda and things in the fridge over there, ladies, and have some of that spinach dip. It's so good," Sheila said. "Be careful if you bring it to the table. You don't want to ruin these photos."

Annie got up to get herself a drink. "Can I get anybody anything?"

Vera gingerly set out all of the dance photos—from the time Grace was four until now, age nine. One fell out of the pile. She picked it up and was surprised to see herself, holding Grace when she was four, posing for the camera. She wondered how many girls she had held in her arms like this, how many pictures were floating around of her and other people's children? Butterflies of jealousy danced in her stomach.

In the picture, she was a brunette, with blond stripes going down either side of her face. She had thought she looked good at the time—but her face, despite the piles of makeup that she wore—looked worn and drawn. She looked like a big sad Kewpie doll. The lines around her eyes were deep, even then. The makeup just wasn't hiding it. And there was a look in her eyes—oh, she didn't know what to call it—but maybe a look of regret. It gave her pause. What was she so regretful about? Could she even remember?

It struck her at that moment that she wasn't happy—and hadn't been for years. Just the expression on her face, the pain in her eyes, all of a sudden, it was too much to bear. It was overwhelming to see this happy little girl, with her mother behind the camera, so proud taking pictures—being held by this sad old woman who would never have children of her own. Now the child, the girl, the little dancer in her class, had lost her mother. Such a loss would never heal completely.

Vera caught her breath as a tear formed in her eye. She took a sip of her wine and thought she would need something stronger than wine . . . soon.

"Well, my goodness, Vera," Paige said to her from across the table as Vera felt the first tear slip down her face. "Are you okay?"

"It's just so damn sad," Vera said. "I mean, this young woman, with these beautiful children. She killed herself, and now they will have to live with that for the rest of their lives. No mother."

"I'm sorry, but it doesn't add up to me," Sheila said.

"Me neither," Annie said from the corner.

"What do you mean?" DeeAnn questioned her.

"It's all just a bit too tidy. Look at this—all of this stuff, out on the sidewalk. I mean, what's that all about?"

The room filled with silence as the scrapbookers dug through their pictures, trying to formulate design and pattern to the children's lives. Annie dropped a scrapbook onto the table; her face was drained of its warm tones. Her hand went to her mouth.

"What is it, Annie?" Sheila asked.

"I found this postcard from a fan of Maggie Rae's."

"Fan?"

"Turns out she did a little writing on the side." Annie grinned. "This was in an envelope addressed to her. Inside is a letter from her publisher. Her pen name was Juicy X."

"Well, now, isn't that something?" DeeAnn remarked.

"Listen to this. 'Dear Ms. Juicy X, I have been a fan for so many years I've lost count. My wife and I love your erotic writing. It helps to keep some spice in our marriage.'"

"What? Obviously they have the wrong person," DeeAnn responded.

"No. It was in this envelope full of letters and cards." Annie held up a huge brown envelope. "Here is the letter from her publisher, and this is a sales report to Maggie Rae Dasher, aka Ms. Juicy X." She placed the sales report on the table for them to ooh and aah over. Thousands of dollars in sales.

Sheila was the first to giggle; then they all started. Even Vera, who was still crying, started to giggle.

"You mean dirty stories? Maggie Rae? Wrote dirty stories?" Sheila wondered aloud.

After they all calmed down, Annie told them, "Yes, but there's more. So much more."

"Well?" Sheila said.

"Here's a card from Robert, her husband. Listen to this," Annie said, and began to read:

"'Maggie, I know you love writing about sex. But I wish you'd stop. It makes me feel like I can't be a man and support you. I'm so sorry that I lost my temper and hurt you last night. I just don't know what gets into me.' And Maggie Rae scrawled across it: 'I'll write want I want to write,' set off with big red X's."

"Well, now, it seems she wasn't the mouse we thought she was," Vera finally said.

Chapter 11

When Vera came into the room, Beatrice was sitting in a chair with her bag packed.

"About damn time," Beatrice said, looking over her daughter's pink sweat suit with a scowl.

"Sorry, Mama. You know Sunday mornings I like to sleep in a bit," Vera said.

"Good morning, Bea," Bill said, walking in the door.

"Morning was over a half an hour ago," she mumbled.

"Are you ready to go home?" he said, sitting on the edge of the bed.

God, could I ask for a more dim-witted son-in-law? Bea just looked at him; then she looked at her bag.

"I'll get the nurse, Mama, so we can get the process under way. You know, they will need to officially discharge you and get you a wheelchair," Vera said, leaving the room.

"Have they figured out who stabbed me yet?" Bea asked Bill.

"I've not heard," he said. "Are you scared to go home?"

"Scared? Just because someone stabbed me in the neck? Hmmph," she said. "Someone comes into my house, I'll shoot the bastard."

"Maybe we should get you an alarm system, just to be on the safe side," he said, smiling, and then smoothing over the blanket.

Alarm system? Bea never thought she'd ever hear about that, but things were changing in her little town, faster than she knew it. She used to know all of the families in town—and most of the farmers and mountain folk on the outskirts, too. With all the new people coming from the cities—like Charlottesville, Lynchburg, and Roanoke—hell, even from Washington, D.C., she didn't know half the people in her town.

It used to be she could walk from one end of the town to the other and smile and greet everybody along the way. Now she found herself searching, sometimes for one familiar face.

She remembered how pleasant it was to live right on Main Street, her end now called Ivy Street, quiet at the appropriate times and with just enough activity throughout the day to keep it interesting. Her house was one in a row of five at one time, though the one at the very end burned in 1965; then the one next to it was purchased by a real estate company just a few years back, after "Old Man" Miller died. Now she had two neighbors on her side of the street, each living in identical Victorian-style houses—all different colors. Hers was pink and blue; on one side was a yellow house trimmed in blue; the other house was blue, trimmed in red.

Across the street were the old brick town houses—some were almost covered by ivy. Betty's place was the prettiest—she was quite a gardener, with something blooming all year long. Beatrice always liked to look out her bedroom window, which faced the front of the street, at Betty's garden.

If she walked across the street and into town, it gave her a different vantage point. She liked to change her path once in a while. Dolly's Beauty Shop was first; then came the post office, expanded to fill almost the whole block. On the other side of the post office was the bakery, and then Vera's dancing school. It had been a big warehouse at one point, until Vera bought it, that is. Her daughter painted it the prettiest shade of yellow Beatrice had ever seen—it reminded her of butter, though it was even prettier than that. The bakery was chocolate brown and pink, with two wrought-iron tables out on the street for people to sit down and eat their muffins and drink coffee. It was so clean and beautiful, with those pink window boxes and cascading petunias in the summers.

Dogwood trees were planted all along Main Street. In the spring, it was a magnificent sight to behold as she walked through her little town. At the end of the business district, she often stood and looked out over the mountains—where she grew up—deep in the hills, nothing but earth and rock and tree and sky. The winding Cumberland Creek started as a trickle in one of the deep caves on Jenkins Mountain.

Across the street from the dancing school was the Wrigley's, which leveled several of the small businesses for that huge parking lot. A few small restaurants were lined up next to it. Mr. Wong's was a Chinese place, and the other place was a greasy hot dog shop.

Lord, what people will put into their bodies these days!

But sometimes Beatrice liked to sit outside of the drugstore, which was between the hot dog shop and the local museum, and watch as people streamed in and out of her daughter's dancing school. Vera was a small-business success—by all definitions. But a great sadness hung over Vera. She thought her mother didn't know this, but mothers always do.

That she could never have a child tore at Vera's heart, so she became a mother to the children she taught. Beatrice always wondered, but never asked, for fear of dipping too far into Vera's business, why didn't they adopt? There were so many children who needed a good home. Biology was only one part of mothering, and any mother worth her salt could second that.

Bea's favorite part of her town was the small park in between the town buildings. This was not the park where the playground was—thank God for that. She loved kids, but there was a place and a time for them. She found a measure of peace, surrounded by beautiful fountains, lovely plants, and good company—this is where the people who were closer to her age gathered. No loud music, no strange modern slang, just pleasant companionship. Some days, she'd sit next to the fountain with two or three other women—men were rare—and just listen to the water trickling, watch the goldfish swim, think about days gone by. In fact, it was always best when they didn't talk: sometimes the small talk nearly drove her mad. But few people were left in her world with whom she could chat about quantum physics. Or history. As she got older, she had learned to appreciate history, and was fluent in the town's past.

Cumberland Creek, at first called Miller's Gap, was settled in 1755 by a group of Pennsylvania farmers of German descent. Pennsylvania was too expensive and crowded. Land in this part of Virginia was still plentiful and cheap then. Sometimes Beatrice liked to imagine what Cumberland Creek would have looked like to the settlers—no buildings, no fences, no real roads, just paths leading horses and wagons around the mountains. She'd read that at one point in Virginia's history, the trees were so large and dense that squirrels could travel from the mountains to the ocean without touching down on the ground.

Imagine the mountains and forests pristine. So dense that the sun barely peeked through. So clean that you could inhale deeply and not get one whiff of another human.

She grimaced. Now the settlers were a different kind. They were coming in droves and getting rid of trees to build their houses on top of one another. They were named Tiffany and Taylor and Reed and Britney. There were no new citizens in the mold of Johann Miller, Peter Baughman, or Mary Jenkins—people of substance. The settlers of the area were of sturdy stock; they fought off harsh winters, survived droughts, and raised families. Of the three founders of Cumberland, of course, Beatrice liked to tell the story of Mary Jenkins. Damn, she wished she could go back and time and chat with her.

When Mary arrived in Cumberland Creek, she was with her husband and three children and expecting her fourth. After a year of settling—house built, land staked, first crops planted—her husband died, leaving Mary and her children vulnerable in this small community.

They settled the farthest out—close to the mountain— and so Mary didn't have much comfort of community as she raised her children, tended her crops, took care of her home and land. Many different stories—legends—existed about her. One claimed that she shot down a Native American whom she found lurking around her property. Another claimed that she later fell in love with a Native American, mothered more children by him, even though they never married. Beatrice liked both stories—though, as with a lot of personal history, nobody could prove a thing.

One thing for sure was that the hills were full of Jenkinses. At one point in time, the Jenkins family owned most of one mountain and the hollows around it. One of Mary's younger sons, Samuel, married a Scotch-Irish girl, who was part of the next wave of settlers in the area. Bridget O'Reilly Jenkins populated the mountain with fifteen children. Hence, Jenkins Mountain and Jenkins Hollow.

* * *

"Are you ready to go, Mama?" As she pushed in a wheelchair, Vera spoke up and interrupted Bea's thoughts.

Bill picked up his mother-in-law's bag.

Well, at least he was good for something.

Chapter 12

After Vera and Bill situated Beatrice at home, they took off for Cumberland Creek Episcopal Church, which was where Maggie Rae's memorial service was being held.

"I didn't know the woman," Beatrice had said earlier that day. "But I wouldn't mind going to pay my respects to her family."

"Oh, Mama, you just had surgery, and the doctor said for you to stay in for about a week. Besides, it's okay for you to miss a memorial or funeral once in a while," Vera said, with a grin, reaching in her bag for a chocolate. Funerals and memorial services were one of Beatrice's favorite events. Not that she liked to see loss and grieving, but she loved the spectacle of them—everybody wearing their best clothes, beautiful music and prayers, sometimes poetry. A good funeral would entertain Beatrice for weeks. She could talk about the strange hat Ellie Pickering was wearing: "I mean, what was the woman thinking?" Or about the fact that some women weren't wearing panty hose or stockings in the church. She wasn't a churchgoer anymore. "But it's the principle of it," she'd maintain.

The best part of any service was the reception, where families laid a huge table filled with food that neighbors, family, and friends brought to them. It was also a cause for Beatrice to mull over for weeks. "I think those deviled eggs went a little bad. I was sick for days." Or "Lord, that red velvet cake was the best I've ever eaten. Who brought that? I need the recipe."

But today, Beatrice was staying home, and Vera would report back to her mother, answering the many questions she was sure would be asked of her. So she planned to pay particular attention to clothes, hats, poems, and songs. But she ached in her heart and in her guts. This memorial service would be like no other, she knew. Nothing like this had ever happened before in Cumberland Creek—a young mother killing herself, leaving behind four children and a husband. Maggie Rae's private burial just took place two days ago. What could a preacher have to say that would make sense of any of it? Provide any comfort to any of the family—especially the children?

Bill placed his arm around Vera's waist as they walked through the church doors together. This was where they had married and attended church, off and on, for their whole married lives. The church grew bigger and bigger—and while they never officially gave up on their membership, neither one liked the direction it seemed to be heading in. The intimacy of worshipping together with people they had known their whole lives was lost.

They walked into the hushed sanctuary, organ music was playing "How Great Thou Art," and people were already seated in clusters. There were more empty spaces in the long pews than not. There was Annie, sitting next to Sheila and her husband, and behind them sat Paige and her husband. Vera and Bill slid over next to Annie.

"Hello," Vera whispered to them.

Annie looked absolutely stunning in a black turtleneck shirt dress, with a simple long gold chain draped down the front. Her long curly hair was pulled into a tight bun, showing off those cheekbones. Gold earrings. So chic.

DeeAnn—wearing a floral dress in navy blue and a matching hat—slid in behind them. "Lord," she breathed out, red-faced. "I don't know how I'm going to make it through this."

Her husband put his arm around her and sat back against the pew. "It's horrible," he said, looking more serious than Vera had ever seen him. Usually quick to laugh and crack a joke, Jacob was the high-school basketball coach and physical education teacher, and Vera had gone to school with him. When he was all dressed up in a dark brown suit, hair slicked back, and shaved, hell, he wasn't a bad-looking guy. Still had those green eyes and most of his hair—unlike Bill, whose hair was long gone—not that it mattered to Vera, not one ounce.

A hush fell over the crowd as the organist stopped playing and the family walked down the center aisle. From where Vera was sitting, she enjoyed a perfect view of the children—the youngest, being held by a woman— Maggie Rae's sister? Next to her sat a dark-haired man whose face she couldn't quite see, but his arm was around her, so perhaps that was her husband. Was he wearing Mennonite plain clothes? Hmm. There were the grandparents—she assumed—huddled around the others, with the husband, holding on to Grace's hand. She sat next to him. Vera wanted to weep as she looked at Grace, so sullen. Would her spark ever return?

It was more than grief. It looked almost like a different child sitting there. Her eyes not only lacked their luster, but they also lacked their youth. Vera's bottom lip began to quiver; a sweaty, trembling Bill handed her his handkerchief. *Well, he was certainly taking this hard— and he barely knew this family.*

Vera turned and briefly looked over the crowd—odd, a Mennonite contingent was there. They looked to be Old Order. Back in the corner, bearded men dressed in dark suits gathered. The women, in the opposite corner, were wearing dark heavy cotton dresses, with their prayer caps tightly around their hair buns, and their faces free of makeup. They traveled a long way off Jenkins Mountain to be here; Vera wondered what the connection was. Perhaps it was Maggie Rae's sister.

But hadn't she heard about a new faction of Mennonites? Perhaps these people were from that group. There was something about them that didn't seem quite right to her—but what did she know. Lord knows, she didn't know much about Mennonites.

Vera looked at Maggie's Rae's blond husband. It was the first time she'd ever seen the man—he never came to the studio or to the recitals. He was tall and thin—not at all what she expected. Now, what was his name? Robert, that's right. While Grace inherited her mother's dark hair, her face was almost an exact replica of his—those ice blue eyes, tiny nose, and heart-shaped face.

Vera wanted to stand up and witness against the man. Strongly suspecting that he beat Maggie Rae, she thought she'd like to humiliate him, just once. But not in front of the children. God knows what they had already seen.

She struggled to see the other children, along with their grandparents, as if one of them could transmit through osmosis what really transpired in that house. Maybe the truth would come pouring from Maggie Rae's sister's swollen eyes—or her other daughter's high forehead. But the truth was never that easy, Vera thought, and probably Maggie Rae's sister was as confused as she and her friends were.

Did they know that Maggie Rae was writing erotica? Did they know her husband "hurt" her? It was hard to imagine in this day and age that any woman would put up with that from any man. But human nature was a complicated thing.

All in due time.

Chapter 13

Annie could count on one hand the number of times she was ever in a church—none of which were like this one. She was in awe of the beautiful stained-glass windows—not so much in awe of the crucifixes everywhere, especially the one on the altar, where Jesus looked like he was in excruciating pain. Awful.

She could barely stand to look at Maggie Rae's family and gave up listening to the preacher, whose voice was a monotone in her ear and made her doze off from time to time. She struggled to listen—but she only slept about four hours. Ben was up and down all night long with a cough—and she had gotten in late, to begin with.

It was difficult to set aside Maggie Rae's papers last night. She felt she had to get at least one scrapbook started—little did she know that she would fill the pages and finish one album last night. Annie loved finding the right space on the page for the pictures, figuring out whether or not to crop them, what kind of stickers and paper to use on the page, and so on. It was deeply satisfying, which surprised her.

And she was piecing together a life, as well as learning how to scrapbook. She used all the pictures from Maggie Rae's youth, right up to her wedding—which was three days after college graduation—an English major, of course, mused Annie.

Eight months later, her first baby girl, Grace, was born.

Smart woman, foolish choices. Life-altering mistakes.

Robert was a devastatingly handsome young man. He looked like he stepped right off the pages of *GQ,* for Chrissake. His clothes hung on him just like a model's, clung in the right places, showing off his thin, muscular physique. Those blue eyes, though, held very little emotion. Annie could not read anything in them—even in the wedding pictures. He was smiling, but his eyes looked the same as when he wasn't smiling. Odd.

Most of the evidence she'd read in Maggie's papers had led her to believe he did beat Maggie Rae; that added to the sense of evil she felt emanating from him. At least it was in writing that he hurt her, though the hurt could've taken many forms. She didn't like the way he was touching his daughter as she sat next to him, listening to the preacher. There was something false about his movements. Had he been hurting them, too? Who knows what they had witnessed?

Annie grimaced, remembering the way her mother and father nearly killed each other. She remembered waking up with her brother clinging to her out of fear because they were screaming at each other and throwing things at one another. When they split, it was a relief.

She took her eyes away from the family. It was too painful to watch them. Even though she hardly knew them, she felt like she knew Maggie—she pasted her baby pictures in a scrapbook last night, along with photos from her vacation Bible school, high-school prom and graduation, college graduation, and then wedding. The hallmarks of her young life were captured in one leather scrapbook for her children to have someday to take in and try to glimpse a mother whom they hardly knew. A mother who was so ill that she shot herself—Annie winced. It didn't feel right.

All of those hopes and dreams she had caught a whiff of while gluing Maggie Rae's pictures in the album—she wanted to write, and she did write. She wanted more out of life; that was obvious. Ah, but depression can hit anyone, especially postpartum. Her youngest child was three. Could she have been struggling for at least three years?

Annie remembered the last time she saw Maggie Rae, who was in the yard and waved across the fence. Maggie Rae was smiling. "Beautiful day, isn't it?" she said; then she shyly looked away before taking off after one of her children who had decided to eat dirt.

It was so difficult when two mothers were trying to carry on a conversation—hell, so many were started and never finished. It was the same in her house. What she wouldn't give sometimes just to have an uninterrupted conversation with Mike.

When they were dating, they often talked late into the night. Just talked. That was what she missed even more than the hot sex, she decided, while half listening to the preacher lead a prayer. She felt a sudden desire to get home to her own children and husband. She should feel free—sitting here without them. Instead, she looked at the family, looked at the preacher, and glanced at Bill, Vera's sobbing husband. *Hmm, I didn't know that Bill knew Maggie Rae.*

Of course, how would she? She barely knew either of them. But how would they even know one another? He was a married lawyer, and she was the busy mother of four children? He appeared cold and standoffish. Annie's stomach churned. She didn't like him—and she had yet to even talk to the man.

She leaned over to Vera. "I have to go," she whispered. Vera nodded her head, as if she understood. Annie slipped quietly out of the pew. She kept her eyes focused on the floor, not wanting to know who was looking at her—the "new" woman in town. Just over a year.

Her heart felt like it would explode as she tried to catch her breath outside, walking home. Was she having a heart attack? She felt no pain, though, just a racing heart. She walked quickly past the cars and the horses and buggies in the parking lot. She held on to a fence to steady herself. She closed her eyes and saw the face of Robert Dasher and a chill came over her. A feeling of dread enveloped her—for Robert surely killed his wife, even if he did not pull that trigger.

"Annie?" said a woman's voice.

She opened her eyes. "Yes?"

"Are you okay?" Beatrice asked her.

"I'm fine. A little dizzy or something. That service—"

"Sad, heh?" she said, putting her arm around Annie.

"Bea, you're supposed to be resting."

"I am. I was just on my front porch and I saw you. Won't you come in and get a glass of iced tea?"

Suddenly she realized how very thirsty she was. Annie smiled. "I'd like that very much."

After Annie sat on the wicker chair on Beatrice's front porch, she took a long drink of the sweetest iced tea she'd ever tasted.

"Mmm, that's good," she said, feeling the cold glass in her hands on this warm spring day. What a typical Virginia spring—cold one day, the next it was warm enough to crave a glass of a cold drink.

"A little tea and sugar is a good thing," Beatrice answered. "Now, how are you feeling?"

"Oh," Annie said, waving her hand. "I'm fine. It was just a bit warm in that church."

The two women sat quietly and listened to the birds and the sound of cars in the distance.

"A bit sad, too," Beatrice said, then cleared her throat.

"I can't imagine that she killed herself. Is that what they are still saying?"

Annie nodded. She took another drink of the tea, felt the caffeine and sugar soaring through her veins. "The thing is, I mean . . . last night I read bits of her letters and other papers and found out her husband hurt her. He uses the term 'hurt' in such a way that it would lead you to believe he hit her."

"I don't know why I'm not surprised," Bea said. "Do you think he killed her?"

A pang of panic seared through Annie again. "Murder?"

But that's what this all had been leading up to, hadn't it? Not a suicide, but a murder. A husband killing his wife.

Happens all the time, Annie reminded herself. *Happens all the time.*

"I don't know what's worse," Bea said.

"At least if she had killed herself, we'd know that was what she wanted, as twisted as that sounds."

"We need to be careful. We can't go around accusing people of murder," Bea said in a lowered voice. She took a drink of her tea and smacked her lips together. "What do Vera and the scrapbook queen have to say about your theory?"

"They don't know it. I just came up with it right this minute," she said.

"Sometimes I think my daughter's brains are all in her feet and hips—but it will hit her, if it hasn't already."

"But what about you? Have they found out who stabbed you?"

Beatrice shrugged. "I've not heard a thing. Pretty damn good. I've been going to that grocery store since way before it was a huge Wrigley's. Here I am, eighty years old; and I get stabbed. And here's the thing—I never felt it."

Annie smiled. "That's a blessing, isn't it?"

"Yes. But now, I keep going over and over in my mind

who I saw that day, and the sad thing is, well, I didn't know most of the people in the store that day. It's hard for you to imagine how that makes me feel. I used to know everybody here."

"I barely know anybody here," Annie said. "And I've been here a whole year."

"A year!" Beatrice exclaimed. "How have I missed you, dear?"

Chapter 14

Vera was entranced by the tables of food. One table held a whole Smithfield ham, all pink and sweet smelling, with glistening chunks of pineapple on top of it. Sitting next to the ham was a huge pan of fried chicken, which she hadn't eaten in several years. But she took a plate and piled it high with ham and chicken—and oh, over there was potato salad, which she also needed to taste.

Another table was full of nothing but "salads"—linguine, pasta, potato, coleslaw, carrot-and-raisin, Cobb, cucumber, both vinegar based and sour cream based. Then there were several kinds of Jell-O salads—red, orange, and green.

Oh, that green pistachio Jell-O salad was one of her favorites. It was so light and fluffy. She only wished the soft lime-green color was a bit more appealing. And those Mennonites were always bringing shoofly pies to events. Vera hated it. Once, she had taken a bite of it and had nearly thrown up.

"Thank you for coming," Vera heard a voice behind her say. She turned to face Robert.

"I'm so sorry for your loss, Mr. Dasher—the children, if there's anything I can do," Vera said, fidgeting with her fork, trying to place it on the plate so it wouldn't fall off.

"Well," he said, looking away from her, "there is

something you can do. But we'll talk about it later, if, ah, that's all right."

Vera was immediately uncomfortable as she noted his difficulty making eye contact with her, or even looking at her while he spoke to her. "Shifty" was the word that came to mind as a chill traveled through her.

"Of course," she said. "You know where to find me. Excuse me, please. I see my husband over there . . . ," she said, and tried to slide through the crowd.

"This is my brother-in-law, Zeb McClain," Robert went on as if he hadn't heard her.

Socially inept.

"Nice to meet you, Mr. McClain." She turned to him and shook his hand, big and calloused. He was dressed in a variation of Old Order Mennonite clothing—a dark plain suit—his funeral clothes, Sunday best? Interestingly, even though he wore the beard with no mustache, which she found extremely unattractive, he was perhaps the prettiest man she'd ever laid her eyes on. His blue eyes were framed with long, dark eyelashes, and his features were chiseled in a face that was set off by a strong, almost square jawline and a beautiful dimple in his chin, as well as around his full mouth.

Very John Travolta-ish, she mused, making a mental note to find out more about this man. Who were his people? He didn't look local at all.

Vera made her way over to her husband. Bill was standing with Sheila and her husband, who both held plates of vegetable dishes—broccoli with cheese, scalloped potatoes, green beans, and deep purple pickled beets. Bill was in hog heaven, for he was already on to the desserts and eating apple crumble when Vera entered the circle.

"I saw you talking with Robert," Bill said, with an edge to his slightly raised voice. He was sweating profusely and was taking his handkerchief to his head. His eyes were red and puffy from the weeping at the service.

"Yes," Vera said. "He's a strange man."

"What do you mean?"

"Mmm. These beets are delicious," Sheila said. Her lips were stained with a slight beet color.

"I'll tell you more when we get home," Vera quickly said, trying to shake the weird feeling Robert had given her. She attempted to focus on her food.

"Yes," Sheila said, "I'll tell you as well."

Steve grinned and lifted his eyebrows. "It sounds so mysterious."

"It's mysterious and sad all at once," Vera said. "Oh, look! Someone brought red velvet cake. Think I'll go and get some."

"I'll come with you," Sheila said. They left their men standing together, as they often did during any special occasion. These two men could not have been any more different. There was Bill and his highbrow, Ivy League, Yankee sensibilities, and Steve, a good old native boy who'd done well in his family's tractor and outdoor sporting-goods business. He'd come up with a mountain-touring idea and branched the company into an expedition group. He often was gone for days leading a group of city folks into the mountain wilderness—all outfitted with goods from his own store.

For all intents and purposes, Vera thought, Bill was the perfect husband—always kind and polite, cleaned up after himself, and he was an attentive lover, for which she had always been grateful. But lately she just didn't want to be bothered. Sex was more trouble than it was worth—so more often than not, she told him no. She explained that she was tired, or not feeling good. And he would never question her. But sometimes the thought of making love with him absolutely just filled her with dread.

"Listen," Sheila said as they were getting their red velvet cake. "I've been thinking."

"Uh-oh," Vera said. "Do I even want to know?" She slid the slice of the cake onto her plate.

Sheila grabbed her by the arm and pulled her into a corner. "Do you know if there was a suicide note?"

"I think I heard someone say that there wasn't, but I'm not sure."

Sheila's voice lowered. "Do you really think she killed herself?"

Vera's heart skipped a beat. "Well, of course, that's what they listed the cause of death as—a self-inflicted gunshot wound to the chest."

Sheila looked at Vera and shook her head. "Think about it. Look around you. We are in her home. Does this place say depressed to you?"

The walls were filled with pictures of her children and one of her parents—maybe that was a grandmother in that old-fashioned round gold frame. But Vera knew that held no meaning if the woman was struggling with depression. It was a chemistry thing in the body—out of whack. The walls were painted bright colors—light blue, almost the shade of the mountains, and sage green in the kitchen. It was kept well—everything in the house was sparkling clean, even the windows.

The green plaid couch and matching chair were a little worn, Vera noticed, but with such a large family, it was entirely excusable. The afghan throw over the back of the couch made Vera sad. Was that what Maggie Rae wrapped around herself while watching television? Or did she wrap it around the children as they dozed off beside her? With all of the children in the house, Maggie Rae probably didn't get much TV time. Still, at the same time, Vera liked to imagine the comfort Maggie Rae might have found beneath that handmade afghan.

"What does depressed look like?" Vera asked.

"Not this," Sheila said, looking very solemn in her black suit. "Look at those plants. She tended them well, even in the midst of having all these children. Look at the beautiful paintings and the lovely drapes."

"Yet, she never filled her scrapbooks," Vera reminded her. "What was that about?"

Sheila shrugged. Vera caught the glare off her tiny rhinestone pin. "Could be she just never had time. But some people are reluctant to put lives onto paper. It can be painful. I went to this session at one of the scrapbook conferences where the teacher talked about the therapeutic nature of scrapbooking. For some people, it's just what they need. For others, it's way too much to really look at."

"And you paid to hear someone tell you that? Honestly, Sheila," Vera chided.

"Sometimes you're just a bitch," Sheila told her, shaking her head.

"I may be a bitch, but I work too hard for my money to go and pay for a pop psychologist to charge me to tell me about the psychological aspect to a hobby. For God's sake. Some people just sap all the fun out of everything," Vera said, taking a bite of the cake.

"Now, listen, I've thought about going and getting the certificate." Sheila's expression became serious. Her jaw clenched and her brown eyes filled with a surge of confidence.

"What? A certificate in what?"

"Therapeutic scrapbooking. It's a form of bibliotherapy," Sheila told her. "It might be a rewarding thing to do."

Vera rolled her heavily lined blue eyes.

"You know, you set up these groups of, say, women who've been abused—"

Vera's eyes met Sheila's. "He killed her, didn't he?" she whispered frantically. "He killed Maggie Rae. My mother always told me that a man who beats a woman would just as soon kill her."

Sheila turned her back on the crowd. "I think . . . you may be right. So what do we do now?"

"I need some air," Vera said, moving toward the door, with Sheila trailing behind her.

The fresh air, while it helped her to breathe, did not prevent the dizziness that overtook her. The columns on the porch looked wobbly and things appeared to be closing in—and then Vera dropped to the wooden porch floor.

"Vera!" she heard before the dark.

Chapter 15

Annie and Bea sat on the porch for a while, watching the hummingbirds and the feeder.

"They are marvelous," Annie said. "I've never seen them anywhere around my place."

"You have to plant some special flowers, and those feeders help," Bea told her. "I love to watch them. It's gotten to be quite a pastime for me."

"Funny," Annie said. "I never have time for a pastime."

"Children keep you busy, but that will change," Bea said. "I just love the beautiful blue color of that bird— I think that one is a male."

"It would figure, wouldn't it?" She was thinking about Robert and Bill, both, for some odd reason.

"Here's what I've been thinking," said Bea. "If we go to the police and they arrest the man for murder, what would happen to those children?"

"Well, I don't know," Annie replied, "but they do have an aunt. She brought them to the park the other day. Maybe she'd take them. Although she seemed, I don't know, like an odd woman. But we can't let him get away with murder—if indeed that's what happened."

"And then," Bea said, placing her glass on a small

wicker table, "I wonder if the police already suspect him. I mean, here we are a bunch of women who aren't police, and we are already concluding that he killed her."

"We have evidence that he probably beat her. They don't, or at least not that we know of," Annie replied.

"If you go to the police with that evidence, you'll have to tell them how you got it," Beatrice said, grinning.

Annie laughed. "Yes, I know. But I'm not too worried about that."

"What are you worried about, Annie?"

"Well," she replied. "There are things that might come up about Maggie Rae that she or her family would not appreciate."

"Like what?" Bea's heavy lids raised up with her eyebrows, revealing penetrating grayish blue eyes.

"Like that she wrote erotica, under another name."

"Oh."

"And, quite honestly, I think this town would have a field day with something like that."

"What do you mean?"

"I mean, once people find out about that, then Maggie Rae's murder may be justified. You know, they will say she was a loose woman and got what she deserved."

Beatrice thought for a moment. "I'd like to say you're wrong, but you may be right. I'm sitting here right now and wondering what kind of a woman writes that trash— not that I think she'd deserve to be killed for it."

"I didn't know her—but she was a beautiful writer and her erotica was good. I mean, it wasn't trashy, you know? The stories are fabulous, even without the sex."

"Like a D. H. Lawrence or an Anaïs Nin, you mean."

"Yes. Well crafted."

"Lawrence is one of my favorite writers. He was one of Ed's favorites, too. Oh, my husband loved to read. I still have some of his books."

"I heard he was a doctor."

"Yes, a fine physician. He practiced right out of this

house. We lived upstairs and he practiced downstairs. It worked out, especially after Vera was born. Sometimes I spent days in Charlottesville at the university and I often traveled to New York, and Ed was able to manage."

"Most women your age didn't have much of a career, I imagine. What did you do?"

"I was a physicist. For many years, I was a practicing researcher. Then I began to be enamored by quantum physics and have been studying it ever since."

"Quantum physics?"

"Yes. Space and time. Matter and energy. Our roles in creating our own reality. Fascinating stuff," Beatrice said. She loved to watch the reaction on people's faces when she told them she studied quantum physics.

"Oh, yes," Annie said, without flinching or seeming surprised. "I recently read a book about that, and I've seen a movie, kind of an odd movie, called *The Life of Quantum Mechanics*. Do you know it?"

Beatrice's mouth dropped open. "Y-yes."

"I really liked it," Annie went on. "I liked the ideas behind it. I'm not sure I understand it or believe it completely, you know."

"Well," Beatrice said, thinking she and Annie were going to be great friends, "many of my students were interviewed for that film."

"Very cool," Annie said.

"Indeed," Beatrice replied. "I've got quite a quantum physics library inside, if you'd care to take a look."

"Oh, sure," Annie said. "But I was sort of expecting some D. H. Lawrence."

Beatrice giggled. "Oh, we've got plenty of that, too."

Just as they got out of their chairs, an ambulance whizzed by and stopped in front of the Dasher home.

"Now, that's odd," Bea said. "An ambulance at a memorial reception."

They stood motionless, watching the red lights, straining to see the crowd gathering around the ambulance.

"Oh, well, guess we'll hear about it soon enough," Bea said. "C'mon in."

Annie's eyes lit up when she saw the built-in bookcases in the library. Bea watched as Annie's long fingers touched the backs of her beautiful books—many of them she had shared with Ed. Bea noticed Annie's nails were cut short, and they were clean. This woman didn't have time to paint her nails. Her hair was loosely contained in a bun gathered at the back of her neck. All business, Bea mused. Yet, she was a stay-at-home mom and gave up a career as a reporter to be a full-time mother. Well, that was according to Vera.

"So you used to be a reporter."

"Yes," Annie said, obviously mesmerized by the books in front of her. "I freelanced for a while, but it just got to be too difficult after Ben was born."

"So you stopped writing?"

Annie looked at her. "For now. I can't seem to manage to put sentences together. But someday I hope to get back to writing."

Interesting young woman, who seemed to have intellect, yet put her kids first. She had a handle on time—that there would be enough of it someday for her to write.

"I hope you do," Beatrice said. "Oh, that's a good book, really. Don't let the title put you off."

Annie laughed. "*Quantum Physics for Dummies,* eh? I like it."

An ambulance flew down the road again, its sirens interrupting a perfectly good conversation.

Then they heard a strange scuffling noise—someone was on the porch. Beatrice opened the door to a winded Sheila, in her stocking feet, with her high heels in her hand.

Chapter 16

Vera was dreaming. She was certain of it. She was sitting on her father's lap, just the way she used to, even as a grown woman. She could feel his arms around her, smell his tobacco, and feel his breath on her neck as she leaned her head down on his shoulder.

"Vera," he said. *"You're not happy. Time is wasting."*

"What do you mean, Daddy?" She wanted to pick up her head, but she was so tired and couldn't manage.

He ran his fingers through her hair and against her forehead. *"Oh, Vera, I wasn't ready to leave you or your mother. And you weren't ready to leave New York."*

"What else could I do?"

"You can't go backward, only forward. Find out what makes you happy now."

She thought about her mother, Sheila, her dancing school, and Bill. None of it seemed to make her happy. In fact, when she thought about the people in her life, she sort of went numb. It wasn't just Bill. It was everybody.

"That's what I mean," her father said. *"Believe me when I tell you, every day is a gift. Don't waste it."*

"Oh, Daddy, I'm not. I'm making a difference here."

* * *

"Forty-one years old and pregnant?" No, it wasn't her father speaking. She struggled to open her eyes. It was a blurry Bill, talking with that same handsome doctor who had operated on her mother.

"Yes," the doctor said. "Vera is pregnant."

Vera thought she was still dreaming and closed her eyes. She could hear voices as she drifted back off to a place that wasn't quite sleep. "Daddy," she said out loud. "Daddy?"

"Vera, are you awake?" Bill rushed to her side and kissed her on the cheek. Tears glistened in his eyes. She nodded. "God, you gave us a scare," he said, voice quavering.

Just then, she could hear her mother's voice.

"Goddamn you, get out of my way! My daughter is in that room," she bellowed. Vera wanted to close her eyes again and now hoped that she was dreaming. But the door flew open.

"Bill, what's going on?" Bea asked, with Annie at her side. Sheila came in on their heels, still carrying her high heels from the memorial service.

"Calm down, Beatrice," Bill said calmly. "She's fine."

"Yes," Vera said weakly, smiling at the crowd of women gathering around her bed.

"You don't pass out if you're fine," Sheila said. "I'm no doctor," she said, looking at the doctor, "but I know that."

He raised his eyebrows, as if to say, *You again?*

"Excuse me, please," he said, and left the room.

"Well, she has a point," Beatrice said.

"Sit down, Beatrice," Bill said, pulling up a chair, close to Vera's bed. "You're going to need to."

"What do you mean?" she asked, slowly sitting in the chair.

"I wanted to give Vera the news alone, you know like all couples at a time like this. But since the day I married her, I knew you two came in a package," he said, looking at Bea and Sheila. "So I want you all to know that Vera and I are expecting a baby."

"That's impossible," Vera said, her heart beginning to race.

"That's what we thought, but that's why you fainted. You're eight weeks pregnant."

"Hot damn," Beatrice finally said. "I'm going to be a grandmother."

Sheila squealed, and Annie's hands went to her mouth.

Bill's eyes caught Vera's. It was a moment of connection, a moment of acknowledgment. They would set their past right. They would have this child. A botched abortion in the Bronx had left Vera with problems her whole life—problems that they said could never be overcome.

She wasn't ready to be a mother, she had told Bill all of those years ago.

"But we can do it. We'll get married and I'll graduate in two semesters. I'll pass the bar," he said to her.

"Bill, I love you. I truly do, but I'm not ready to get married and have a baby. I've been working my whole life to be here and work as a dancer. I can't do this right now," Vera told him.

What she hadn't told him was that it was only a fifty-fifty chance that he was the father. She had met a dancer from Brooklyn during her last show, and Tony was long gone by the time she knew she was pregnant. He was on the road with a Broadway show. He called her a few times and sent a couple of scorching letters.

She and Bill had been going steady for years when she met Tony. From the minute she saw his huge, deep brown eyes, she knew she wanted to sleep with him, but she would not admit that to herself. It was the late 1980s, and she was in the thick of the arts and dance communities. Even though sex was everywhere—she had only slept with Bill. She always believed sex was part of love. It was the Southern good girl in her. She could never shake it. As much as she wanted to be young, hip, and loose, she was who she was. So love came with sex.

But love had nothing to do with the way she felt about Tony. It was as if something reached inside her and made her insides twist. When they were partnered for a very sensual dance, every move was like torture. He held her hand and she felt sparks. He touched her hip and she just wanted to wrap her strong legs around him. When their eyes met, her heart leaped—just like in the romance novels she used to read. When he smiled, showing off deep dimples, it hurt so much that she sometimes could not look at him. When she leaned against him one night—they were all alone in the studio and it was late— she felt his erection. And there was no denying it. She reached up and touched his dark hair, which was soft, even though it was wet with sweat.

"Tony—"

"From the minute we touched, I felt something. Did you?" he asked breathlessly.

She nodded her head. She was sweating and her heart was racing. They had been dancing all night. But as he lifted her to him and lodged her against the wall, her legs automatically found their place around him. Effortless. Sublime.

There was a reason they were partnered in the show— their bodies suited one another's. And as they found out that night, no partnering could have ever been more sweet.

As she looked into her husband's eyes now, she wished she could dwell in the comfort of knowing she had made the right choice. She touched his face, now streaming with tears. "Oh, Bill," she said. Suddenly she realized everybody else had left the room, including her mother. He was the one she chose; the one who chose her. She made a life with him and never really regretted it, but she sometimes longed for the abandon she had felt in Tony's arms. And now she would be blessed with a child. It was the child she should have had years ago.

Chapter 17

Ben and Sam were running around in the front yard with no clothes on. Completely naked. Annie couldn't help but laugh as she saw her husband chasing them around the yard. He wielded a huge water pistol, which was squirting them.

"Ahh," he said, noticing her at the gate. "Finally. Help!" He fell down on the grass and the boys pounced on him.

Annie opened the gate and jumped on her boys, rolling over the grass.

"Mommy! Mommy!" She smiled, feeling the cool grass on her skin. It had been quite a day. The memorial service, almost passing out, visiting with Beatrice, and then heading to the hospital to see a pregnant Vera.

"Who's hungry?" she said to them. Of course, they all were.

They started to file into the house, and Mike grabbed her, kissed her, and patted her on the behind. "I missed you," he said.

"I bet," she said. "It's been all of four hours, Mike. And I've had a day and a half."

"Really? I saw an ambulance and wondered about that."

"It was Vera. She passed out at the reception. It turns

out she's pregnant. Quite the miracle story," she said,
with her eyes meeting Mike's. Having babies still felt
like a privilege to them—whereas so many of their
friends just took it in stride.

It took Annie and Mike years of trying to get pregnant.
Finally, after a diagnosis and treatment of endometriosis,
Annie became pregnant, only to suffer a series of miscar-
riages. Finally her Sam was born. Such a blessing to carry
him to term—and she wished for the same joy for Vera.

"And I also chatted for a while with Vera's mom. You
know, the woman who owns that beautiful pink-and-blue
Victorian house? We sat out in her garden. Speaking of
gardens, I'd like to plant one."

"What? What kind of garden?"

"A hummingbird garden. We sat and watched them on
her porch. It was fascinating. Oh, and she lent me this
book," she said, and held up the book as they walked into
the house. She glanced around her home and looked at
her husband. "Quite a day, huh?"

Clothes and toys were scattered all over the living
room, and dishes were piled in the sink—why not the
dishwasher? It was less than a foot from the sink.

Mike looked at her sheepishly. "I wanted to spend
time with the boys," he said. "I'm sorry I didn't pick up,
but we had good quality time together."

Annie wanted to scream. Did he not think she had
good quality time together with the boys? How did he
think the dishes got into the dishwasher? The towels got
folded and put away? She managed to do that stuff when
they were napping or eating or in front of the television.
It took careful maneuvering.

She took a deep breath. "I'll get supper as soon as I
clean up the kitchen a bit," she said flatly, and left Mike
standing in the living room.

"C'mon, boys," she heard him say. "We need to pick
up these clothes and toys."

Why did she have to get angry in order to force him into action?

She started running water over the cereal bowls, with bits and pieces of cereal already hardened on them, and the sippy cups, smelling like grape juice. Sweet, sickening smell, she thought. And the stickiness drove her mad. After she placed the dishes in the dishwasher, she looked out the window.

Yes, that's where I'll plant my hummingbird garden, in that corner. Just a small space at first. Nasturtiums along the fence. Foxgloves. Cosmos.

What else did Bea tell her? Dahlia. Oh, yes, Annie loved dahlias. She thought she'd get some red dahlias if she could find them. A bright little red feeder in the middle of it all.

"Annie, I wanted to tell you that I enjoyed looking at that scrapbook," Mike said as he brought in more dishes and handed them to her. She stopped herself from rolling her eyes. "Dishwasher," she said, pointing to it.

"Oh, yeah," he said, and smiled weakly. "But you're standing right there."

"So are you, Mike," she said.

"Well, okay," he said, and put the dishes in the dishwasher. "Ta-Da! There."

"So," she said, ignoring his sarcasm, leaning on the kitchen sink, "you liked the scrapbook."

"Yes, I thought you did a great job on it. I liked the way you tore off pieces of postcards that related to the things in her book. The wedding journal entry was a classic, eh?"

"Yes, sort of heartbreaking, considering that her husband probably beat her," she said, turning to fill a pan with water.

Spaghetti, she thought, *is going to be my savior tonight. Everybody will eat it. It's easy to make, and it will go really well with the bottle of wine I'm going to down.*

"She had to know that before she married him," he said.

"I dunno. You'd think so, wouldn't you? They were married right out of college. She was probably already pregnant."

"Aha," he said.

"Maybe it all just happened after they were married, living in the same place together, with all of the stresses of—" she began to share her observations, but was interrupted by a knock on the door. The boys ran, giggling, to the door. They hardly ever received company.

When Annie and Mike came to the door, a stranger awaited, wearing a sharp dark-blue suit. Had Annie seen him at the memorial service? He held up a police badge.

"Good afternoon, I'm Detective Adam Bryant. May I come in?"

Chapter 18

When Annie told the Cumberland Creek scrapbookers that Detective Bryant was coming to the next crop, they decided to meet a little earlier than usual. Sheila ordered Chinese and they skipped out on dinner at home.

"Now, can someone fill me in on what happened at the reception? I mean, all I remember is talking about murder, feeling like I needed fresh air, and then nothing," Vera said.

"Murder?" DeeAnn said, placing her plastic fork down.

Sheila grimaced. And the women looked at one another.

"You and your big mouth," Sheila said under her breath, brushing a noodle from her burgundy Virginia Tech sweatshirt.

"Sheila?" Annie said.

"It's all right. You should hear the way she talks to me sometimes. God knows why I put up with her," Vera said, smoothing over her place mat.

"Don't try to change the subject," DeeAnn said. "What's going on?"

"It's just that after we found out that Maggie Rae's

husband hurt her, we wondered if he more than hurt her, you know?" Vera said.

"It's a long way from beating to killing—if he, indeed, beat her. Hurting could mean anything," Paige said.

"Is it a long way?" Sheila wondered. "Can you pass me the fried noodles, please?"

They sat in silence eating their Chinese food when Detective Bryant rang the doorbell. Sheila glanced at her watch. "He's not supposed to be here yet."

"We have nothing to hide. Just let him in," Vera said.

Greetings exchanged, the detective walked into the room filled with pretty scrapbooking doodads, paper, and food. He was a large man, tall, about six-five, and broad at the shoulders, narrow at the hips. He was manly-looking enough to look out of place in this group of women, who were all looking at him—a decent-looking, clean-shaven man in a blue suit, with eyes to match. Shoes polished to a shine. Spiffy. Maybe an ex-military man? Hadn't Vera seen him at the funeral?

"I'm Detective Adam Bryant," he said, flashing his badge. "I just have a few questions for you. Now, what's going on here?" He gestured at the table.

Vera cleared her throat. "Dinner," she said, smiling. "Would you like some?"

"No thanks. Let's cut to the chase, shall we?" he said, smiling politely, revealing one deep dimple on the left side of his mouth.

"He knows everything," Annie said. "One of the family members saw us taking the scrapbooks."

"Well, now, if that don't beat all," Sheila said, setting down her fork. "Saw us taking the scrapbooks, yet never said a word. That's how much it meant to them!"

"And you are?" he said to her as he held up his recorder in her direction.

"Sheila Rogers. I own Creative Scrapbooking, where Maggie Rae bought those supplies from. We saw the boxes on the street for the trashman and we took them.

If that's illegal, then I'm sorry. We just wanted to make some scrapbooks for her family!"

"Calm down, Sheila," Vera said, touching her arm. "Please sit down, Detective."

He pulled up a chair and glanced around at the stacks of scrapbooking materials.

"Well, now," the detective said, lifting one of his eyebrows. "I'm not so much interested in you ladies stealing the trash as I am in what's actually in her stuff, and what you are doing with it."

Annie cleared her throat. "I've made a folder for you of her letters, notes, and other personal papers. I'd like it back at some point, if it's possible. There may be things I can use in her scrapbooks."

"Thanks, Mrs. Chamovitz," he said. "And what about the rest? The photos?"

Vera shrugged. "I've already finished a dance scrapbook for Grace. Annie's finished one about Maggie Rae, and the others are almost done, too. We're making scrapbooks to give her children. Her papers just happened to be in the pile of stuff waiting for the trash—later, the very same day she died, I might add."

"Bastard," Sheila said.

The detective lurched backward, eyebrows shot up. He folded his arms. "Such strong language, Ms. Rogers."

"I think he killed her," Sheila said.

"Now, wait a minute. You're making a lot of assumptions," Detective Bryant said. "Dangerous assumptions."

"But it does seem suspicious," Annie said. "Why would he get rid of that stuff the day she died? That's odd."

"If he actually killed her, it would be an incredibly stupid move on his part," Bryant said.

"Could you pass me the duck sauce, please?" Vera asked. "Robert doesn't strike me as being very bright."

Sheila rolled her eyes. "I know what you mean."

The detective crossed his arms.

"That's a mean thing to say. The man is obviously grieving," DeeAnn said, glancing at Bryant and smiling.

"Maybe," Vera said. "Maybe that's it. But he gave me a weird feeling. I don't know. He's just odd."

"Hmm," Bryant said, leaning forward. "How well do you know him?"

"I don't know him at all. He never came into the studio or came to any of the recitals," she told him. "I've gotten to know many of the other fathers, but not him. The first time we spoke was at the reception."

"Still, just because we think he hit her, and he is a bit strange," Annie began, "I mean . . . to actually kill her?"

Chills crept up Vera's back. She felt the blood drain from her face. "You know," she said, "I just remembered something. On the night before Maggie Rae supposedly killed herself, she called the dance studio to set up an appointment to talk to me about the youngest daughter taking dance class. I thought it was odd, because a woman who's planning to kill herself probably wouldn't be doing that."

"That may be true," Bryant said. "But everything is fine sometimes and then one thing happens to set a depressed person off, you know? Did you happen to save that message?"

"I think so. Come down to the studio anytime," Vera said.

"I think you need to be careful, ladies," Bryant said. "Nobody's talking about a murder investigation. People don't like being accused of murder." Just then, his beeper went off. "Excuse me, ladies. I'm sorry," he said, getting up from the table. "I need to get going. Thanks for the information, ladies." He held up the envelope and walked toward the door. "I'll be seeing you around."

"Good Lord," DeeAnn said after he left. "I hope so. What a man to feast your eyes upon."

"DeeAnn! Really," Sheila said, then laughed.

Chapter 19

Vera sat back on her couch and took another sip of her decaf. Damn, she already missed coffee, but she was determined to eat and drink what was best for her unborn baby. Her mind sifted through the possibilities this child brought to her and Bill. Was it true that babies brought couples closer together? Was it true that pregnant women craved strange food, and their husbands hunted down whatever they wanted at all hours of the night? Was it true that pregnant women couldn't get enough sex?

She smiled as she heard Bill coming down the stairs.

"Morning," he grumbled. "Coffee?"

"Yes, but it's decaf. I can make you some," she said, picking up the paper to read more about Maggie Rae's husband, Robert Dasher, who evidently was a person of interest in what was now a murder investigation.

"Don't worry about it," he said, leaned over, and kissed her forehead. "I'll get it."

She loved the way he looked in the morning, unshaven and unkempt. His stubble now as much gray as brown, and with a little bit of a double chin since he'd gained a bit of weight and was working on quite the beer belly. It took at least a cup of strong coffee for him to get that spark she loved into his green eyes.

She heard him scrambling around in the kitchen as she read over the newspaper. He was emptying out the leftover coffee from the decanter, putting the pot back in its place; now he was pitching the grounds and scooping in new coffee. God, could she smell that from here? It seemed as if all of her senses were heightened with this pregnancy.

Her attention snapped back to the newspaper. She skipped to the part about Robert:

> *Thirty-two-year-old Robert Dasher, Maggie Rae's husband, has a history of domestic violence. He is currently not an official suspect in the case. According to statistics on murder cases within the home, the partner is usually the first suspect.*
>
> *Dasher, a former long-distance runner, holding statewide titles, works as an accountant for Brett & Hughes. A spokesperson for the company said he is a model employee, rarely missing a day's work.*

"According to the Cumberland Creek Police Department, Dasher was questioned and let go," Vera said out loud as Bill entered the room with a steaming cup of coffee in his hands, his fingers curled through the blue handle.

"For what?" Bill said, spilling his coffee as he set it down on the table. "Damn. I'll be right back." He went off to get a towel.

"They are now saying that Maggie Rae's death was a murder, not a suicide," she said, raising her voice as he left the room.

"Murder?" he said, cleaning up the spill. "Really?"

His eyes were suddenly bigger and brighter. It was the lawyer in him, she supposed, excited about the possibility of a murder case in their sleepy little town.

"And—and did you say they let Robert go?" he asked, stuttering.

Goodness, he is excited.

"They have no evidence to hold him, I suppose. They are calling him a 'person of interest' and they mention several other 'persons of interest.'"

"Did they, um, mention any names?"

"Only two, but they claim there are more. Local resident Leo Shirley and Maggie Rae's brother-in-law, Zeb. Do you remember him? He was at the funeral."

"Kind of. Usually in these cases, it is the husband," he said, sitting down in his favorite overstuffed chair. He lifted his coffee to his lips.

Is that a tremor in his hands?

He set his cup down on the table beside him, then took the remote in his hand, flipping on the television.

Soon Vera would leave the room because she couldn't stand to watch television with her husband. His constant flipping of the channels drove her to distraction—it was almost like fingernails screeching across a blackboard.

"You seem excited," Vera said.

"Now that they know it wasn't a suicide and are saying it's a murder, it is exciting, " he said after taking another sip of his steaming black coffee.

"They'll find evidence, I bet," he said. "He's a strange guy, don't you think?"

"I don't know," she said. "He does seem odd. Maybe just very different from the men around here."

"I bet he did it," he said after a few minutes. "Just a feeling."

Vera believed in the justice system and had absolute confidence that both the killer of Maggie Rae and the person who stabbed Bea would be brought to justice. So her thoughts already moved on to what colors she was going to use in the nursery. She noted, however, that Bill seemed to be taking quite an interest in this case. Maybe he'd offer to take up Robert's defense.

"I'd like to start fixing up the extra room for the baby," she said. "I'm thinking we should paint the walls yellow. Um, I don't know. Maybe purple? But whatever we choose, we need to be careful of what kind of paint we use. You know, some of it emits harmful gases for a baby to breathe, so we need to be careful."

Bill looked at her. "I'm leaving that all up to you, darling. I trust you to take care of it." He turned back to the television.

"I'm going to need your help," she said.

"What?" he said, clearly not paying attention. He smoothed what hair he had left down onto his head. "I'm sorry. I was trying to watch the news."

"I said I'm going to need your help, Bill," Vera said.

"Oh, sure, just let me know what you want done and when," he said, smiling at her.

"I better get dressed. I've got a class this morning."

As she walked up the stairs, she stopped momentarily to watch the weather, caught a glimpse of her husband biting his lip—a habit he only indulged in when he was worried.

Is he worried about the baby? About Maggie Rae's husband? About what?

After brushing her hair thoroughly and placing a headband on it to keep the bangs off her face, Vera smeared red lipstick from corner to corner of her mouth. Then she took a sideways glance at herself in her full-length bedroom mirror. Of course, she was being silly. She wouldn't be showing yet. But soon. She couldn't wait for that beautiful baby bump to appear. Everybody would know she was going to be a mom. Finally. A mom.

Suddenly Bill was behind her, his arms wrapped around her.

"We are going to be parents," he said quietly.

They looked at themselves in the mirror. Bill's thin lips kissed the nape of her neck, sending shivers through her. His kisses were as light and soft as rose petals brushing her skin. He held her tighter in his arms, placing his chin on her shoulder.

"I, ah, have a little time to spare this morning. Do you?"

The doorbell rang, intruding on their Monday.

"I'll get it," he said. "You stay right there."

Vera sat on the edge of the bed and began to disrobe. She heard the muffled voices of men. "Detective Bryant," she had heard that. Those Cumberland Creek police just couldn't leave her lawyer husband alone sometimes.

Chapter 20

Annie placed another picture of Ben in the scrapbook on her kitchen table. The boys were fed and watching *Sesame Street,* and all that she could think about was the potential murder case. She needed to think about something else, so she started working on her scrapbooks.

Even if Robert Dasher wasn't an official suspect, the police talked to him, along with a few other men. That was enough, she knew, for the police to start investigating his background in earnest. And, unfortunately, in a town like Cumberland Creek, it was more than enough to start the rumor mill going. Three phone calls came for her already this morning—one from DeeAnn, one from Paige, and one from Sheila.

"I really think he did it," Sheila said. "He gives me weird vibes. Imagine, your own husband killing you. What must her last thought have been? Oh, I just can't think about it."

Annie didn't know what to think. She hated to jump to conclusions. But at the same time, she had been reading Maggie Rae's own letters and cards. The way he "hurt" her was just a part of it. Their relationship was full of tension—it appeared that way right from the start.

Countless apology letters from Robert were stacked up in the box—definitely a part of an abuse cycle.

In one of his early notes, he mentioned that he knew her family was not keen on him—they didn't know his people. He was Unitarian, and to their way of thinking, he thought a little too highly of himself: *We've overcome that. Don't let them tear us apart.*

Annie pasted the picture of Ben in the bathtub on the page, which was decorated with bubble stickers and a piece of journal paper, where Annie wrote about Ben and his baths—the way he always hated them and cried and sobbed through the whole thing. So different from his brother.

And that was one of the shocking things about having a second child—often he or she was nothing like the first one. They were their own little people right from the start.

Annie and her brother, Josh, were different—he was always much more studious and quiet. She was gregarious and popular. Maggie Rae and her sister were different, too.

Annie remembered a note written on the back of a picture of Maggie Rae and Tina Sue: *"I sometimes wish I could be good as Tina Sue. More pious."* Sometimes Annie felt that way about a couple of her cousins whose family was Orthodox—but never felt bad enough to really investigate that part of her faith further.

"Mommy!" Sam's voice called in from the living room. "Potty!"

Annie ran into the living room, where Ben had just peed in the potty chair.

"Yay!" she said, and Sam patted his little brother on the back. "What a big boy!" Oh, wouldn't it be great to have two boys out of diapers completely? She was so tired of changing diapers—not to mention the expense, and having to drag around the damn diaper bag everywhere she went.

Annie cleaned up after it and sat down in front of the computer. She turned it on and clicked on the icon for the Internet. "Hmm. Let's look up Robert Dasher."

Robert Dasher was a runner and that was clearly documented—so many titles and interesting "running" photos where you could barely recognize him because of the contortions of his face.

There was an honor he received from his employer, the Employee of the Year Award. *Wow. That's interesting.*

"Mommy! Potty!"

Annie's heart leaped. So quickly . . . again? She ran into the living room—the scent greeting her first. Her hands went to her mouth and nose. Both of her boys were covered in it.

Chapter 21

"So they think it's her husband, huh?" Rose said when Beatrice picked up her phone.

"What the hell are you talking about?"

"Such a foul mouth on you, Beatrice Matthews," Rose, her cousin, said.

"It can get even raunchier. Push my buttons," she said, laughing. "Now, what are you all up in arms about this morning?"

"Have you read the paper?"

"Not yet. I just got up and am having my breakfast. I try to wait until after I eat to read that lousy paper."

"The police are questioning young Robert Dasher about his wife's murder," she said.

"Well, well, well," Beatrice said, sitting down. "It's true then. They think she was murdered."

"Heavens, yes. You knew that, didn't you? If she shot herself, she wouldn't still be holding on to the gun like that—and in her right hand, yet."

"She was left-handed?"

"That's what it says in the paper."

"What's the world coming to?"

"It's always been like this. Where've you been? Remember the Jackson family? Oh, now, that was a horrible thing."

Just thinking about the Jacksons made Beatrice's stomach churn, and she swore she felt a chill travel up her spine. Rose and Beatrice had found them—the young lovers, killed by the girl's father. Rose and Beatrice had been only thirteen or fourteen years old. They were wandering through the woods, looking for the orange conelike morel mushroom, which grew on the ridge overlooking the creek, underneath a dense patch of oaks. They had been singing a spiritual, "I'll Fly Away."

Between the thick shadows and pockets of mist in the mountains, the girls were used to their eyes playing tricks on them—or thinking they saw something that wasn't really visible. A shadow could look like a bear or a witch or the Grim Reaper. So when they saw the shadow of a human foot, they had noted it but kept walking—but when they saw the booted foot sticking up from a tree trunk, they dropped their half-full baskets and went running to find their mothers.

"What is wrong with men?" Rose said suddenly into the phone.

"Stupid, I guess," Beatrice said, and chuckled. "But I loved mine."

"Yours was a good one," Rose said. "Mine? Well, that's another story for another day. So what do you think of this Dasher fella?"

"I don't know him," Beatrice said. "But they say he beat her. A man who beats his woman would just as soon kill her."

"Unless she kills him first," Rose said quietly.

"You did what you had to do," Beatrice said. They had been over this several times throughout the years.

"I wish things were different," Rose said. "I didn't mean to kill him. Just meant to defend myself."

Beatrice kept her thoughts to herself—but if ever a man deserved to die by the hand of his wife, it was Samuel. Everybody knew that—even the local sheriff and coroner. "Official" cause of death? *Accident.*

"I know, darling," Beatrice said.

"I had a dream about him the other night. Bastard's still in my dreams. He mentioned the legend to me. You know the one about the woman lost in time. She walks the mountains, lives in the caves, eats the earth, drinks the air."

"And suffers great sorrows."

"I'd like to know more about this time business, Ms. Quantum Physicist."

Beatrice cackled. "Me too. But it is true that the caves are in geographic alignment with other places on the planet that are supposed to be 'magic.'"

"Odd, isn't it? I mean, I'm sure that story is older than the hills, and for us to find out that part of the legend is true, well, it makes you wonder about the other parts."

"I don't know, Rose. I'm fairly sure nobody is walking through time. We've yet to figure that out. They've been successful experimenting with some animals, but people? It's just too dangerous to try right now, until we have a few more things figured out, like what happens at the cellular level when time travel occurs."

"Jesus. I'm sorry I brought it up," Rose said, and laughed. "Now, I better go. But be careful. Watch out for that Robert character."

"He's a skinny bag of bones. I can take him."

"I'd think your gun would be more useful than your fists."

"Depends on who you talk to," Beatrice said, and smiled.

"By the way, did they find out who stabbed you, dear?"

Beatrice's stomach sank. She'd never get over it—

being intentionally hurt by someone in her community. Who would do such a thing?

"No. But it happened on the same day as Maggie Rae's murder. And the brilliant Cumberland Creek police think there's a link," she replied.

"But why would Robert Dasher hurt you?"

"I told the police I didn't think he was in the store that day, but I can't be sure."

"It's the oddest thing," Rose said. "You being stabbed the same day as Maggie Rae being murdered."

After hanging up from talking with Rose, Beatrice placed her dishes in the sink and heard a strange noise on her front porch. Sounded like a cat. She rinsed her dishes off and placed them in the dishwasher. There it was again.

Oh, well, bother.

The sound was eerie. Maybe it was hurt. She padded to her front door and opened it.

She grabbed her chest and gasped. There, in front of her door, was a baby doll, crying, with a knife sticking in its neck. It was naked. Its big blue eyes stared up at her. Someone had smeared lipstick across her puckered mouth. Her red hair was a tattered mess. The knife was placed through her neck and came out of the chest, where it was evidently pressed upon the voice box, making the doll cry that fake little doll cry.

"What sicko did this?" she asked, stepping out onto her porch and looking around. She saw nothing out of the ordinary in either direction. At this time of day, it was pretty quiet on Ivy Street.

Her heart raced with anger. *Who would do something like this?*

Someone wanted to scare her. Someone thought she knew something. Well, the joke was on them. For once in her life, she was fairly certain she knew nothing at all.

She left the doll sitting on her porch as she went to phone the police.

"This is Beatrice Matthews on Ivy. You need to send someone over here. There's a baby doll, with a knife sticking out of its neck, on my porch."

"There's a what?"

"You heard me. Someone better get over here and do something about it. The sound of it is driving me mad and I'm about ready to pitch the damn thing."

Chapter 22

Vera sat at her desk, drumming her fingers. It was Tuesday afternoon, just like any other Tuesday afternoon—a pile of paperwork and a class in an hour—except for one thing: she was pregnant. She didn't feel any different, maybe queasy or light-headed at times, but that could be because she had stopped drinking her morning coffee. Since when did caffeine get to be bad for fetuses? Still, she was determined to do everything right for the baby she was carrying.

She faced the computer screen, looking over the accounting on her computer. Something wasn't quite adding up. *Is that the right number?* She was so deep in thought that she didn't hear Robert coming up behind her.

"Ms. Vera?" he said quietly, and she about jumped out of her skin, squealing.

"Oh, Lord, you scared me. I didn't hear you coming. This damn accounting program," she said.

He laughed. "Ah, I know it well. I'm an accountant."

"Please have a seat," Vera said, trying to remember her manners, even though she was scared to death of Robert Dasher. According to the newspaper, he was a strong person of interest in his wife's murder.

Now she looked across her desk at Robert Dasher.

What did a murderer look like? Like this? His blond hair could have used a wash, and he was in sore need of a shave. He was thin-lipped and pointy-chinned. His eyes were as ice blue as ever, even though they were red and a little puffy.

"What can I help you with?" she said, her heart racing.

"I wanted to let you know that Gracie will be continuing on with her dancing this year. I've spoken to a friend of mine, a counselor"—his voice cracked—"and he says that continuity is important, you know." His eyes went to the floor. "The children all need to keep on with their same activities. Need to keep that continuity," he said again, with a peculiar twitch of an eyelid.

Vera's heart slipped a bit as she looked at this young man. She didn't know whether to be frightened or feel sorry for him. Something about the way the light was hitting his face . . . Suddenly he looked so young and vulnerable, like a grown-up child. How could he have killed anybody? Still, he did probably beat Maggie Rae—and that was hard to imagine now, in this moment. Maybe they were jumping to conclusions by thinking he beat her. Maybe he just "hurt" her feelings. *But the newspaper said he had a history of domestic violence.*

Robert was soft spoken, obviously in pain, and was trying to do what was best for the children. Still, he did not make eye contact. A flash of those bony hands slapping Maggie Rae across the face popped into Vera's head.

He lifted one of his hands, then balled it up and placed it on the desk. What did he want? She jumped a little.

His feet shuffled around a bit on the floor. "The thing is, the payment this month might be a little late. There's some mix-up with the finances and I can't get into some accounts yet until the estate is settled."

"Oh," Vera said with relief. So the crop's assumption was true—Maggie Rae was paying for the dance lessons.

Perhaps he didn't make much money. "Well, we will work with you on that, Mr. Dasher."

She'd been in this position before—when a crisis hit a family, often it was dance classes they were forced to give up. When it was a struggle to put food on the table, who could blame them? But clearly this man knew how important dance was to Grace. It could be the very thing that helped pull her through this horrible time.

Vera had seen it before. She was more than willing to wait for money—and even foot the bill if necessary. Gracie needed to dance, and her father could see that.

Still, as Vera placed the paper she was holding onto her desk, she saw that her hand was trembling. She could be sitting across the desk from a cold-blooded murderer; she couldn't shake that fear.

He noticed her tremor, too. Their eyes locked.

"Vera," he said, his voice cracking again, dropping his balled-up hand on her desk hard. "I didn't kill my wife."

"Of c-course, you d-didn't," she responded.

He placed his hand on his forehead, avoiding eye contact. He suddenly reminded Vera of an eagle or some other large bird. His movements were jolted. His eyes shifted around, as if hunting or searching for something.

"I know that detectives have been nosing around here," he finally said. "But I gotta tell you, I still think she killed herself. I've been over this in my mind, again and again. I don't know what I could have done to stop her. I don't know why they think I killed her. I was at work."

"Well, now," Vera said, trying to soothe this obviously tortured, probably dangerous person. "My mama always said that if you're innocent, you've got nothing to worry about."

"The thing is," he went on, "I wasn't the best husband. I know I could've been a better husband. I've lost my temper a few times with her. But I loved her. I was crazy about her."

She reached out and patted his hand, still unsure of his innocence or guilt, but she could see he was in turmoil and needed help. She couldn't get over how young he looked at that moment, just like a boy sitting across from her, except for the razor stubble.

"Now, you say you have a counselor?" she managed to say.

"Yes." He sat up and pulled his hand away. "And I'm looking for a sitter. Maggie Rae's sister can help a little, but I need a full-time sitter. If you can put the word out, or if you know anybody . . ."

No, indeed, thought Vera. *I won't be sending any young girl to your house.*

Later that night, over a supper of beef stew and crusty bread, she mentioned it to Bill.

"Robert Dasher came by the studio today."

"What for?"

"He wanted to chat," she said, breaking off a piece of bread. "He's creepy, but at the same time, I feel sorry for him. Odd."

Bill pounded his fist on the table.

"He's playing your sympathies, and I won't have it. He needs to stay away from you!"

"Now, Bill, he is the father of one of my students. It's unrealistic to think I'd never be talking to him. And he's right, Grace needs to continue with her dance lessons."

"Yes, but he should not be talking to you about the case at all. Or sitting across the desk from you, crying. Son of a bitch!" His face turned bright red.

Vera laughed. "Calm down, Bill. It's nothing for you to have a heart attack over. You're sounding like a jealous man, and we've been married too long for that."

He slid his chair over next to her, wrapped his arms

around her. "God, woman, I love you. You're going to be the mother of my child. I don't want that man near you."

Vera sank into a warm bliss that carried her through the rest of her night—alone with her husband in the bedroom.

Chapter 23

Murder comes to Cumberland Creek?—Yolonda

How did you hear about that?

Don't you ever read your paper? There are letters to the editor accusing Maggie Rae's husband.

REALLY?

So what do you think?

They said it was a suicide. Now, there seems to be an investigation going on. And we think that he beat her from time to time.

Really? That's terrible. I didn't think women put up with that stuff anymore.

Don't be so naïve.

Nobody's ever called me that before. (SMIRK)

The blue of the computer screen suddenly made Annie very tired. Yolonda's ignorance swept through her, too. If someone as smart as Yolonda didn't think abuse still went on, how would the court ever prove its case against Robert?

I need to go. Sorry. So tired.

Annie! It's only 9:30.

That late! ;-) Good night.

Good night.

Before she switched off the computer, Annie decided to Google Robert Dasher, again—jeez, there were a million of them. How about Robert and Maggie Rae Dasher?

There they were at some kind of a business function. Interesting.

There were pictures from their wedding.

There were some Facebook and LinkedIn accounts.

Hmm. This guy looked as ordinary as could be. Yet, she knew from Maggie Rae's cards and papers that he was a tyrant.

She decided to look up Juicy X—Maggie Rae's pseudonym.

Wow, what a website. Gorgeous graphics. And was that Maggie Rae in a platinum blond wig? Good Lord, the woman was built. A visitor would never know she had birthed four children. Of course, there could be touch-ups. Thank God, she wasn't naked, but just almost naked. Annie didn't want to see the rest of her. She read the site's text:

About Juicy
Juicy is a woman with a passion for words and

*sex. She has won every award, including the highly
regarded ALLEROTICA, the HOT LUNCH award,
and the ZIPPY awards. She is an acclaimed author
who says there is nothing she'd rather write about
than love and sex—the kinkier the better.*

Annie clicked on the Amazon link. All twelve of her
books were at the top of the romance charts. Jesus.
Annie knew the woman was making a lot of money—yet
they lived in what was probably the smallest house in
Cumberland Creek. It was odd.

She clicked off the monitor—she'd have to explore
more tomorrow, if she could. Right now, her eyes were
burning with strain.

So rumors were already spreading about Robert
Dasher. She wondered if that would affect his trial at all.
She wondered if he would ever make it to trial. . . . If
a community like this thinks he killed his wife, who
knew what would become of him?

Mike was already in bed—she could hear him snoring
from where she sat at her desk. She climbed into bed and
felt the weariness of the day rest in her body. Soft blankets, sheets, on her warm skin. She lay in her bed, looking at the ceiling, thinking about Maggie Rae's papers
that she gave to the detective. When she ran into him at
the gas station, he said he'd give them back to her.

"Oh, that's not necessary," Annie stated. "I picked
them up by mistake. We just wanted to make scrapbooks
for her kids. They were among her things. I'm not sure
any of it can be used in her scrapbooks."

"Oh, still, I'll need to give them to somebody. Might
as well be you," he said. "Obviously, her husband doesn't
want them."

He looked at her with an uncomfortable acknowledgment and shrugged his large shoulders before walking away. She almost invited him over for coffee. The reporter in her would not allow it—neither would the wife in her. She never really trusted cops. She'd seen too many shady ones and had been involved in a number of stories with good cops gone bad. Maybe Bryant was one of the good ones, but maybe not. And she knew her husband would not appreciate her inviting a man in for coffee, even if he was a detective.

Now that Annie had finished the scrapbook, she was really unsure of whom to give it to. Maggie Rae's husband left it out for the trashman; her children were still quite young; maybe her sister? What did she say her name was again? Tina Sue, in the purple ski jacket, sitting at the park bench. Did she give her last name? If she did, Annie couldn't remember.

She rolled over on her side and closed her eyes. What a day. What a weekend. All of a sudden, she was in the thick of this small town. She had acquaintances, if not friends, and she'd been to a scrapbooking party, as well as a hospital room and a memorial service. Life was surely getting a bit more interesting. Two weeks ago, it was just Annie and her boys, and she didn't know that she lived down the street from a murderer. She was saddened and shocked by Maggie Rae's death when she thought it was a suicide. But a murder frightened her. Is any place safe? God, if a family wasn't safe in their own home—where could they be safe? And with her own husband? She couldn't imagine the thoughts going through Maggie Rae's mind as her husband pointed a gun at her. Did she beg and plead for her life? Did she have time? Or was it over so quick that she had no time to make sense of anything? No chance to think of her children? Her husband killing her?

A cold chill ran through her and she pulled the blankets closer around her shoulders. Cumberland Creek was a strange place. It was quaint and beautiful on the outside—but underneath the surface was something dark, foreboding, and sinister.

One of the sights she was afraid she'd never get used to was the parade of Mennonite horses and buggies that came through the town, especially on Wednesdays, when they held a farmers' market in the town square, which was tomorrow. She would just never get used to the plain way the women and men dressed, and the way in which the women seemed to be subservient to their men. Then she smiled—her aunt Ida could have written the book on subservience, and she was an Orthodox Jew, which irritated Annie's mother to no end. "How could two women be raised in the same house and be so different?"

Annie rolled over again and saw the sky—just as blue as a perfect sky could be. The sun warmed her skin and she realized she had forgotten her sunblock. She reached for a drink—it was pink, with a fancy little umbrella plopped in it. She sipped on it—whew, a strong cool drink was just what she needed. A masculine hand reached for hers, sending ripples through her body. It was as if a shard of electricity zipped through her. She looked into his eyes. Wes.

The next thing she knew, they were making love on the sand. They started out on a blanket, but as was usually the case when the two of them had sex, it got a little, well, active. As he pushed into her, she could feel the gritty sand and waves kissing her toes. They were alone on the beach, just them and the expanse of white sand, turquoise water, and their bodies—young, firm, lithe. She felt as if the sand had begun to sink, but she and Wes somehow became a part of the sky. She woke up, shivering in orgasm.

She rolled over and closed her eyes, hoping she hadn't disturbed Mike. There was a smile on her face, though, as she remembered reading Maggie Rae's story about a hot young couple on the beach.

* * *

The next day, Annie dressed Ben for an outing at the farmers' market. Ben loved walking through the town—that in itself was cause for exploring and keeping him quite happy. They were a bit rushed because Sam would be home soon from the new preschool program he was trying out.

Annie loved the produce at the Mennonite Farmers Market—tables of spring greens, spinach, and rhubarb lined the town square. And, oh, the strawberries! She never saw such beautiful, big berries. So perfectly shaped.

"These are so beautiful!" she exclaimed aloud, perhaps a bit too enthusiastically, for the Mennonite woman behind the tables sort of sat back and looked suspiciously at her. She forced a smile.

The woman's alabaster skin almost matched her white cotton blouse. Her piercing blue eyes scanned Annie. She looked around—they were all fair. Had she never seen an olive complexion?

Suddenly Annie felt awkward. "I—I'll take this basket," she stammered.

"Thank you," the woman said, handing Annie her change and her basket of strawberries.

Annie bent over to give Ben a taste of a ripe strawberry and he reached for her necklace—the Star of David in her child's tiny hand.

Chapter 24

Beatrice was awakened by a glow on the edge of her bed. It was her husband again.

"Beatrice?"

"Yes," she strained to say, for she was so tired. She opened her eyes and saw her dead husband as clear as she could.

"It's Maggie Rae," he said.

"What?" Her heart skipped a beat as she struggled to sit up.

"Maggie Rae is lost," he told her, looking very perplexed. *"Something holds her here, but it's not like with us."*

"What do you mean, Doc?"

"It's bad. She's in pain and is hovering in a darkness."

"What do you mean?" Beatrice said, frightened, feeling a tingling travel up her spine.

"I'm not sure I can explain this—but there seems to be a vacuum created by some of us when we are alive, where all this darkness goes. Dark thoughts, dark dreams. She is filled with them," he said. *"It's frightening, even to us."*

"Can you help?"

He shook his head.

"You will have to take care of this, Beatrice, and I

wish I could tell you how. But I'm confused by it. Oh, there she is," he said, and disappeared.

Just then, Beatrice heard a loud, crashing sound.

"What was that?" she said aloud, and reached into her drawer for her gun. This time, she'd be prepared. She turned off the safety, feeling the cold, hard metal in her hand. It was a window breaking downstairs. She was sure of it. Go downstairs? Or call the police?

She locked the bedroom door quietly, her hands shaking suddenly, breath shallow. She imagined her bedroom as being filled with light, just as her cousin had taught her to do in times of stress. She picked up the phone and dialed 911.

"This is Beatrice Matthews, at 610 Ivy Street," she said softly into the phone. "I believe there's an intruder in my house."

"We'll dispatch someone immediately, Beatrice. Where are you physically located?"

"Upstairs in my bedroom. Door is locked."

"Stay where you are."

"I plan to," she said, and hung up the phone.

Soon she heard the sirens and looked out the front window. She heard the police shuffling around outside for what seemed like hours, then someone yelling about glass.

Then her phone rang. "Mrs. Matthews, it's safe for you to come downstairs. Please come down and open the door for us. Just like the doll, this incident seems like a simple vandalism. Be careful of the glass."

A simple vandalism? She took a deep breath and tried to quiet her pounding heart. *A simple vandalism.* She'd never had so many acts of weirdness and violence directed at her.

Bea decided to take her gun with her, just to be on the safe side. As she opened her bedroom door, she felt the cold rush to her. It was a cool spring morning—but heavens, this was a down-deep cold, getting into her bones. Goodness, she wished the changing spring weather patterns would settle. One day warm, the next cool. She went back in her room and grabbed her shawl from the chair.

As she descended the stairs, the breeze in her home disturbed her sensibilities. She wrapped the shawl closer to her. Even though she heard the officers in the distance, she felt alone, and the house felt utterly empty and cavernous. A fine layer of dust—or was it glass—covered everything. The sun was just rising, with streams of pinkish gold flecks of light coming through the windows. Bits of leaves and branches were scattered in her living room, along with shards of glass, shining, sparkling, reflecting. One piece was reflecting so strongly that she found herself shielding her eyes with her hands. As she did so, a cold wind shook her curtains, and something black flew across the room. What the hell was that? A bird? A bat? No, it was too big for that. Too big and too fast. She swore she could feel every little hair on the back of her neck stand at attention, and a putrid scent filled her nose and mouth.

"Mrs. Matthews? Please open the door," came the voice from outside.

She slipped her gun into a closeby drawer and opened the door and saw a young officer, looking like he was about twelve. Could they have sent a *more* inexperienced young dweeb?

"Good morning, ma'am."

"What's so damn good about it?"

He ignored her. "We need to look around in here. We figure someone threw a rock or something. Might be in the house. It would help if we found the instrument. Maybe we could find who did it."

"I doubt it," she retorted in a clipped tone. "You still haven't found who stabbed me. Or who left the doll on my porch."

"You're the same lady?"

"Indeed I am," she said, pointing at her neck, still bandaged, exasperated.

"I need to make a phone call. Excuse me."

In the meantime, two other officers came in and took pictures and looked through the glass shards for a rock or a brick—anything. They found nothing. It was almost as if the window had shattered on its own.

"Good Lord, where is my mother?" Beatrice heard Vera ask as she ran up the porch stairs.

Then an officer's voice, telling her where Bea could be found, responded.

Vera opened the door and looked at her mom.

"I believe I'd like a cup of coffee. Could you, dear?" Beatrice said, grabbing Vera's hand and leading her into the kitchen.

"Are you okay?"

"I'm fine," she replied. "Just need that cup of coffee." She sat at her kitchen table and watched Vera make coffee and listened to the officers traipse around in her living room.

The scent of brewing coffee filled the kitchen and soothed her. It was one of those smells that Beatrice never grew tired of—here she was, eighty years old, and the smell of coffee still held immense comfort for her. It took her right back to her childhood on the mountain, sitting at her mother's table, with not a worry in the world. In her mind's eye, she could see her mother's blue curtains waving in the Virginia breeze, her weary mom pouring the coffee into her dad's cup, then into her own. She could almost feel her mother's touch right here this moment. She closed her eyes, swimming in this feeling.

"Mama," Vera said, disrupting her thoughts. "Between the stabbing in your neck and now this, I'm beginning to think someone has it in for you. Why don't you come and stay with us?"

Beatrice did not reply. *If she only knew about the doll.* Sometimes her daughter's love felt like a noose. Today, here, in the kitchen where Vera was raised, Beatrice wondered if her daughter would ever really know who she was. How many times did Bea have to assert her independence?

Beatrice smiled, then rolled her eyes. "I don't think so, Vera. This is my home."

"I'd feel more comfortable until they find out who stabbed you," Vera said. "I just want you to be careful. Maggie Rae's husband . . . well, he could be dangerous."

"He could be, but nothing my pistol can't handle."

"Now, Mama, that's just what I mean. I really wish you'd get rid of that thing."

"Your daddy bought it for me and taught me how to use it. I feel safe with it here next to me in my nightstand. So over my dead body will I get rid of it. In fact, you can bury me with my gun in one hand and a book in the other," Beatrice said, pausing. "I'm glad to know you're concerned about me, but I'm not going anywhere. I'll be damned if I'm leaving my home over some vandal."

"It's more than vandalism, Mama. You were stabbed. Maggie Rae was murdered earlier that same morning. Seriously. Think about coming to stay with us until this blows over, and call me if you need me for anything." Then with a concerned hug, Vera left the house.

Now alone, Beatrice immediately thought about her cousin Rose, who knew more than most people about ghosts. The more she thought about the dark thing in her home, and what Ed had said, the more she believed it was Maggie Rae. What to do about it? And why her? She decided to give Rose a call.

"How do, cousin?" Rose said. "Seems like we just got off the phone." She chuckled.

"I'm not so good today, Rose. A lot has been happening here."

"Well, we have the Internet out here now," said Rose. "Have everything you do, except the crowds and the murders and the stabbings."

"Well, then, let's get right to it," Beatrice said, laughing.

Beatrice told her story to her cousin. Rose had never left the mountains—never traveled anywhere. Her sons brought her groceries once a week from town and she made her own clothes—mostly cotton skirts and dresses. She had no use for "dungarees," as she called them— nor did she have a use for cosmetics. Her face was weathered and worn—but a subtle beauty clung to it, like a faded jewel.

She learned her skills as an herbalist as a child from her and Beatrice's grandmother, who was a skilled midwife, much in demand. She also knew the old healing ways with herbs.

Beatrice used to talk with Ed about crazy old Rose talking to her plants and to her spirit friends. But the older Beatrice got, the more she herself turned to her mountain heritage, which seemed to be mostly in the form of chats with Rose—whether on the phone or occasionally in person. They were in close contact.

The mountains could close in on a person. When she was growing up, she wanted nothing more than to escape. Rose was one of those individuals closed off to anything but the mountains. But, Beatrice acknowledged, Rose's wisdom with herbs was vast, and was proving to be right on target with what some of the newest herbalists and doctors were claiming. In fact, one of the ways Rose earned money was by selling her mountain herbs and teaching classes twice a year.

Beatrice explained what had happened that morning.

"You need to do a cleansing of your house, first," Rose was saying. "I'll send you the dried sage. I want you to burn it, go through your house, clockwise in each room. When you're doing that, picture a white light wrapping around each room, then expand it in your mind and wrap your whole house in this light."

"Hmph," Beatrice said. "Is that all there is to it?"

"I don't know," Rose said. "Maybe not, but that's the place to start."

"So, can you make sense of any of this?"

"I think Ed was warning you. I think there is a darkness around you and your house. If it's this Maggie Rae's spirit, I'd suggest you find out more about her. Also, just tell her to leave you alone. She can't hurt you."

"But she broke my window," Beatrice reminded her.

"Oh, yes, ghosts can break things. Windows are their favorite way of letting you know they are not happy. They can also attack you—but their attacks don't last long enough to really hurt."

"What? Ghosts can hurt you? Well, I have heard of everything now." Beatrice felt a sudden panic.

"I thought we might go to the caves the next time you visit, but the boys didn't think it was such a good idea," Rose said, changing the subject as if they had just been talking about the weather, instead of ghosts.

"Why not?" Beatrice asked.

"They tell me there's a group of suspicious characters up there these days."

Beatrice harrumphed. "More suspicious than usual?"

"Yes," Rose said, suddenly serious. "You know about all the stories about the caves?"

"Well, some of them."

"As long as I've known about the place, there's been stories about it," she said, and paused. Beatrice heard her sipping a drink. "There's the one about the lovers."

"Oh, yes, I remember that one," Bea said. "An Appalachian Romeo and Juliet story."

"Then there's the one that claims that our caves are located on some kind of special axis and have magical properties. The water there comes from a pure spring and runs along those beautiful quartz and calcite rocks—"

"Yes, I remember. . . ."

Beatrice still dreamed of the place sometimes. For a child, it was like a fairy kingdom full of sparkling rocks and mushrooms, not to mention the wildflowers and herbs that grew outside the caves. In fact, in her dreams, she danced with and spoke to fairies often. And she always thought, *I need to remember this,* and would forget what the fairies told her upon awakening.

"It's a perfect place for ritual, really," Rose went on. "According to the boys, someone is doing ritual—and not in a good way."

"Animal sacrifices?" Bea said, and laughed.

"No, Bea," she said. "It's really very serious. They are trying to manipulate the 'energy.'"

"For what?" Beatrice said. "Can you be more specific?"

"I wish I could. All I know is they have several holy books and are picking and choosing what they like and creating a sort of cult. Maybe a Mennonite faction. I was up there a few days ago and I can tell you, the energy is different. It feels dead."

Beatrice's heart sank. "It was so vibrant. I still dream about it."

"We all do," Rose said, as if Beatrice should have known that. "We are a part of this land. And it's a part of us."

Chapter 25

Paige laid the thick yellow scrapbook on Vera's desk. "I'm done with it," she said. "I don't know how I managed."

Vera looked up from her paperwork. Her friends just flat-out refused to acknowledge that she actually worked for a living. They just stopped by and interrupted her every chance they got.

"What do you mean?" Vera finally asked, looking directly into Paige's big doll-like blue eyes.

"Daniel. He reminds me a lot of my boy. The soccer games, the art projects, that funny little crooked smile . . ." Her huge blue eyes reminded Vera of saucers as they widened.

"Well, maybe you should call him," Vera said, bracing herself. Still, it needed to be said—but it wasn't as if she hadn't said it before over the years.

"Goddamn you, Vera," Paige said. "He knows where I am, and phones work both ways."

"I know, dear," Vera said, turning to her computer because she didn't want to see Paige's fair complexion turning angry red. "But he thinks you're ashamed of him."

"Well," Paige said, her blue eyes flaring. She pushed a strand of her blond hair behind her ear while she tapped her manicured nails on the desk. "How would you feel if your son was gay?"

"I don't know, Paige," Vera answered, looking back at her. "Randy is a wonderful young man. Has a great job, and is doing well for himself. Why is his sexuality such a big deal?"

Paige looked crushed. Her thin lips turned down. Her face flamed red.

"Can you just put this behind you? Pick up the phone and call him."

"The Bible says—"

"It says nothing," Vera finished. "As far as I remember my Bible, it celebrates love, in all forms. Are you willing to go to your grave not having a wonderful close relationship with your son—all because of whom he chooses to love?"

"Well," Paige finally said after a few moments. "I hadn't thought of it quite like that. Still, there's Earl. He will never accept his son being gay. I just know it."

"Earl is Earl, and you are you. Time goes so fast, dear. I think we need to hold on to the people we love, don't you? This thing with Maggie Rae, you know, should make us all sit up and take notice."

"I suppose you're right." She sighed, and then spoke again after a moment. "Maybe I'll call him later today. But now, Vera, what happened to your mom's house? I saw the broken window when I drove by."

"Nobody knows," Vera said. "Vandals. They never could find the rock or the brick that was thrown, though. And they still don't know who stabbed her."

"Boy, your Mom's having kind of a rough time of it."

"Can't get her to admit that, though. Old fool," Vera said, smiling. "Can't get her to stay with us for a while, just until things calm down. She won't let me stay there, either. It's so frustrating."

* * *

What Vera didn't tell Paige was that she thought her mother was finally losing a little bit of her mind. She'd always been an odd bird. Had always insisted that her daddy was still with her and talked to him frequently. All of the quantum physics stuff played into it. Vera couldn't understand the language of it, but she knew it had to do with a separate reality or creating your own reality, and she always felt like maybe Beatrice was creating her father's ghost, at least in her mind.

But today, her mother talked about Maggie Rae. And she was concerned because her late husband had warned her, and then the incident with her window had occurred almost immediately afterward.

"I swear I saw something very dark in my living room," Beatrice said. "It flew out the window so quickly."

"A bird?"

"No, I don't think so," Beatrice said. "I've been thinking about what your father said—that Maggie Rae's caught in some dark void. Something is holding her here and that it's not good."

"Mama, what are you saying? That Maggie Rae's ghost broke your window? That she was the dark thing you saw?" Vera questioned, with a chill traveling through her.

"I know it sounds crazy, girl. I know it. But I've also known my whole life that's there more to this life and the next than what we know."

"Oh, now, Mama, you're scaring me," Vera said. It was true. Her mother scared her frequently—for her whole life—talking about such things. Vera wanted nothing to do with ghosts or the spirit world. This world was what mattered. Flesh. Bones. The child inside her.

"I have to tell you, Vera, for the first time in years, I'm a little scared, too." Her mother's eyes were wide, and her hair was uncombed. She looked a little scared. That frightened Vera even more.

"I don't believe in any of this nonsense, you know

that," Vera said, biting into a cinnamon roll. "Mmm, this is good."

"Thanks, I think there's more in the freezer."

Did her mother really believe it was Maggie Rae who had broken her window? Did she really think her husband came to her and talked to her—even though he'd been dead for twenty years? Well, if it was Maggie's Rae's ghost—and that was a big *if* in Vera's mind—why would she be at Beatrice's house and breaking her windows?

"That would be the mystery to solve," Beatrice said when Vera asked her. "I didn't really know the woman."

"We're finding that none of us really did," Vera replied.

"How about that Maggie Rae?" Paige said, sitting down. She took off her blue cardigan sweater and hung it over the chair. Her large bosom was poking out of a too-small V-necked T-shirt. "Writing dirty stories. How about that?"

"Shocking," Vera said, flipping through a file.

"What would possess a woman?" She leaned forward on Vera's desk. Her thin shoulders rested on bony arms.

"I wondered that, too. I'm sure everything will be revealed in due time. Don't you think so?"

"I asked Earl about it. He said he's read some of her stuff—he's quite the porn guy, my husband." She rolled her eyes. "He said it was good, but kind of kinky and violent."

"Really?" A brief image of her old lover, Tony, smacking her bottom flashed in Vera's mind—no matter where their lovemaking took them, she found it pleasurable. Even a little pain added to the pleasure. Bill would never do such a thing—he was too much of a gentleman.

"Yes, evidently, we are talking whips and chains and everything."

"Oy," Vera said. "That's kind of embarrassing that we know that. Poor woman. I'm afraid all of her secrets will be revealed as time goes by. Honestly, who wants to know all of that?"

"Honestly?" Paige said, with a wide grin. "I do."

Chapter 26

Annie was compelled to look away from the computer screen as she read about sadism and masochism—commonly known as S&M. She was surprised to find tears lurking at the edge of her eyes, thinking about Maggie Rae. As one drop slipped down her cheek, she took a deep breath. Why would a woman want to be humiliated and hurt? With so much pleasure to be found in sex, in life, why the pain?

She looked up "submissive" on the Internet. On Wikipedia, she found:

> **Dominance and submission** (also known as **D&s, Ds** or **D/s**) is a set of behaviors, customs and rituals involving the giving by one individual to another individual of control over them in an erotic episode or as a lifestyle.

Hmm. Interesting, but not quite what she was looking for—what she wanted to know was why would a person be attracted to being hurt, what kind of psychology was behind it. Then Annie keyed in, *Psychology of Submissives.* One website came up and said:

According to Freud, people become masochistic as a way of regulating their desire to sexually dominate others. The desire to submit, on the other hand, he said, arises from guilt feelings over the desire to dominate.

Hmm, Annie thought, feeling as if she was dipping into murky waters. Freud? What a nut.

Another website said:

Despite the research indicating that S&M does no real harm and is not associated with pathology, Freud's successors in psychoanalysis continue to use mental illness overtones when discussing S&M. Addiction, for one thing.

Addicted to S&M? Annie groaned. Addiction seemed to be the modern epidemic. Everyone wanted that easy fix, instant gratification—drugs, alcohol, and even sex. She read further.

According to a sex magazine, *masochism is a set of techniques for helping people temporarily lose their normal identity . . . that stress makes forgetting who you are an appealing escape.* That was the essence of the "escape" theory, one of the main reasons people turned to S&M.

Fascinating, thought Annie. *A form of escape. To want to be hurt.*

Annie turned away from the computer and looked at her boys, who were napping in her bed. One of them sighed in his sleep.

She picked up the brown envelope that the detective had left on her doorstep with Maggie Rae's papers inside. She stuck her hand into it and pulled out a birthday card from Gracie to Maggie Rae. *Love you, Mommy* was written in purple ink, smelling slightly of grape. She

smiled. Her boys loved those scented pens, which were
scattered throughout her house.

A note slipped out of the envelope. It was from
Maggie Rae to Grace:

> *I always wanted to be a mom, but I want you to
> know there's more to life than marriage and
> family. Oh, it can be good, sometimes. But mostly
> it's thankless. Thank God, I have my writing, my
> fantasies, my friends. Otherwise, I fear I'd slip
> into absolute nothingness. . . .*

Annie's heart felt like it stopped for one moment.
There in the midst of something she couldn't relate to at
all—the S&M—Maggie's words reached out to her and
Annie felt a deep sense of compassion and connection.
She took a deep breath. *There but for the grace of God.*

For generations, women had lived their lives simply
tending to their children and their husbands. Why wasn't
it enough for all women? Why did Annie get bored with
her kids? Want something more?

The S&M made Annie uncomfortable. She'd always
been pretty straight with her sex life. Still, it was within
the realm of "normal" sexual behavior. She admitted that
reading about S&M helped her to understand Maggie
Rae's personality. She was more certain than ever that
Maggie Rae's story held more richness and depth than
she'd ever know. She was not just about sex or even erotica. She was a person who was responding to a pivotal
event in her life. But what was it?

Annie meditated on a picture she found of the young
Maggie Rae, her sister, Tina Sue, their mother, and their
father; all were seated on a porch swing, with an apple
tree behind them. Tina Sue was smiling at her sister. The
mother looked stern, staring straight ahead at the camera.
Maggie Rae was tucked under her father's arm and

smiled adoringly at him. He smiled back. Nothing was menacing about this faded Polaroid snapshot with a diagonal jagged edge. Still, she stared at it, wishing she could step into it, take the hand of young Maggie Rae, and listen to her secrets.

Chapter 27

Sheila explained to Annie that vellum paper was a little difficult to use—but it was so beautiful. "You just have to be a little more careful when you cut it. It tears and frays so easily."

Annie ran her long fingers over the smooth milky paper. "So this adhesive won't show behind it, if I put it on the back? It will still hold?"

"Yes, it will hold. When it dries, it becomes invisible," Sheila said. She was sitting next to Annie, but on the other side of her was a pile of new scrapbook paper—beautiful shades of orange and yellow and brown.

Vera loved to watch Sheila explaining some technique to a newbie. She held a certain "I know my business" look on her face—almost the same look she would get when they were young girls playing at being bank tellers. That thought made Vera smile. She looked at Sheila's face, which was just now beginning to show wrinkles at the corners of her eyes and mouth. That one tiny mole on her cheek had vexed Sheila for years. Finally she just gave up and accepted it. That was one of the blessings of aging—acceptance.

Here she was, thinking like an old woman, and yet a life grew inside her. She already began a journal for the baby, writing about her thoughts and feelings over the past two weeks since she'd found out that she was expecting. It was such a shock to her that it was taking time to get used to. And she had other things on her mind—like her dance recital next week and all the upcoming rehearsals.

"I wish Paige were here," said DeeAnn suddenly. "I think she'd love those cheese biscuits I brought."

"Oh, yes, she would. Who wouldn't?" Sheila said.

"I guess we take a backseat to her boy," Vera said.

"It's about time," DeeAnn said. "I mean, Lord, who cares if the boy is gay? It's been years since they've even talked."

"Plenty of catching up to do," Sheila said.

"You know," Annie spoke up quietly, "I don't think it would be easy to be the mother of a gay person."

They all looked at her.

"What I mean is, they have it rough and it would be difficult to see that," she said.

"Oh, yes, I agree," DeeAnn said, biting into a cheese biscuit. "Besides that, nobody wants to think of their kids having sex—at all."

Annie raised her eyebrows. Her mother said the same thing to her when Annie became sexually active at sixteen.

"My daughter started way too early," DeeAnn said while cutting a picture. The sound of the squeaky scissors was drowned out by her voice. "But it turned out okay. I mean, she went to college, is becoming a nurse, getting married next year. It all comes out in the wash."

"If we're lucky," Sheila said. "I'm afraid my Donna will make me a grandmother before I'm ready," she said, and laughed.

Vera's heart sank. Sheila was thinking about becoming a grandmother, and she was preparing for her first baby.

Donna was Sheila's oldest daughter. At fifteen, she

was beautiful and was built like she was twenty-five, turning the heads of older boys—and of men, too. "God, that girl!"

"Speaking of sex," Annie said after gluing down a picture of Sam in his Halloween costume—dressed as a bunny. "I've been reading . . . digging through Maggie Rae's papers again."

"And?" Vera said, wondering if she really wanted to know.

Annie took a long drink of her wine. "Some of this stuff is painful to read. But riveting. I think after looking at her picture, reading some of her notes and trying to piece it together, I think she was just lonely, basically. Her husband was never around to help. He was working long hours, traveled extensively. Four kids. That's tough. She couldn't handle it. The truth is, I'm not sure I could."

"So, do you still think she was murdered, rather than killed herself?" Vera wondered.

"I don't know. It seems to be complicated. I wonder what the detective is making of this. He made copies and dropped the papers back off with me because he said it didn't seem like her husband wanted them."

"That says it all, as far as I'm concerned," Sheila said, looking up from her cutting.

"Calm down," Vera said. "Not everybody cares about this stuff like you do, for God's sake."

"What do you think, Vera?" DeeAnn asked. "I mean, he came in to talk to you."

She took a deep breath. "I've really not thought about it too much. I've had a lot on my mind with Mama and the baby. But it was a strange conversation. He seemed genuinely distraught, and I have to say he also seemed like he was trying to do good by his children."

The women sat in silence for a few seconds.

"I think the situation is complex," Annie volunteered. "Maggie Rae wrote this beautiful erotic stuff—and she had a thing for S and M. Maybe he didn't like it. Maybe he killed her and doesn't remember doing it. Maybe she *did* kill herself. I mean, I've thought about so many possibilities."

"It doesn't make sense to me at all that she killed herself," Sheila said.

"It also doesn't make sense that she never placed any of her pictures in her scrapbooks," Vera said.

"You know, I wondered about that, too," Annie said. "Why would somebody buy all that stuff and never do anything with it? I mean, was she waiting for something? Was it too painful for her to mull over her life, to look at it on scrapbook pages?"

"Maybe she was just busy. Gosh, all those children, and the writing she did. It makes sense to me now that she couldn't make it to a crop," Sheila said. "But still to buy one scrapbook and a few things and never use them is one thing—but boxes of it? I don't know."

"God, I wish I'd known her better," DeeAnn said.

"I think we all do," Vera said, looking around the table, wondering how well she knew any of them. Even as close as she and Sheila were, she would not be surprised to find out about secrets in her past as well. She hadn't known DeeAnn as long as she knew Sheila. DeeAnn was a transplant from Minnesota, who married a local man, the principal and football coach at the high school. DeeAnn barely mentioned her life growing up in Minnesota. Of course, there was Annie—the most different of all of them. All of them could be into strange sexual practices or witchcraft, for all Vera knew. Some things are better left that way.

"There's nothing wrong with a little healthy repression," she could hear her mother's voice saying in her mind. Vera wondered if all forty-one-year-old women still heard their mother's voices in their head as strongly as she did.

"What are you working on, Annie? That's beautiful," Vera said.

Annie held up the page with one photo of Maggie Rae holding Grace as a baby. She framed it in turquoise vellum paper against a glitter pink page, pasted the note she had found written from Maggie Rae to her daughter, and used buttons as embellishments in the corner of the notes. She pulled out the word "confidence" and used it as a headline for the page. She handwrote it in large letters in purple archival ink. The women read the note. Vera held back tears. Damn, she was just so emotional these days.

"That's pretty powerful words coming from your mama," DeeAnn said.

"Depressing too," Sheila mumbled.

Chapter 28

Annie dumped the contents of the huge envelope onto the table.

"Let's see what we come up with here," she said.

Papers, postcards, certificates, cards, notes of all shapes and sizes, were splayed across the table. There were ticket stubs to movies, plays, and ballets. "I'll take those," Vera said. "Oh, look, she wrote something on the back of this ballet ticket stub. It was the Richmond Ballet. She wrote 'first anniversary' on the back of one."

"Sweet," DeeAnn said. "Look at this. A recipe card with her mom's recipe for red velvet cake. She wrote, 'I can't make it as good as mama, but I try.' Oh, red velvet!"

The women quieted as they searched through her papers. Inspiration sparked from these fibers and pieces of Maggie Rae's life.

"Oh, my. Look at this. It's from Zeb, Tina Sue's husband. A postcard with a quote from the Bible, handwritten on the front of the card. 'You shall not bring the wages of a harlot, or the price of a dog, to the house of the Lord your God for any vowed offering, for both of these are an abomination to the Lord your God.' And then on the back of the card . . . um . . . let's just say X-rated material," Sheila said, and blushed.

"Let me see." DeeAnn grabbed it from her and howled in laughter. "Yep. X-rated, indeed."

"That's just creepy—a Bible quote on one side and that on the back," Vera said.

"Perhaps that's why he's a person of interest," Annie said. "Her brother-in-law. And it would seem he didn't like her writing erotica, either. Maybe they were having an affair. Seems like an intimate and strange thing to keep."

"Lord, truth is stranger than fiction," Sheila said. "Can you imagine if it was her brother-in-law who killed her? What if they'd been having an affair and she cut him off? Or his wife found out and he needed to choose? I don't know. He was so strange at the funeral, dressed in Mennonite garb like that. But I don't think they were even Mennonite."

Annie held a thick letter envelope, with a handwritten address in black ink on it. The return address was Leo Shirley's and she recognized his name as a "person of interest" also listed in the paper, next to Zeb McClain's name.

She opened the envelope to a stack of letters folded neatly into one another. One glance told her they were love letters. No wonder he was a person of interest. This man loved Maggie Rae, or may have been obsessed with her.

"What do you-all know about Leo Shirley?" Annie said.

They all stopped and looked at her.

"Did you say Leo Shirley?" Sheila asked.

Annie nodded.

"Bad news," Sheila said, and grimaced.

"Why? How do you know him?" Vera asked, setting down her glass of wine.

"I just remembered that he was listed in the paper as a person of interest, and here's some letters from him. He and Maggie Rae were having an affair."

"What? Are you sure? He's a married man!" Vera said.

Annie held up the letters. "He was deeply in love with her."

"*In lust* is more like it, and it doesn't surprise me. He's always been trouble—him and his brother, Harv, the postman," Sheila said. "They went to school with us and were just bad news."

"What do you mean?"Annie asked.

"I mean, they were always in trouble. You name it; they did it. Drugs. Vandalism. DUIs. In and out of juvenile detention homes. Rape. Assault and battery. Just as mean as they could be."

"Add adultery to the list," Vera said. "What a slimeball."

"He seems very sweet in his letters. Here, read them," she said, and handed them out to the women.

Annie read over the next letter. "Oh, so much for sweetness. Listen to this. 'I love you, Maggie Rae, I always have. If I can't have you, nobody else will, either.' Seems like she was breaking it off. Here's one that's warning her, again."

"Did you say the detective copied all of this?" DeeAnn asked after a few minutes.

"Yes, so he's seen this, and they already have him on their list. But as far as I know, they've not made any arrests."

"There's no doubt in my mind he's capable of murder," Sheila said. "I'll never forget the time when we were kids and he took Mrs. Laskowski's cat and set it on fire. Oh, that gave me nightmares for years."

"Wow! Look at this," Annie said, peeling a stuck photo from in between the notes. An almost naked Maggie Rae was cuffed to a chair, a man behind her licking her neck. "Is this him?"

"Yep," Sheila said. "Why don't we just throw that away?"

"I wonder if his wife knew about him and Maggie Rae," Vera said, taking the picture from her. "Some men just can't control themselves. Cheating on their wives!" She flung the picture to the table.

"I never understood why his wife married him, anyway," DeeAnn said. "He's never even held a job, has he?"

"Love is blind. But it ain't deaf and dumb, too," Sheila said.

"Regardless," Annie said. "Cheating on your wife is one thing. Murder is another."

"I bet he killed Maggie Rae," Sheila said.

"Now, hold on, you were convinced that Robert killed her, weren't you?" Annie laughed.

Sheila chuckled, too. "I guess it's a good thing I'm not a cop. I'd go around arresting men whom I already know way too much about just to get them off the streets."

"So, do we tell his wife?" Vera wondered out loud as she sorted papers.

"I say we stay out of that," DeeAnn said, taking a sip of wine, then setting her glass down. "Besides, if he's been called in for questioning, I'm sure she knows by now, if she didn't before. Can I see that purple pen? I just want to write a little something on this page."

"So," Annie said, "we have three possible suspects. Robert. Leo. And Maggie Rae's brother-in-law, Zeb. Any of them could have killed her. Plus the newspaper claimed there were more. I wonder who else is on their list."

Chapter 29

"Annie, why all these questions about S and M?" Joshua said to her over the phone.

"I told you. I'm reading the stories written by this woman who was really into it. I read that it could be an escape."

"Yes, that's one of the theories, and I have to tell you it's widely practiced and it's considered within the norm of accepted sexual practices within the psychiatric community."

"What's not accepted?"

"Rape. Bestiality. Sex with kids. That's about it," he said.

Annie could hear him blowing smoke into the phone. Her brother, the psychiatrist, had smoked since he was seventeen. One of his many habits that she despised. She hated the way he bit his fingernails down to the nubs and the way he could never sit still. But most of all, she hated the way he analyzed everything. She smiled. He could probably say the same about her.

"I guess I was trying to figure out what kind of person would want to be hurt."

"Why? Where is that going to lead you?"

"I don't know, really. It's just that it's all so mysterious.

Her death. The circumstances. I'm just trying to piece it all together."

"Why don't you talk to her husband about her?"

"Oh, God, Josh, I couldn't do that. He's the lead suspect in the case. And he creeps me out."

"Oh, c'mon. You've questioned worse. What's happening to you in Cumberland Creek? Are you losing your edge?"

She thought for a moment. "Maybe I am. But this is close to home. I'm a mother now. She lived two doors down. He lives there. I don't want him showing up here when Mike's not home—which is a lot these days, you know. What premise would I have in talking to him?"

"I don't know. Think of something. I have to go. Be careful, Annie. Love you."

"Love you, too, Josh," she said into the phone, and went back to folding clothes, which is what she was doing before Joshua had called to check on her.

Mike had been gone for two days. He wasn't scheduled to be home for another two. Her brother often called to check on her, as did her mom and dad. Now, of course, the scrapbook club members also called. It was hard being a single mom—she couldn't imagine doing it all by herself, every day. Everything, from taking the trash out, to tucking the boys in at night—it was exhausting. God bless the women and men who were single parents.

One more load of laundry today and she would be finished—at least for the day. Tomorrow there would be another pile. The piles never stopped.

The phone rang. "Hello," Annie said.

"Ms. Chamovitz?"

"Yes."

"This is Jim Carlson from the *Washington Tribune*."

"Oh, yes, Jim. I know your work. How are you?"

The boys started running through the house. In a panic, she took the phone into the bathroom and shut the door.

"What can I help you with, Jim?"

"We're doing a story on domestic violence that leads to murder. I've got reporters all over the country looking into local situations. We sent a reporter to Cumberland Creek a few days ago. He's not getting anywhere. You know, nobody will really talk to him. We've gotten some basic facts from the cops, but that's all. I'd like to get a story about the possible murder of Maggie Rae Dasher. I'm looking for a series, perhaps. You know, profiles of the people involved. Her husband, maybe. Someone else in the family as well. Maybe even one of the kids. I don't know. I just need someone to get in there and poke around. Someone the locals trust. Are you up for it?"

Annie's heart was pounding—and then leaped. Could she manage to do this story? "I'm not sure how much they trust me, either. But I can give it a go. When is the deadline?"

"Work like this takes time. The deadline is flexible. But I do want the scoop on it, if you can manage."

"Well," she said. "I already kind of have a head start on it."

"What do you mean?"

"I have Maggie Rae's papers, photos, and scrap-books," she told him.

"How did you get those?"

"They were left on the curb for the trash, and my friends and I took them. Nobody from the family has even asked after them. The cops know I have them. They already copied them and then gave it back to me."

"Well, what do you know? Life in a small town. It looks like I called the right person, after all," he said.

She could hear the boys squealing in the background as they raced through the house. Could he hear them? She began to sweat.

"I'll e-mail the details on pay and how to reach me, and so on," he told her. "I have your e-mail."

"Great, I'll look for it, and I'll get busy on this right away," she said.

After they hung up the phone, she opened the door to all of the clothes she had just folded—they were strewn about the house as if a party was going down. And there seemed to be. Sam wandered through the room with a pair of her underwear on his head.

How would she ever think clearly enough to write these stories? Why didn't she tell him no, that she had retired several years ago at the ripe old age of thirty-two? Why couldn't she?

Chapter 30

"Thank God, it's Saturday night and I have only one more week to the recital," Vera said after taking a drink of wine. She was finishing up a scrapbook for her star dancer, Nancy Mayhew. She'd just gotten the letter in the mail—Nancy would be attending Juilliard in the fall. One more picture to place, and it was a lovely one—when Nancy was dancing the part of Clara in their annual production of *The Nutcracker*.

There was Nancy—such beautiful lines—in a full arabesque, brown hair undone, adding to the youthful costume. She was gazing at the camera with confidence; yet she maintained character. The best dancers were always excellent actors. Their eyes were as much a part of dance as their perfectly pointed, turned-out toes.

She stuck the photo onto shimmery silver paper, which framed it beautifully, and watched as it brought out the delicate blushes—the pinks and the sages—from the photo. She placed glue dots on the back of the paper and stuck it in the center of the deep purple page.

"I hear you," DeeAnn said. "It's been a hell of a week at the bakery. 'Tis the wedding season, and I'm exhausted."

"I bet you are," Sheila said, placing paper onto her

cutting plastic board. Then she placed her circular template over a picture and began to cut it with her X-ACTO blade. Vera loved watching Sheila wield an X-ACTO blade.

"Some of the cakes are gorgeous, though. There was one we decorated for today that was red, gold, and white. It was stunning!"

Vera flipped her scrapbook back to the beginning to check through the pages to make sure everything was still where it should be. The glue dots and other adhesives now were so good that she rarely found anything—but she wanted to be careful, especially since this album would be a gift. She loved the little-girl photos of Nancy. She was always so sweet, but she was such a serious dancer. Just the way she pointed her toe suggested maturity beyond her years—even as her face still held sweet, chubby, soft baby cheeks.

Suddenly her stomach lit with tingles. Maybe she would have a daughter. Maybe someday she would be working on her own daughter's dancing scrapbooks. A tear stung at her eyes. Could it be? Would that she could choose, it would be, of course, just to have a healthy child. But to have a girl? A girl to dance? Could she be one of those mothers who sees her dreams come true through her daughter? Did she really want that?

When Vera thought about her own mother—well, no two women could be more different. Beatrice had tried to ignore Vera's commitment to dance for years. She just wrote it off as "good exercise." She supported her and made sure she had what she needed—the shoes, the tights, the leotards, the countless hairnets, the bobby pins, and so on. But when Vera hit high school, Beatrice talked with her about college and her future.

"Your dance—and your dance performance and teaching at such a young age—is going to help you get into college. But what will you study? Law? Medicine?"

"Law?" Vera said. "Law? No, Mother, I'm a dancer. I'd rather just find a company to audition for. But if you insist I go to school, I'm studying dance."

"Study dance in college? Well, I've heard of everything now! You don't go to college for dance."

"You can. And I will," Vera said.

Her mother waved her off, shook her head, and walked away.

Vera knew she had disappointed Beatrice by not studying something like physics or medicine, but dance was the only thing that interested her. At least, even at that young age, she knew herself. And knew that she could live with her mother's profound disappointment. Even her father had found it hard not to disapprove.

"We love you very much and will support whatever decision you make. But dance is not a good way to make a living, you know?" he said.

Thinking back to the way that made her feel, Vera decided right then and there that she would never put pressure on her child to dance—or not to dance. Or to do or be anything. Life was tough enough without having to live your life to please someone else.

Yes, she would help her son or daughter discover his or her own passion, and would support him or her in no matter what it was. Soccer. Painting. Baking. Whatever. She'd keep her mouth shut about it and let them choose.

But she was getting ahead of herself. Her first concern was delivering a healthy baby, carrying it to term, and taking care of it, which seemed complicated enough. There were thousands of books about how to take care of babies. She'd never have all of the time she needed to read every book on the subject, of course, but she did go to the library today and checked out a few. She also heard a ridiculous story about her mother finding a baby doll on her front porch.

"Who told you about that?"

The librarian shrugged. "I can't remember."

"If it were true, I'd know about it," Vera said, and took her books out the front door.

But now, she wondered about it. Her mother was surely not herself these days. Darn, she wished they would find the person who stabbed Bea. Was it the same person who had killed Maggie Rae? The police suggested that. It was too coincidental. But why Beatrice? Did she know something about the murder? She had been known not to tell Vera things because she didn't want her to worry. Suddenly the thought of Beatrice as a grandmother made Vera smile.

"What are you doing over there?" Sheila interrupted Vera's thoughts.

"Thinking about the baby," Vera said, and smiled.

"Me too. I'm actually knitting a blanket. I've not knitted in years," Paige said. "It's going to be great to have a baby around."

"You're onto something other than the murder," DeeAnn said. "But I can't get over there being a murder in our little town. It makes me so angry and so sad."

"Really?" Annie spoke up after setting down her plate, which was smeared in hummus. "It frightens me. Who killed her? Where is he? Or she?"

Vera felt a coldness come over her and then travel along her spine. She shivered. Here she was—bringing a baby into this increasingly complicated world. At least she could protect and love him or her. And that is what she and Bill would do. She and Bill were going to be wonderful parents. She was sure of it. She hadn't felt so good—so happy—in years. It was as if her cells were exploding with life, energy, and happiness. She noticed a difference with Bill as well. This baby was already bringing magic into their lives.

"I know. Once you start to think about it, it could be anybody," Sheila said. "You know, the way she was, well, I hate to say it, but she could be entertaining absolute strangers. Bring them to our town for a little sex, and who knows what else? Question is, are they gone or still hanging around?"

"Sheila!" Vera said, closing the dancing scrapbook. "You've got a hell of an imagination."

"Thank God for it, too. Or else I'd have lost my mind years ago," Sheila said; after a moment, she laughed. "Could you please pass me one of those chocolate cupcakes?"

"What do you have there, Annie?" Vera asked.

"It's a picture of Maggie Rae's mother. What a pretty calico dress."

"They all wore those dresses in those days," DeeAnn said, looking over Annie's shoulder. "And look at those hands. They look like they belong to a much older woman. These women in the Hollow in those days . . . about worked themselves to death."

"Oh, now, look at that," Sheila said, taking the photo out of Annie's hand. "There's something on the back. 'I ache for you, Mama.'"

"Bless her heart," Vera said.

Chapter 31

Annie sank into the warm bliss of her fourth beer and looked around the table. DeeAnn was intent on the page in front of her, moving pictures around, tilting her head. Paige just closed her scrapbook and was eating the last chocolate-and-peanut-butter cupcake. Sheila was straightening books on her bookshelves piled with scrapbook materials. Vera was stretched out on the floral couch, asleep. She had been for about an hour. Annie's eyes were beginning to droop.

Above the couch were beautiful pictures of Sheila's four kids. And the corner cabinet held even more pictures, along with trophies and ribbons. Thank God, there were no paintings of barns. Annie was a bit sick of the barn scenes everywhere she went. There was not much décor at all in the basement scrapbooking room that didn't revolve around Sheila's children. Annie wondered what Sheila would fill the room with if she didn't have children.

Annie loved these rub-ons that she had recently purchased from Sheila. She worked her stick across the paper until she was sure that the fancy scripted word "Magic" came out perfectly. She pulled the paper back slowly, until she saw the word on the page. Nice. Underneath the word was a photo of Maggie Rae and her husband, Robert. They looked so happy. His arms were around her. Both of them were smiling for the camera, taking a break from a family game of soccer. Someone's foot was kicking the ball in the background. A flying braid was part of the picture. Scattered pieces of their children. Imagining them now, with no mother, broke Annie's heart.

She looked at the snoozing Vera and thought how blessed she was to be expecting a baby. Vera had all of it in front of her. Annie loved the boys when they were babies—she didn't mind the sleep loss or the nursing. Somehow she found the energy to take care of them and the fortitude not to care how tired she was. In fact, she remembered rocking Sam in her arms until they ached, not wanting to lay him in his crib.

Annie closed the album. "I need to get going," she said after draining her last beer.

Paige looked at her. "I'm leaving, too. Need a ride?"

"Nah," she said. "I'll walk."

"Walk? Haven't you heard there's a murderer on the loose?"

"I'll be all right. I've got my pepper spray," she said, pulling it out of her bag. "And I just live right around the corner and down the street."

"Well, okay," Paige said. "You be careful." She was still gathering her things and shoving them in her scrapbooking tote when Annie said her good-byes.

Annie didn't have that much to carry, amazed that all of these scrapbookers had special equipment to carry all of their stuff in. DeeAnn and Paige both had cases on wheels. The cases had equipped compartments made just for scrapbooking supplies—a space for stickers, a space for sticky tape, a space for scissors, and drawers for paper. It was an amazing sight to behold.

She flung her bag over her back as she turned the

corner, and heard something. She wondered if she herself had caused the noise, or if someone else was out at this hour of night—or morning. What was it? One thirty-five, her watch said. She rolled her sleepy eyes. She'd pay for this tomorrow.

She heard the rustling noise again. Maybe it was one of the many neighborhood cats prowling around. Still, she moved forward through the darkest spot on the street as quickly as she could, heading to a more well-lit area. The moon was not quite full and clouds began to glide across it. The sidewalks gave off a little sparkle, and the streets were completely quiet—which Annie always found a little unsettling. The town had long rows of streets, with quiet houses on either side. Trees took on an ominous quality and they shadowed over the sidewalks.

Is that the thump of a foot?

Annie's heart raced and she felt sudden beads of sweat form on her forehead. It was all she could do to stop from running. And she wished she had not drunk that fourth beer. She just then realized that she was more than a little tipsy, just about tripping over her sneakers.

She reached in her bag and pulled out her pepper spray. Whoever it was would get an eyeful. A rustle again. She turned quickly—was that a man behind that bush? She tried to focus her somewhat drunken eyes. She held up her spray and saw the rhododendron shimmy as a figure moved behind it. A tall man was definitely crouching behind the bush. She blinked.

Confront him? Yank him out from behind the bush? Her heart beat madly in her chest. There was a day she would not have thought twice about it. But tonight, all she could think about was her two boys and getting home safely to them. She did not want to leave her children motherless—not if she could help it. *Don't be foolish,* she told herself, *just get home.*

But if a man was following her, should she really lead

him to her house? She stood paralyzed in that moment. *Go home? Confront him?*

The pull of her home won in the end. She thought that if he followed her, he'd have to deal with Mike and possibly the police.

When she opened the door of their tiny bungalow, she had never been so grateful to be at home in her life. Her eyes took it all in: the faded brown couch sitting against the wall with toys piled in the corner, the finger-smeared screen on the television; the big plaid chair, with the cushions beginning to wear out; the old blue afghan thrown over Mike's chair; the potty chair sitting in the corner; the tiny 1940s pink kitchen; her snoring husband; her sleeping boys. Yes. She was home.

The next day, as she was pouring Mike's coffee, she felt her heart jump as she thought about last night.

"I think someone followed me home last night," Annie told her husband.

"You think?" he said, putting down his fork.

"Well, someone was outside. It was one-thirty. I could hear him behind me every once in a while. And once, I think I saw a man behind a bush or something."

"You think?"

"I drank four beers, Mike, you know? But I'm positive someone was there. I wasn't *that* drunk."

"What? From now on, don't walk home. Get a ride from somebody, okay? Who knows what kind of creep that was? There's a murderer out there, Annie!"

"Yes, I know that," she said, sipping her coffee. "But I really hate to be bullied into driving instead of walking the two blocks to Sheila's. I mean, how crazy is that? I was armed with my pepper spray. And I'm fine."

"Don't be stupid, Annie. Until we find out who this

killer is, please don't go walking around the town alone with pepper spray to protect you. I mean, holy shit."

"Mike, I've been in worse situations. I can handle myself."

"That was then," he said, raising his eyebrows and his voice. "This is now. I love you. The boys love you. No more, Annie, do you hear me?"

Chapter 32

Vera's recital was another smash. All of the parents and children were happy with it. She was at home, relaxing on her baby blue soft couch in the middle of her let-down-after-the-show time—where she felt completely exhausted and exhilarated simultaneously—when the phone rang. It was Officer Bryant on the other end.

"Do you mind if I ask you a few questions, Ms. Matthews?"

"I don't mind at all," she said.

"Can you tell me where you were the morning of Maggie Rae's death?"

"I was home," she said, digging her feet between the plush cushions.

"Where was your husband?"

"He was away on business," she said.

"Do you know where your mother was?"

"Hmm. No. I don't really think I do. I imagine she was at home," she said, wondering what her mother or husband had to do with any of this. "That morning is when she was stabbed, of course."

"How well did you know Maggie Rae?"

She didn't answer right away.

"I knew her as well as anybody else did, I suppose. She kept to herself. But I saw her once a week for Grace's ballet class. And she was going to sign her younger one up," Vera answered, looking over at Bill's empty chair, feeling a pang of missing him.

"How do you know that?"

"She left a message at the studio the night before she died. She was going to bring her daughter in."

"Interesting. Oh, that's right. You mentioned that earlier. Very interesting."

"That's what I thought. It doesn't sound like something a woman would do if she were planning to kill herself."

"That sounds about right," he said. "Well, thanks for chatting a bit with me, Vera. Have a good night."

"Thank you. You too," she said. Strange for him to call her on a Saturday night. She dug for the remote and flipped the television on, pulling a green throw over the top of her. She switched the channels, looking for something decent to watch. She stopped on the public television station that was showing a lineup of British comedies.

It was quite a night. She leaned her head back onto the couch cushion and sank in. Then she heard the doorknob rattle. A key went into the socket, and the door opened. What the—she shot up off the couch—it couldn't be Bill. He wasn't supposed to be home until Monday. But there he was, standing in his raincoat, half soaked.

"Came home early, Vera," he said.

"I see that."

He slipped off his raincoat. "It's coming down out there."

"Yep," she said, getting off the couch and wrapping her arms around him. "Nice to see you."

He stiffened.

"Vera, I need for you to sit down and listen to me," he said, cupping her hands in his.

"What is it? Oh, God, is it Mama?" she said, sitting down, grasping her chest.

He smiled his worried smile. "No, darlin'. Nothing like that."

He sat next to her on the baby blue couch, where she had just been resting and thinking over her life.

"There's no easy way to say this. But, uh, I had an affair with someone."

"What? I don't believe that, Bill. What kind of sick joke is this?"

His face dropped and a tear formed in his eye. As he took off his glasses, he rubbed the tear away.

"Vera, I need you to listen with an open heart. Please."

She nodded. "What's going on?" She felt her heart sinking, and her stomach felt as if it would roll off into oblivion.

"I'd been seeing a young woman—"

"Young?"

He nodded. "Look. I have to tell you because it's going to come out eventually. I don't know of any other way to tell you this."

"Good God, Bill, what have you done?"

Was she dreaming? Was her perfect husband telling her he had been cheating on her? She couldn't believe what she was hearing. She felt the room spin.

"I don't know. She was so young and beautiful and willing. I feel like an old fool, really."

"Screw you, Bill, if you think I care how you're feeling." She just wanted to hit him. She sat on the edge of the couch and held herself back from clobbering him.

"The woman was . . . Maggie Rae."

Her hands went to her mouth; she gasped and felt sharp pangs in her chest.

"I'm sorry, Vera. You don't know how sorry I am."

"Sorry? Jesus, Bill. Did you . . . kill her, too?" she

barely asked. The wind, the energy, suddenly sapped from her.

"No," he said, looking like he'd been slapped. "But I am a suspect, which is why I'm home. I got a call from the police. I was with her the night she was killed, but I left around two in the morning. She was murdered around four."

Vera's thoughts were running at warp speed in her brain. The recital. The phone call from the detective. Her husband home early now. Telling her he cheated on her. Now he's a murder suspect. He cheated on her with a much younger woman. He cheated on her.

"Vera? You are angry, I'm sure. But you need to know that with Maggie, it was just about the sex. No emotions. No love. No relationship."

"Christ, Bill. Do you think that makes me feel any better?" she shot at him. What to do? Leave? Make him leave? Forgive him? Pretend it didn't happen? Here she was, expecting his child.

"What's going on in that mind of yours, Vera?"

She was thinking that they already had the room upstairs picked out for the nursery and had chosen the color—a beautiful butter yellow. They were trying to make up their minds about the cribs they had been seeing and had decided on a lamb theme. Funny what you think of in times like this.

But a resolve formed hard in her guts—in that moment, she knew she hadn't loved her husband in years. A good friend and companion, yes, but there was no love between them. It wasn't her heart that he was breaking—it was her pride, her integrity, their commitment to one another, which somehow seemed to be deeper than the word "love" could even get to. No point in bringing a child into this. It would work out somehow, but it would have to work out differently from what she'd thought.

"Bill, I think you need to leave."

"Vera!"

She put up her hand. "Really? Really? Are you going to argue with me about this now?" She stood up and stomped up the stairs, stopping halfway up. "I want you out of this house."

Chapter 33

Beatrice had just gotten into bed when the doorbell rang.

"God, who could it be at ten-thirty?" she muttered.

Bea felt a stab of fear and reached for her pistol. She pulled off the safety. She didn't know much these days, but one thing she did know: that was no ghost at her front door.

"Who is it?" Beatrice called to the door.

"It's me, Bea. Bill," the muffled voice said.

"Oh, for heaven's sake," she said, opening the door. "What's going on?" Her heart was racing, wondering about her daughter.

When she saw the dejected look on his face, she knew it was serious.

"Beatrice, she's fine. She just kicked me out. I wish there were someplace else I could stay, but the hotel is filled. Can I stay here tonight?"

Beatrice stifled a laugh. *Vera kicked Bill out?*

"Well," she said, clearing her throat. "C'mon in, Bill."

"Thanks," he said, bringing in his bag.

"Good Lord, how long are you staying?"

"Well," he said, looking at his bag. "I was still packed for the business trip. You see, I needed to get home . . . and . . ."

Beatrice watched her son-in-law of almost twenty years tripping over his words. She saw the sick pallor on him.

"Can I get you a sandwich?" she asked.

"I don't want to be a bother."

"Oh, heavens, it's no bother. Was just thinking of getting myself one," she told him. "You know, a little snack before bed. I've got some chocolate chip cookies here, too. Fresh batch."

"I sure could use a bite. I don't know when I last ate today. Maybe it was breakfast . . . I don't know."

He sat down at her turquoise table as Beatrice fixed him a ham sandwich with mustard and mayonnaise— just the way she knew he liked it. She knew him almost as well as her own daughter did. She knew him so well that she had an immediate sense of foreboding as she handed him the sandwich.

"Must be serious," she said, sitting down on the chair next to him. He suddenly looked old. How long had he had those gray hairs, those wrinkles at the corner of his eyes, those droopy eyelids?

He swallowed his first bite and shook his head. His lip started to quiver.

Good gracious, is he going to cry while sitting at my kitchen table? Bea shifted around in her seat, her eyes dropping to the floor. Maybe he didn't need to know she saw him cry. Then came the sob. She reached out and grabbed his hand.

"Now, Bill, it can't be that bad. What has Vera done?" His hand was clammy.

He looked her straight in the eye. "It's not Vera. It's me. And I can't talk to you about this. It's very personal. I don't think Vera would appreciate it."

Without realizing it, he just told Beatrice everything she needed to know—except the details.

Suddenly she felt a cold air sweeping over her. She pulled her robe tighter around her. "It's so cold."

"It's not cold in here at all," he told her.

"I must have a chill," she said; then she smelled the rotten smell again, briefly. Her hand went to cover her mouth and nose—what a putrid scent—was this Maggie Rae? This smell? This cold? Suddenly the cold went, as did the smell, and her son-in-law was crouched next to her on the floor.

"Are you all right?" he said to her. "What's wrong?"

"I'm fine now," she said. "Just caught a chill, I guess."

He sat back in the chair. "Now," he said after a moment, "this is a damn fine ham sandwich."

She cleared her throat. "Now, Bill, I've known you a long time. I've also known my daughter since before she was born. I've always wondered about you two. You've always seemed mismatched to me, but it's really not my business."

"I knew you felt that way. We both did."

"I know Vera well enough to know that there are only a couple of things that would drive her to throw her husband out of the house. Cheating or murder. Maybe both."

His mouth dropped open.

"You don't need to know the details, but I've been putting this together, sitting here, right now. How did you know Maggie Rae?" *The smell, the cold. Of course, it was Maggie Rae.*

He sighed. "I've been seeing her off and on for a few years."

"And you told Vera tonight?"

"Yes. I had to. I'm now a suspect in the suicide-turned-murder case. I figured it was best that she hear it from me."

"That was mighty decent," she said with a sarcastic tone. "How is she?"

"She's in bed. She won't let me near the room."

Beatrice stood up and headed for the phone.

"Where are you going?"

"I'm going to call her."

"Let her sleep."

"Do you really think she's sleeping? Her husband of nearly twenty years comes home, tells her he's been cheating and is a suspect in a murder case, and you think she's sleeping?"

Some smart lawyer he is, she thought, and grunted. He knew what she was thinking.

She dialed the phone. "Pick up, Vera."

She hung up and dialed another number. "Scrapbook lady, you still partying over there? Can you come and pick me up? We need to go and see Vera. Well, now, don't ask questions. Just come and get me, would you?"

"Now, Bea, does the whole town need to know about this?" Bill asked.

"I didn't call the whole town, Bill. I called Sheila, who happens to be Vera's best friend. I think she's going to need us. Do you have something to say about it?"

"No, ma'am," he told her.

"Now, Bill, this isn't the worst thing to happen in the world," she told him as she started up the steps. "She may be able to forgive you, someday. After all, she's carrying your child."

"You don't understand," Bill said. "Vera will never forgive me. She's got too much pride. Damn. I just couldn't help myself with Maggie. I didn't love her. I swear. I just wanted . . . sex . . . to feel young and hot and sexy again. That's it. It was just sex."

Beatrice stopped in her tracks. "I hear you, Bill. I'm an old lady, so maybe my observations don't mean a damn thing in this world. But it's really never just sex, is it?"

"No," he finally said. "I suppose you're right. Things haven't been right with us for a long time. There's nothing wrong . . . just not right. Do you know what I mean?"

Beatrice didn't know what to say. Why did they stay together all these years? What held people in the same situations if they were not happy? If she could be blessed with another eighty years on the planet, she'd still never know. She loved her husband, and he loved her. Sex was never an issue. Neither was cheating nor murder.

"No, I can't say as I know what you mean, Bill. But it seems to me that you've got bigger problems than my daughter if you're under suspicion for murder."

"That will resolve itself, I'm sure," he said. "I'm innocent. I didn't kill her. I left her around two. She died around four—just about the time I was getting on the plane. That's a sound alibi. But they found my DNA on-site."

Beatrice continued on her journey up the stairs. Sound alibi. Maybe he didn't shoot Maggie Rae, but she had a feeling he may as well have.

Chapter 34

"Did you have to call him her *lover,* I mean right there in the newspaper for everybody and their brother to see?" Vera shot at Annie, who was sitting across the table from her. Annie's first article had been published, both in the newspaper and online versions.

"Well, that's what he was, dear," Sheila spoke up. "You need to accept that. Everybody knows it. Just seeing it in print is hard."

"Yes, I'm sorry," Annie said after cutting a picture of Ben and reaching for the sticky dots to place on the back of the photo before sticking it on the paper.

"It's humiliating," Vera said, throwing her pen down on the table, which was covered in bits of paper, archival-grade colored pens, and photos.

"It's more humiliating for him than for you. He's made quite an ass of himself," DeeAnn said.

"I never knew he wanted to . . . you know . . . ," Vera began.

"Oh, now, don't go down that road," Sheila said.

"Yeah, really," DeeAnn agreed.

"But I've been sleeping with the man for an eternity. He never once pinched me, slapped me, or asked me to let him tie me up. Nothing."

Sheila smiled. "Listen to yourself, darling."

Vera cracked a smile and laughed. "Yes, I know it sounds ridiculous."

"It really does," Annie said. "When it comes to human sexuality, well, it's very complicated. I've been reading a lot about it. Part of the whole S and M thing is escape. We are different people with different lovers, that's all."

Still, Vera mused, why did Bill feel like he needed to sleep with Maggie Rae to wear that mask? Well, he knew Vera well—or at least he thought he did—and he knew she would not have submitted to him. But she would have at least liked to be asked—or even not asked—just for him to assert himself while in the act. That would have been decent.

Vera sighed. He was gone—out of the house, and almost out of her life, even as his baby grew within her. God, she hoped she was carrying a girl. She'd teach her to be strong and follow her dreams—no matter what fool of a man came along. Sort of like what Bea had tried to do with her.

But still, Bea knew nothing about the terminated pregnancy or how that unraveled her, nor how it had brought her and Bill together like two wounded birds, clinging for life. Or not for life. She realized recently that she'd been mourning the death of her first baby all of these years. Those right-to-lifers had no idea how difficult it was to go through an abortion, how hard it was to even come to the decision. But then once you did, how it haunted you. Tormented you. If they knew it, they'd realize, perhaps, how cruel they were. Still, if she hadn't gotten the abortion, who knows what would have happened?

As it was, it seemed as if she'd wasted half her life with the wrong man, in the wrong town, with the wrong dream. Nothing left to do but move on and hope that her child would learn something from her life and not make the same mistakes. Maggie Rae's husband, at least, knew who she was. After all these years, she found that Bill was a different person altogether. But Vera found out—quite by accident—that Robert supported Maggie Rae—up to a point.

It was the morning she'd gone for a drive after a restless night. She ended up at Harmony Bakery, on the outskirts of town, and bumped into Robert, who asked her to join him. She was too tired to argue and figured there was nothing wrong about sharing doughnuts and coffee with the man whose wife cheated with her husband.

"I knew she had boyfriends," he told Vera after they started commiserating about their cheating spouses.

"Didn't it bother you?" Vera asked him.

He shrugged. "I figured as long as she kept coming back to me, it was okay. It was better to be honest about it with each other than to lie, you know? She had this incredible drive. And that had nothing to do with me."

"I think I admire your attitude, though I'm not sure I understand it," Vera said after sipping her coffee. She wished she could find a way to change the subject gracefully. "I mean, the way I was brought up, sex is about love."

"It should be," he said, looking at her shyly. "Now," he continued, "the only thing we ever really fought about was her writing."

"Why is that?"

"Because I felt that she could really write. You know, Maggie Rae was gifted. Why she used her gift that way, well, it used to bother me," he said.

"Still, it was what called her to write, yes?"

"Oh, yeah, I guess so. I just wish I could find her papers, cards, and things. Maybe it would explain some things to me."

"Robert, we have them," Vera blurted out.

"What? How?"

"We found them on the street the day she died, along

with her scrapbooks. We rescued them and have been working on putting books together for your kids. We figured you didn't want them."

He looked perplexed. "I had no idea. How did they get on the street? I didn't put them there."

Vera shrugged.

And so the plot thickened.

"Why would you meet with him?" Sheila wanted to know. "He probably killed his wife."

"We met to discuss Grace, at first. Then I felt more comfortable with him at the bakery. I mean we were out in public. After getting to know him, I don't know about him killing Maggie Rae," Vera said. "I'm not so sure anymore."

"What makes you say that?"

"I can't say, really. It's just a feeling I have."

"At least now we know he didn't put her scrapbooks on the curb," DeeAnn chimed in.

"Well, if he didn't—and I'm not so sure I believe that—then who did?" Sheila asked.

"Perhaps the killer put them on the curb, but why?" Annie wondered. "Is there something in all that stuff that would implicate the killer?"

"Maybe it was Maggie Rae, herself," Vera said.

"Or maybe it was Bill," Annie said.

Vera looked daggers at her. "Okay. A week ago, I never would have imagined my husband in bed with another woman, I'll give you that. But I know there's no more surprises with Bill. I know he doesn't have it in him to kill someone."

"Maybe the S and M thing got out of hand. Not that people who are into S and M are also into guns and killing. But maybe the emotions of it all just sort of exploded," DeeAnn said. "I'm sorry to say that, Vera. But it's something you need to think about. Once the trial opens, who knows what they will dig up. Prepare yourself for anything."

Vera's blue-lined eyes grew wide with disbelief to hear such a thing coming out of DeeAnn's mouth.

"That might be best," Sheila said. "You know I've always loved Bill, like a brother. But I've always wondered about him."

"What do you mean?" Vera asked.

"He was always a bit too placid. I always wondered what would happen if he lost his temper. You know, what's underneath that calm, composed self of his."

"That's just who he is," Vera said. "I've only seen him lose his temper once or twice the whole time I've known him."

"Really?" Annie chimed in. "How long have you been married?"

"Almost twenty years, but I knew him all through college," Vera said. "All right, now, I'm beginning to resent this line of questioning. How many of you could kill someone?"

She was met with an awkward silence.

"I think if we are all pushed hard enough, we are capable of murder. If someone hurt a member of my family . . . ," DeeAnn began.

"Now, that's not what I'm talking about. Whoever killed Maggie Rae meant to do it. It was very personal. Bill doesn't have it in him," Vera said as the other women turned back to their scrapbooks.

"So, if Bill couldn't kill someone, and you think that her husband didn't do it, who did it? Leo? Zeb? I don't know. The police questioned them, but were not able to hold them. They both have solid alibis. We are missing a huge piece of the puzzle," Annie said.

Chapter 35

Annie checked through her bag one more time: notebook, check; tape recorder, check; water bottle, check; camera, check. Three hours for getting to Harmony Bakery, interviewing Tina Sue—Maggie Rae's sister—and returning home in time to pick up Sam from preschool and Ben from daycare.

Tina Sue lived in Jenkins Hollow and suggested they meet at the bakery because it was easy for "nonlocals" to get lost in the hills. The bakery had a quiet café adjoining it.

Ben fussed a bit when Annie dropped him off at day care—and she wondered if he'd gotten enough sleep. He was always more clingy when he was tired. His sobs made her ache as she forced herself to walk away from him. The best thing to do was to keep walking, Janet, the teacher, had told her when this first happened. It was only two half-days a week that he was there. But, God, it was hard. How did she not know if she was damaging her child forever by leaving him there?

She took a deep breath and willed away her tears. She had no idea that parenting was going to be so painful, so fraught with moments of just not knowing if she was doing the right thing.

She sat in her car and started it up. Jeez, what was she doing? Was this interview that important? This job? She wanted to run back into the daycare and grab her son. Her cell phone beeped. It was her editor.

"Yes?"

"Great piece, Annie. We all want more. Are you taking your camera today?"

"Yes, sure."

"Okay, great. We need a few more photos with this piece. Okay?"

"Sure. I'm on my way," she said, then put the car into gear.

She was being foolish. Ben would be fine. Taking another deep breath, hoping to settle her stomach, she pressed her foot on the gas pedal.

It was one of those clear spring days that made Annie feel like she and Mike made the right move by picking up their lives and moving their family here. The farther she drove toward the outskirts, with the mountains looming in the distance, green fields on either side of her, the more at peace she felt. She wanted her boys surrounded by fields, mountains, and breathing fresh air.

She was unprepared for the size of the bakery, though DeeAnn had told her it was a tourist trap. It definitely catered to tourists, with all the cutesy Mennonite cookbooks, trinkets, and "handmade" items, like quilts and crocheted blankets. Just the scent of sugar and lard that met people when they opened the door of the bakery was enough to put twenty pounds on a person.

Tina Sue was already sitting with a doughnut and a cup of hot chocolate on the wood table in front of her. Annie ordered a cup of tea and a cheese biscuit. *Four dollars for a biscuit?*

This was the second time she spoke with Tina Sue; the first was at the playground, after Maggie Rae's death. Tina Sue looked better today, eyes less swollen and red, with just a bit of pink lipstick to give her a little color.

"Thanks for agreeing to do the interview," Annie said.

"You're quite welcome," Tina Sue replied after sipping her cocoa. Her expression held something innocent, almost childlike as she sipped her chocolate drink. "I'm happy to help."

"There's a lot of controversy surrounding your sister's death. It must make it difficult on the family. How are you-all doing?"

"We miss her. Especially the children do, of course. We're trying to be strong for them. I'm glad school is almost out, because that will make it a little easier for them to manage. I teach school in Lynchburg and will be off for the summer, so I can stay with them until we find someone else."

"What do you think of all the controversy?" Annie asked, and bit into her dry biscuit. How disappointing. The biscuit was so beautiful, yet tasteless.

"I'm not sure what you mean. A murder always has controversy, doesn't it?"

"Is that what you think happened?"

"I never believed my sister would kill herself," Tina Sue said after a long pause.

"Why?"

"She wasn't depressed. She was one of the most happy, well-adjusted people I knew. A great mom. Loved being a wife."

"But you know, of course, that she had many lovers?"

Tina Sue squirmed in her seat and brought a napkin to her mouth as she looked out the window.

"Yes. I knew that. And maybe that's one of the reasons she was so happy. I mean, so many of us might think about taking a lover and don't have the guts. Some people just don't believe in monogamy, and many of those people are happy and well adjusted in their lives," she said, as if rehearsed.

She is saying all the right things. Who has she been coached by?

"Why would a woman with a dedicated husband, four beautiful children, a successful writing career, albeit secret, take on so many lovers? Why would she allow herself to be used by men who obviously did not care about her, while her children were asleep upstairs?"

"It's really about your viewpoint. She didn't see it that way at all," said Tina Sue, now twisting her napkin. Her pink nail polish was chipped and her nails were uneven.

"That is not the societal standard. Would you not agree to that?"

"I would. But there was nothing standard about my sister. For example, she went to the high-school prom with two dates. Oh, that gave folks something to talk about for years," she said, and laughed. "I just came to accept and love her for who she was. And really, that's the best we can do for ourselves and anybody else in our lives, isn't it?"

"What about her husband?"

"What about him?" she said, her well-shaped eyebrows knitted.

"What do you think about him?"

"I always thought my sister could do better. But that wasn't up to me, of course. But if you're asking me if I think he killed her, I have to say, I really don't know. Sometimes I think he's capable of murder. Other times, I think, 'Good God, could this man really have killed my sister?'"

"How well do you know him?"

"Well enough to know about his temper and that he hit my sister several times through the years."

So much for the "theory." It just became a fact—as far as Annie was concerned.

"How did you know?"

"Once, she came to visit with a black eye. She liked to

be submissive in sexual relationships, but she didn't want it so rough that she'd be bruised, especially not on her face. So I asked her about it."

"And?"

"Robert didn't like her writing erotica. Actually, I don't think it was because she was writing erotica. I think it hurt his pride that she made more money than he did," she said, taking a bite of her doughnut.

Annie sat back and drank her tea. "You know, Maggie Rae's papers are full of evidence her husband hurt her frequently. He's denied those allegations and maintains his innocence. But why else would he write apologetic cards about saying that he hurt her?"

"I really can't say," Tina Sue said, and blinked.

"I wondered why she'd put up with that. But sometimes the pattern of abuse reaches back into childhood," Annie said, treading as lightly as she could.

Tina Sue sat up straighter in her seat. "Oh, no, there was nothing like that in our house. As a child, Maggie Rae was so happy. She really invented her own world. She spent a lot of time alone. Didn't seem to bother her at all. She filled notebooks with her thoughts, stories, and poems. Maggie Rae also loved to dance, was quite a good dancer," Tina Sue said, her voice cracking as she looked out the window.

Annie took a deep breath. "Forgive me for asking, but did she have any darker tendencies. Violent?"

Tina Sue nodded and looked at her hands, which were twisting the napkin furiously now. This was the worst part about being a reporter. Here was Maggie Rae's sister, obviously distraught, and it was Annie's job to keep probing. She took a deep breath and watched her subject.

"Yes, come to think of it. Maggie Rae had a dark side to her—she mutilated her Barbie dolls, for example, and had gotten into more fights at school than most children. My parents had a time with her."

"What did your parents think of her writing erotica?"

"They never knew. Of course, our real father died when we were still kids. He was a good man, very devout. My mom remarried several years after, and then she died. We were raised, basically, by my stepfather and a stepmother, later."

"I didn't know that."

"Oh, yeah. Well, many people don't, why would you? He was a great stepfather and just stepped right into our family. And, well, he married Shelby after we were older. You know, teens."

"Did you and Maggie Rae get along okay?" Annie asked after a moment of letting that news sink in.

A winsome smile came across Tina Sue's face.

"We did have our moments. She accused me of being the good sister, the devout one. She said she could never be as good as me, so why try? She couldn't wait to get off the mountain, and I never understood it. She was surrounded by family who loved her, but their love didn't comfort her. I've never understood her choice to live in Cumberland Creek, to marry an outsider. But I think that's pretty typical of siblings. We were raised as good Christian girls and tried to get along."

Annie tried to ignore her last statement. Was that a slam because she was Jewish? Surely not. Still, she found the hair on the back of her neck standing at attention. She decided to change the subject.

"What would you like people to remember about your sister?" Annie asked.

"I really hate that this murder investigation has become about her sex life. She was much more than that. A good and kind person. A gifted writer. Really wonderful mother. Excellent cook. The best sister ever. But, you know, she'd really not mind the sex part. She was a free thinker and lived her life honestly. She just had this intense sexual drive. Funny, if she were a man, I'm not sure we'd even be discussing this."

Her last statement gave Annie pause. She thought about it all the way to pick up Ben and Sam. It was true that she'd probably not be asking very much about a man's sex life, even if it had been revealed that he had several lovers. But then again, it wasn't really Maggie Rae's sex life that interested her—it was the impulse that lay beneath it.

Chapter 36

"Randy and I just had the best visit," Paige told the Saturday-night croppers. "You just can't believe how much I've missed him."

She was now working on a new album for him—a mother-and-son album, filled with photos of their activities through the years and mementos, such as ticket stubs, programs, ribbons from awards he'd gotten. She was also doing a good bit of journaling—writing alongside the pictures.

"I love these journaling boxes. You just write on them, place them next to the picture, and voila!" Paige said.

"That's going to be an amazing gift for your son to have," Sheila said.

"How's Earl taking it?" Vera asked.

"He's not thrilled," she said. "But I'm working on him."

"Good," Vera said, turning to Annie. "How's the writing and the interviews coming?"

Annie finished eating her chip and held her finger up. "You know, I'm glad you brought that up. I wanted to run this by you. I'm getting a lot of conflicting reports about Maggie Rae. It's interesting."

She pulled out her recorder from her bag and set it on

the table. "Here's my interview with Mary Miller, one of Maggie Rae's teachers."

Annie pushed the play button:

Annie: I'm so sorry about Maggie Rae.

Mary: Yes, me too.

Annie: I understand she was an unusual child.

Mary: Very creative. But other than that, I don't know.

Annie: What about her teenage years?

Mary: What about them? I hope you're not referring to all those wild rumors.

Annie: Was that all they were?

Mary: Of course. She was gifted with a vivid imagination and a bit of a big mouth. But she was a good Christian girl, from a good family.

Annie: What exactly do you mean by that?

Mary: What I mean is, she was raised right. Respectful of her elders. Went to church. Studied hard. Had a good and kind spirit. She was not the bad girl that people claim she was.

Annie: How do you know?

Mary: I watched her, you see. I was fascinated by her and her sister, how they looked alike but were so different. Tina Sue just never was as bright as Maggie Rae. Maggie Rae just shone like a bright light. Tina Sue was, and is, a good person, but never was bright—in any way. I always wondered how their parents felt about that. It was so obvious. And I always wondered how the sisters really felt about it. I'll always remember this poem Maggie Rae wrote. It was called "No Questions, Just Faith." And it was about the way her father raised her. She was not allowed to question him. Very old-school upbringing. In the poem, she was praying to find a way to make peace, within herself, with all of her questions. Her brain never seemed to rest. Her family didn't quite know how to deal with it.

Annie clicked the recorder off.

"Maggie Rae *wasn't* the bad girl?" Vera said. "I beg to differ."

"Well, of course, you would, dear," Sheila said, and patted her hand.

"I mean, there she was, sleeping with my husband and God knows who else," Vera said.

"Mary was talking about when she was a teenager," Paige said. "Right?"

"Yes. And keep in mind that Tina Sue said she slept around a lot as a teenager," Annie said. "I'm not sure what to make of it."

"I'm a teacher and I can pretty much tell you who is a bad girl and who isn't in our high school. But every once in a while, I'm surprised. I was shocked when Penny Taylor showed up for school this year pregnant. Maybe Mary didn't know them as well as she thought."

"That's what I thought," Annie said. "But I thought that her other observations were interesting. Tina Sue led me to believe that there wasn't much sibling rivalry. I mean, there were some little issues, like Maggie moving from Jenkins Hollow—"

"Little?" Sheila interrupted. "That would not be a little issue to those folks. It was traitorous. For generations, if you lived up there, you married there, had your family there. You just didn't consider leaving."

"So when she married Robert, who wasn't from the

area, and moved to Cumberland Creek, it probably upset a lot of people," Annie said.

"Indeed," Vera said, setting down her photos. "But you know what upsets me? They still have not found who stabbed my mother. I mean, good God. What are we? A major city? I just can't believe the police have found nothing. No fingerprints on the knife. Nothing."

"I can't believe Bea doesn't remember anything. Or that she didn't feel anything. It's so strange," Paige said, gluing down a photo of her and her son in front of a tent at a campground.

"She's pretty sure that she didn't see Robert that morning," Vera said. "So if the killer is also the person who stabbed Mama, that leaves him out."

"Oh," Annie said. "I also have Robert's interview on this tape. Such as it was. Do you want to hear?"

She hit the play button again:

> Annie: Nice to see you again, Robert.
>
> Robert: Same here, Annie. I don't know what we have to talk about. I've told everybody everything I know.
>
> Annie: I've not heard you mention that you beat Maggie Rae.
>
> Robert: What?
>
> Jeff Myers: Don't react to that. I think you should leave, Ms., uh, Cham-o-vitz, is it?
>
> Annie: I'm sorry, Mr. Myers. I thought your client would like to get on the record about his wife beatings.
>
> Jeff Myers: Alleged wife beatings, Ms. Chamovitz.
>
> Robert: Jeez!
>
> Annie: There's nothing alleged about it.
>
> Jeff Myers: We'll see about that.

Annie: My mother always told me not to trust
        a man wearing a bow tie. Are you sure
        you want this attorney to represent you,
        Robert?

She shut off the recorder.

"That didn't get far," Vera said. "You were kind of mean, Annie."

"Mean? He beat his wife, for God's sake. What's wrong with you?" Sheila said.

"Regardless," Annie answered, "I have another interview scheduled with him on Monday. I hope it leads somewhere. I also have one scheduled with Bill and Detective Bryant."

DeeAnn lurched back in her chair, brought her hand to her head, holding her forefinger and thumb in the shape of an *L.* "Losers," she said, and laughed.

Chapter 37

The only time that Robert Dasher could meet with Annie was at night. He worked during the day. Now that Tina Sue was staying with his children a lot, he arranged to meet Annie at Patty's Pie Palace, which sat at the edge of town, before the long trek to Lynchburg—the opposite side of town than the long trek to Jenkins Mountain.

"Good Lord," Mike said. "These people love their pie."

"I like it, too," Annie said, and smiled as she reached for her keys. "I have no idea how long I'll be. I'm glad the boys went down easy tonight. Maybe you can get some rest."

"Nah, I think I'm going to look at some Internet porn," he said, and grinned.

She smacked him playfully. "Good night," she said.

"G'night," he said as she was walking through the door.

Her stomach suddenly felt like a lead weight had landed in it. Leaving her home at eight-thirty at night, with both boys snug in their beds, and her husband alone with them, felt akin to abandoning them. A part of her would much rather be with them, in bed with Mike, or snuggled next to him on the couch watching a movie. But Robert Dasher—and the story—pulled at her.

It was a short drive on the mostly dark roads. Did these folks not believe in streetlights? Suddenly, a brightly lit, pie-wedge-shaped diner shone in the not too far-off distance. It looked out of place on the long, winding road against the mountainside. Goodness. Annie wasn't sure if it was tacky or kitschy. Maybe it was both.

Patty's Pie Palace was crowded. It was one of the few places around that was open until eleven at night, proving that there was a nightlife in the area. The rest of Cumberland Creek proper rolled up the sidewalks at seven. Annie was surprised to see so many people. She laughed at herself. *There is a life after eight-thirty; I remember it.*

Robert was sitting in a corner booth. He lifted his head and nodded at her. He was alone—left his lawyer behind. Annie breathed a sigh of relief as she walked across the black-and-white tile floor, her sneakers squeaking against it. She paused momentarily to feast her eyes on the pies in the display case. Huge mounds of meringue, slightly browned, ignited her curiosity as to what was beneath them.

"That's some pie, eh?" Robert called out to her.

She walked over. "What's good?"

A grin spread across his face. Annie was slightly taken aback. She didn't think she'd ever seen the man smile. "Anything," he said. "I've eaten just about every kind they have, but I think the butterscotch is my favorite."

"Oh, that sounds good," she said, setting her bag on the cherry-red vinyl seat. She dug out her recorder and notebook and slid the bag over the seat, next to the wall. A strange, New Age, sort of jazzy music played more loudly than what Annie would like. She hoped that it wouldn't interfere with her recording.

"How are you doing?" she asked, tucking a wayward piece of hair behind her ear.

He looked down at his hands, which were folded on

the table, next to the upside down coffee cup waiting to be turned and filled. "I miss her every day."

He seemed sincere.

"I'm sure you do," Annie said, thinking it was probably true—even if he had killed her. "Can you tell me a little about Maggie Rae's family?" She clicked on the tape recorder.

"Sure. What do you want to know?" He smiled at the waitress, who had just come to their table and set tall glasses of water in front of them. "I'll have the butterscotch and a cup of decaf."

"Me too," Annie said, smiling at the waitress, and then watching her walk away. "I understand that it was a little controversial for her to marry someone who didn't grow up on the mountain."

Robert tapped his finger on the table. *Drum. Tap. Drum. Tap. Drum.* He looked out the window. "Yeah," he finally said. "Maggie Rae had a bit of a rough time with her family over it. She used to say she wished her mom were still around. You see, her mom was a Baptist who married a Mennonite man. Even though he was from the area, it was still considered a strange thing to do. Maggie Rae used to say her mom would understand and would defend us."

"You didn't think twice about marrying her?"

"No," he said, not quite looking Annie in the eye.

"Vera told me that you knew about Maggie Rae's affairs."

"Yes," he said, looking off to the server, who was heading toward them with their pie. She set the plates down on the table, along with the carafe of coffee, turned over their cups, and poured the coffee

"Anything else I can get for you?" she said.

"No thanks. This is fine," Annie said.

"I'm a married woman, Robert. I don't think I'd go for my husband sleeping around," Annie said in a lowered voice as the waitress walked away.

"So?" he said, picking up his fork and cutting a piece of his pie with it.

"So what's that about? Why would you allow your woman to have lovers?" She looked directly at him. He looked at the pie, then scooped his forkful into his mouth.

"Mmm," he said, and shrugged. "You know, people can have different arrangements."

"What's that supposed to mean?"

He looked at her in a funny way—was that a flirtatious look? She wanted to laugh—or smack him.

"I mean Maggie Rae and I had an agreement—an open marriage. We could both have sex outside of our relationship, as long as we kept our relationship the priority."

"C'mon, Robert, that kind of thing never works."

"It worked for us, for years. Until now."

"Are you suggesting . . . that it was one of her lovers that killed her?"

"Look," he said, putting his fork on his plate, making a clanking noise. "I don't know who killed my wife. But I know it wasn't me."

"But what about one of your lovers?"

His face reddened; his already thin lips flattened with tension. "I, uh, didn't have any lovers."

"But you said—"

"Yeah. I know what I said, but I was just not interested in anybody else." He scooted around in his seat. The vinyl squeaked.

Annie looked away and took a bite of her pie. The flavor exploded in her mouth. Sugar. Fat. Creamy butter-scotch. What was there not to like?

She handed Robert the postcard that Tina Sue's husband had sent Maggie Rae. "What do you make of that?"

"Zeb," he said, and smiled. "What a nut. Thinks he's some kind of prophet or something. I don't know why he sent her this card. He must have known about her writing and thought she was an 'evil' woman."

"What do you mean that he thinks he's a prophet?"

"He claims to get messages from God, and he even has some followers," he said. "Sad sorts, really. 'Lost souls,' Maggie used to call them. Homeless people. Drug addicts. Criminals on the run, maybe. All looking for God, and all thinking Zeb McClain has a direct line to him."

"Whoa," Annie said, her stomach sinking and the hair on the back of her neck prickling. "This is the first I've heard of that. So bizarre."

"Speaking of bizarre. There's Leo Shirley and he's walking this way," Robert said. "Looks like he's on something."

Leo Shirley? Who was that? Annie was filing through her brain. Oh, yes. One of Maggie Rae's lovers—the one in the picture. She felt her face flame and looked out the window.

"Well, if it ain't Robert Dasher," the man said. "And look there, he's sitting with a new broad. Maggie Rae's grave ain't even cold yet."

"Excuse me?" Annie said, just as Robert started to say something.

Leo lurched back, as if he wasn't expecting her to speak, and grabbed his chest. "Good God, Robert, this one is gorgeous."

"Now, hold on there," Robert said, his face reddening.

"Or what?" The man leaned on the table and sidled up to Robert in a clear challenge. He held himself almost like an ape, slightly hunched-over shoulders, long arms hanging down.

"Now, just calm down, both of you," Annie said. *Were people looking at them—or did she just feel like they were?*

"Honey, he ain't got what it takes to satisfy a woman," Leo said, tilting his head toward Robert.

Robert stood and reached for the man's collar. "You best be getting out of here," he said quietly, but forcefully.

"A woman like that . . . needs a real man," Leo said, his eye ablaze, pupils dilated. He grabbed his crotch. Annie looked away, momentarily, in embarrassment— both for herself and Robert. When she looked back, Robert was growling as he slugged Leo; then she watched him fall over.

"Robert!" Annie yelled, but the manager was coming over as Robert straddled the man and let him have it again. Robert's face was contorted with anger and grief—she was struck by the complete sudden change of his mannerism—like Jekyll and Hyde. The aggression sent her heart racing.

Two men shoved Robert to the door; another two men picked Leo off the floor. He brushed himself off, and before turning back around in the direction he was heading, he looked at Annie with an approving leer.

Chapter 38

"I'm sorry to wake you up, Mike, but I'm going to be late," Annie said. "I wanted to let you know."

"Thanks," he said, sounding like he wasn't completely awake. "Be safe, love."

"I'm at the police station. Can't get much safer than that," Annie said as Detective Bryant walked into the interrogation room, where she was sitting. "Better go."

"Checking in with the husband?" the detective said, sitting down across the table from her.

She nodded as a wave of weariness came over her. She really wanted to be in bed, asleep, next to Mike, but the police asked her to come to the station and answer a few questions.

"What were you doing with Robert Dasher?" Detective Bryant asked, lurching forward in his chair.

"I was interviewing him. You know I'm working on a series of articles," she replied.

"Without his lawyer present?"

"I'm a reporter, not a cop. He can talk to me without his lawyer, even if his lawyer doesn't want him to. You know that."

"I'd have been more comfortable if someone else were there."

"We were at the Pie Palace, not in a dark alley," Annie said, trying to seem more lighthearted about his concern than what she actually was. She was downright angry.

"I don't want to offend your modern sensibilities, Mrs. Chamovitz, but a beautiful woman has no business meeting with a murder suspect anywhere, alone, especially in this weird case. Understood?"

"Detective, I appreciate your concern, but I can handle myself," she said. "But what do you mean by 'weird'?"

He looked away from her, his hands rubbing his face. "You know. All the sex stuff." He shifted in his seat, leaned back, and crossed his legs.

She held back laughter. Bryant was a big, tough guy, embarrassed about the kinky-sex issues brought up by this case. As she looked at him incredulously, his face began to redden and he looked away.

He finally met her eyes. "It's just that a woman like you needs to be careful, reporter or not. I'm surprised your husband lets you go out to meet men like Robert Dasher."

"I don't need my husband's permission, Detective, just his support. This is the twenty-first century," Annie said.

"I'm s-sorry," Bryant responded, stammering slightly. "I didn't mean—oh, never mind. Back to Dasher and what happened tonight. What exactly did you see?"

Annie crossed her arms in front of her and sat back in the uncomfortable chair. "I was looking out the window when it first happened. When I glanced away from the window, Robert was already on top of Leo. I thought it was interesting. Scary, but interesting."

"Why's that?"

"We were just talking about their open marriage. Robert said he was okay with Maggie Rae having lovers. The next thing I knew, he was trying to beat one of them up."

"Interesting observation," the detective said. "But maybe Leo came after him."

"Could be. Is that what Robert says?"

He nodded.

"What's this Leo like? I mean, I've heard that he's got a record and has been a problem for years," Annie said.

"Correct. That's a matter of public record."

"Are you going to make me look it up, or are you just going to confirm that?"

"He has a troubled background. I can't comment on family situations, but he does have a record. If you want details, you'll have to look it up. Who's questioning who here?" he countered, smiling weakly.

Annie smiled back.

"But, once again, I'm warning you to be careful if you go snooping around in his background. My impression is, he's nobody to mess with."

"Yet, Maggie Rae did. She was so smart and talented in every other way—except she slept with these creeps. I just don't get it," Annie said, almost to herself.

"Smart? Talented?"

"Sure. Her writing was remarkable."

"Remarkably dirty," he said, smirking.

A knock on the door interrupted.

"Detective?" A uniformed officer came into the harshly lit room and handed him a folder.

"Thanks," he said as the officer left the room.

"Any breaks in Maggie Rae's case?" Annie asked, thinking she might as well take advantage of this opportunity.

"Here's what we know," he said, leafing through his papers. "She did not kill herself. As we learn more about who she was and who she hung out with, we are questioning each and every person who came into contact with her, especially these men she slept with and her writing fans. Leo has been eliminated as a suspect in the case because he has a sound alibi. He was in a local bar and has about five witnesses who saw him . Bill says he was on an airplane at the time of her death. We're waiting on confirmation on that. And we continue to sort through the others."

"What exactly led you to believe she was murdered?" She'd read about it in the newspaper, but she wanted to be sure.

"I suspected it right away because the gun was still in her hand. Besides, it was in her right hand. Maggie Rae was left-handed. It really took very little investigating for us to see that this was not a suicide."

"And so you suspected Robert right away?"

"Usually, in these cases, it's the husband who murders his wife. A sad fact, but true," said the detective. "There was nothing taken from the house. Nothing showed that it had been broken into. All clues lead to someone who knew Maggie Rae. Someone who knew her quite well. Whether that's her husband or a lover, I can't say."

"What about a lover who happens to be her brother-in-law?" Annie asked.

"We've questioned Zeb," the detective said, not missing a beat.

"I'd think he's looking like your number one suspect, then," Annie said, just to see his reaction. This was a viable interview technique.

"What?" Bryant said with a raised voice. "Zeb Mc-Clain might be half crazy, but he's got a solid alibi. I think you should leave the detective work to us, Mrs. Chamovitz."

"I wish I could, Detective, but there is a killer out there, who might have tried to kill Beatrice Matthews, and might kill someone again. And it doesn't appear that you've made any progress at all in getting the killer off the streets."

The detective stood.

"I think you should go," he told her, and opened the door.

Chapter 39

"Annie!" Vera said, when she finished telling the scrapbookers about her evening with Robert Dasher. "Unbelievable!"

Annie was digging in Maggie Rae's boxes of photos, organizing them in piles, hoping to find a photo of Zeb. "I just really want to see what this guy looks like."

"He's beautiful. Didn't you see him at the funeral?" Vera said. "He looks like John Travolta."

"Interesting. A John Travolta look-alike married to Tina Sue?" Annie said. "And no, I didn't see him at the funeral. I think I'd have remembered. Is this Zeb?" Annie showed a picture to Vera. "He kind of looks like Travolta."

"Yes! But that's not a good picture of him," Vera said. "In person, well—"

"Almost as handsome as Bryant," DeeAnn chimed in. She was at the die-cut machine, feeding in paper, which the machine then spit out as perforated designs. She began to gently punch out the tree shapes.

"What an ass," Annie said.

"Who, Bryant?" DeeAnn asked.

"Yes. I saw him at the station. They wanted me to answer questions about Robert and Leo. I couldn't be much help. I was looking out the window when it first happened. Bryant was really cocky with me, wanted to know what I was doing with Robert, why wasn't I home at that time of night. What the hell? It's none of his business what I do."

"Hmm," Sheila said while pouring a glass of wine. "Sounds like he either really likes you or has it in for you."

"The police generally think of reporters as pains," Annie said. "So I'm betting it's not that he likes me. I mean, what is this? Second grade?" She laughed.

"But why?" Sheila wondered. "Aren't you both trying to do some good?"

"Yes, but sometimes there's a conflict between the public's right to know and the police wanting to protect them. I've known some really wonderful cops in my day, but I've also known some lousy ones," Annie said, sifting through photos.

She found three photos of Zeb: The first one was kind of blurry. He was sitting on a porch in a rocking chair—his shirt was off, showing well-sculpted abs and arms. The other picture was of him at a picnic, eating a watermelon. The last picture she found was a wedding picture. He and Tina Sue, dressed in a traditional white wedding dress, were standing at the altar, looking into each other's eyes.

She set them down on the table, one beside the other.

"He's at a church here," she said out loud, almost talking to herself.

"Well, of course," DeeAnn said. "That's their wedding photo."

"Yes, I see that, DeeAnn," she said, and looked at her, with her eyebrows lifted. "But Robert said that Zeb thinks of himself as some kind of prophet. I'm not sure how that jibes with being a churchgoer."

Sheila almost choked on her wine. "Zeb? He's just a bone-stupid redneck."

"Sheila!" Vera said. "Honestly, if I didn't know you better, I'd say you were a Yankee. No offense, Annie."

"None taken," she said, even though she was a bit startled to hear the word "Yankee" in this day and time. Besides, many Marylanders considered themselves Southern, even though Virginians did not. That was a subject she didn't want to broach.

"Now, listen, I've heard that Zeb gets visions," Paige said, finishing her glass of wine. "One of my students is a cousin or something. They say he believes these visions are from God."

"And we have a postcard from him, along with photos. How many of you keep pictures of your brother-in-law?" Annie asked.

"I certainly don't," Sheila replied. "Anybody want more popcorn?"

"I have a few wedding pictures of my brother-in-law and sister," Paige said, "but I don't think I'd keep any of just him. That is kind of strange. But Maggie Rae didn't seem to be very organized. Maybe she'd meant to give them to Tina Sue."

"I think Zeb and Maggie Rae had an affair," Annie said. "Imagine, with your own sister's husband."

"He killed her," Sheila said. "I know he did. I can feel it in my bones."

"Sheila, dear, you've said that about three men now," Vera said, and laughed.

"I just want them to find the murderer. I want them to find who stabbed your mother, too. This is getting a little ridiculous. The more we dig into her life, the more I wonder how one woman could really be with all these men. Most of them have issues. I mean, gee, look at that Leo."

"I did get a chance to look at him really closely, and I say there is something wrong with him. Robert said he was on drugs—maybe that's it," Annie said. "And Maggie Rae had a few issues of her own. I mean the S and M is one thing, but the sex drive is another. Maybe she was an addict."

Vera turned the page on her scrapbook—the style of which was frilly, with a lot of floral stickers and feminine colors. DeeAnn was back at the die-cut machine; she preferred a simple, but colorful, country flavor to her scrapbooks. Paige, who used a lot of funky embellishments in her scrapbooks, was cutting photos. Sheila, Annie mused, was a scrapbook artist, leaning back and surveying her page.

Annie stared at the photos in front of her. She was mentally leafing through the scrapbooks she'd already made of Maggie Rae's life. She had been more than piecing together a life in those pages. She'd been piecing together an illness and a murder. Who would have thought that scrapbooking would lead Annie and the others into such murky depths? S&M, open marriage, perhaps sexual addiction, murder? Scrapbooking was a lot like piecing a news story together, except with just images— and it also had a good deal in common with investigating murder, it turned out. Gathering information, digging into the past, putting the pieces together, checking out the research, coming to a hypothesis, and proving or disproving it. Interesting.

Okay, maybe that was a stretch, and maybe it didn't happen often—but it was absolutely happening now. Annie wondered if she died tomorrow, what would her pictures and papers say about her?

Chapter 40

Annie sat back in her chair and looked at the words on her computer screen. Robert Dasher's gaunt face played in her mind. Her boys were sleeping, finally. She glanced at the clock—eleven forty-five, too late for her to be awake. Mike was gone for the night—a short business trip. It was so quiet—she stopped keying in her transcript and reveled in the silence. The glow of one light on her desk, while the rest of the house was dark. Just then, she swore that she heard a noise in her yard. Like the soft thumping of a foot against the grass at the front of her house.

A chill ran up her spine and her heart lurched as she heard the sound again. Someone was in her front yard. Why would someone be there this late at night?

She sat for a moment, completely paralyzed, trying to catch her breath. She then rose and walked quietly through her hallway. She slowly pulled the boys' door shut. *Click.* The door closed. She walked into the kitchen, where she could see out the sheer-curtained window—perhaps without someone noticing her.

She could hear her pulse rushing through her ears as she tried to see out her window. Was she being silly? Was this in her imagination? All of this writing about murder and sex might just be getting to her. The streetlights shone on her front stoop as she heard the footfall again.

Suddenly an arm swung into her view and a flash of blond hair. Nobody else she knew had that exact color of hair: it was Robert Dasher.

He knocked on her door.

She stood quietly, not moving. Why would he be at her house this late? Should she answer? Tell him to go home?

"Ms. Annie? Please, Ms. Annie. Open the door. I know you're awake. I saw your light on."

That doesn't mean I'm taking visitors, idiot. No. No good can come of this.

He knocked louder. "Annie!" he said louder. "I need to talk to you."

"Robert?" she said through the door. "You need to go home. My children are sleeping in here."

"Okay," he said with a lower voice. "I just don't want you to think I killed Maggie Rae. We can talk, can't we?"

"It's late, Robert," she said sternly. "You need to go home."

She could hear him press his body into the door and turn the knob. Oh, God, please—had she remembered to lock the door? Yes!

"Annie . . . Annie . . . you have no idea about Maggie . . . the things she did . . . ," he mumbled. "I don't want a decent and pretty woman like you to get the wrong idea. You're so pretty, you know that . . . don't you?"

Okay. That did it. "If you don't leave now, I'm calling the police," she said. Right afterward, Ben cried out into the night, a night that would prove to be sleepless for Annie, even after she got Ben back to sleep. Like a madwoman, she went through their home, making sure all of the doors and the windows were secure. And then she did it again.

When she was done, she called Beatrice.

"I'm sorry to wake you, but can you please come over and stay with the boys? I need to go to the police station."

"I'll be right there."

"Be careful. Robert Dasher is out there somewhere."

"Hmph. I hear you," she said groggily.

When Beatrice arrived at Annie's door, she was dressed in her robe. She held her pistol in her hand. When she saw Annie raise her eyebrows, she casually slipped the gun into the pocket of her blue fuzzy robe.

"That bastard best not come back," Beatrice said.

"The boys are asleep. Please make yourself at home," Annie told her.

"Erratic behavior," Beatrice said, almost to herself.

"My thoughts, exactly. It was almost as if he were a different man."

"Careful, dear," Beatrice said as Annie walked out the door.

When Annie walked into the police station, she was surprised to see Detective Bryant holding the arm of a very drunk Robert Dasher. The detective looked up at Annie; Robert did not. It looked as though he was having a hard time staying awake.

"I'll be right with you, Mrs. Chamovitz," Bryant said.

She sat on the hard wooden chair in the waiting room and folded her arms. Robert was drunk, which explained a lot. Or maybe not—maybe it just muddled things even more. She'd seen drunks in her day—and even knew some alcoholics. As she thought about Robert—the redness to his face—it was the way a lot of alcoholics looked. Did he have a problem?

"Sorry, Mrs. Chamovitz," the detective said as he walked back into the room. "How can I help you?"

"I think you just did."

"What?"

"Robert Dasher was at my house tonight."

"What?"

"Trying to get inside. He was concerned that I thought he killed his wife."

"And?" Bryant was on the move again and gestured for her to follow him.

"And he said I was such a pretty and decent woman that he didn't want me to think bad of him," she replied, walking into his office.

He smiled, sat down on his chair, then leaned back in it. "The poor schmuck. He probably didn't kill her. But he really acts like he did."

"'He *probably* didn't kill her'?"

"He does have a sound alibi. He was working."

"It doesn't take too long to get from Richmond to Cumberland Creek, especially when there's no traffic in the middle of the night."

"Yes, I know that. Thank you very much," he said sarcastically. "But Bill says he was there around two, left at three. Robert has a witness that saw him at four in the hotel in Richmond, which is about the time she was murdered."

"Oh."

"And we have evidence that someone else was there."

Annie noted the college degree framed on his wall. Harvard. *What is he doing in Cumberland Creek?* She'd be damned if she'd ask him.

"The missing link?" she asked.

"Indeed."

"Care to share?"

"With you? No. I've been patient with you, helping you out with your stories. But I think it's time for you to back off."

"Why?"

"It could get dangerous. I warned you. Look at what happened tonight."

"Yeah, but you said he probably—"

"I know what I said," the detective said harshly. "Even if he didn't kill his wife, he is a man with a temper, and he could have hurt you tonight. Last time I checked, you have two little boys who need you at home. Maybe you should concentrate on them."

Annie's face heated with rage and humiliation.

He rose from the chair.

"Excuse me," Annie said. "My children are none of your concern. And I'll have you know they are well tended."

"Yeah, well, whatever," he said, walking away, leaving Annie burning with fury.

Chapter 41

Vera finished loading the dishwasher and poured the soap into the dispenser. She felt the baby flutter in her again. Strong. She flipped the on switch and heard the doorbell. Who could it be at nine in the morning?

She opened the door to her soon-to-be ex-husband and mother. Boxes filled their arms.

"What on earth?"

Bill shrugged.

"I've been cleaning," Beatrice said. "These are yours. I've been hanging on to them for all these years."

"C'mon in and set them down on the table. What's in them?"

"There's more," Bill said as he headed for the door. "I'll get them, Beatrice. You sit down."

Beatrice smiled at him. "Thanks, Bill."

She sat down. "What does a person have to do to get a cup of coffee around here?"

"Just made a fresh pot. It's decaf, Mom. I'll get you some. What on earth got into you?" Vera asked, pouring her mother a cup of coffee.

"I've no idea what you're talking about."

"I mean, with the boxes and everything."

"I talked to Annie this morning—she's pretty shaken

up. You may want to give her a call. But, anyway, about last night, after I got home and into bed, I was awakened by that Maggie Rae again. Or at least that's what I thought it was. I told it to leave me alone and closed my eyes, and then I heard this crash in the attic," she said, slurping her coffee. "Bill heard it, too, so we went up to investigate."

"And?"

Bill was dropping off the last of the boxes and piling them into the corner of the dining room.

"He saw Maggie Rae, too."

"What?"

"Now, Beatrice," he said, walking into the kitchen. "I'm not sure what I saw. It was dark and whirling around the attic, like a little tornado. You could barely see it because the moon only half shines in that room. And it left very quickly, shattering your mother's attic window when we turned on the lights." He leaned against the door frame, still wearing his pajama shirt.

Vera's mouth fell open. She was used to her mother talking like that—but Bill? So steady? So intelligent?

"So Bill taped up the window with some cardboard until we can get replacement glass. And I made some coffee and thought I'd keep him company and go through some things. I found all of your scrapbooks—since the time you were a baby. And I've been going through them."

"Me too." Bill smiled. "I hope our baby looks like you did. You were so cute."

Vera warmed. "Have a seat, Bill. Coffee?"

He nodded.

She poured his coffee. "I've got some peach cobbler in the fridge. Who wants some?"

"Who doesn't?" Beatrice replied.

The three of them sat at Vera's table talking about how good the peaches were this year.

"I think you're showing a bit," Bill interjected.

Vera nodded. "Maybe. You saw a ghost," she replied. "What the hell is that about?"

He shook his head. "I don't know, Vera. I really don't know. But it scared the shit out of me, I can tell you. Your mom's not the crazy old fool I always thought she was."

Beatrice laughed. "And you are not the boring fart I always thought you were."

"Well, now. Isn't this just a big love fest?" Vera said. "Just as our divorce is to be final, you two hit it off like two peas in a pod."

"Your divorce has nothing to do with me," Beatrice said.

"I really wish there were another way, Vera, if you could find it in your heart to forgive me," he said, reaching for her hand.

For the first time in years, Vera felt a stirring in her heart as she looked at Bill. She didn't know if she was capable of forgiving him—a forty-five-year-old man acting a fool with a young woman, whose body was firm and ripe, while her own was beginning to show signs of age. It felt cruel. A woman had her pride, after all.

"I'm leaving," Beatrice said. "You two need to talk."

"I'm not sure there's much to say," Vera said, but Beatrice left, anyway.

Bill was still holding her hand.

"I love you, Vera, with everything in me," he said. "We've been together forever. Can we just give it one more chance?"

"I don't know, Bill. . . . I . . . the whole Maggie Rae thing."

"Can you understand that I never felt for her anything near what I felt for you? She hired me to look over some contracts. I was intrigued by her writing and stopped by the house one day, and the next thing you know . . . I don't know. I suppose I was behaving in that clichéd midlife way. I was so flattered by this young woman's attention. So stupid of me."

He brought her hand to his mouth and kissed it tenderly, then bit it gently, sending shivers through her. God, it had been a long time, and the pregnancy left her hormones in such a state. He pulled her to his lap as she sighed.

"Bill, I don't know. . . ."

But he kissed her then, and she drew away from him. He kissed her again, pulling her closer to him. Her heart began to race and her resolve melted. She tried to squirm her way out of his arms—but he held her steady as he gently bit and sucked at her neck. His breath sent tingles through her. Was this really happening?

His hands began to wander all over her—she tried to stop herself from responding—but it was no good. She found herself hungering for more, hungering for her husband.

The next thing she knew, she was pulling him closer as she lay back on the kitchen table. Her cotton nightgown was above her waist, and the coffee cups rattled as plates, forks, and knives fell to the floor.

Chapter 42

DeeAnn almost choked on her wine when Vera told them what had happened. Annie ran over to pat her on the back. "Are you okay?"

Her face was red and she continued to cough, even though she nodded yes —she was fine.

"Good God," said Sheila. "How could you let him touch you?"

"I don't know, Sheila. I guess . . . I was horny."

The reply led to fits of giggles.

"Oh, for God's sake," Sheila said, trying not to laugh. "Right there on your table?"

"It was the best sex we've had in years," Vera said, brushing off crumbs from her purple T-shirt that had *I'd rather be scrapping* on it.

"Don't invite me over for dinner. That's all I have to say," DeeAnn said, her face red from laughing.

"So?" Annie asked after everyone calmed down. "Is the divorce off?"

"I don't know," Vera said, lining up her ruler so that she could cut a straight edge.

"Of course, you'll get back with him," Sheila said. "Isn't that what the sex meant?"

"I'm not prepared to let him back into the house," Vera said.

"It's just too confusing," Sheila stated. "I can't keep up with this."

"It's just the baby," Annie offered. "Every time I've been pregnant, I was incredibly horny and could not get enough sex. Poor Mike. He couldn't keep up."

"Well, I could have lived without knowing that," Sheila said. "I never felt horny when I was pregnant. I was always so tired and miserable."

"I feel great," Vera said. "And, in fact, Bill is coming over later tonight for another little chat."

"Be careful, Vera, this just might be, you know, divorce sex. It happens all the time," Paige said.

"How do you know?" DeeAnn asked.

She shrugged. "I guess I've read about it."

"So what if it is?" Vera responded. "I'm going to enjoy every minute of it." She bit into a lemon bar. "Goodness, this is delish, DeeAnn."

"Thanks. We're thinking of trying that recipe with some other ingredients—like blackberry, lime, and orange."

"Oh, that would be very good," Vera said.

Annie concentrated on cutting out the star figure from the template with her X-ACTO blade. She was thinking about her interview with Bill, which was two nights ago, the evening of the day he and Vera had made love on the kitchen table. He told her he was sure they would be getting back together.

"I feel confident that she will take me back," he had said. "I think she's beginning to realize that sex and love can be two different things. They are for men—and for some women. For Maggie Rae, for example. I wasn't her only lover."

"Did you know that at the time you were seeing her?"

"We never discussed it, but every once in while, she hurried me along because someone else was on his way."

"That must have hurt a little," Annie said.

"Not really." He shrugged. "I didn't care for her. I just wanted to sleep with her. Hasn't that ever happened with you?"

He looked at her with his piercing green eyes and she felt a ripple of embarrassment.

"I'm not the one being interviewed here, Bill," she told him, resenting his assumption that it was okay to talk to her about this.

"No. But I hope, dear, that you've experienced that passionate release with a man you didn't care about, whom you just wanted to sleep with. It's satisfying in the strangest way."

Of course, she had, but it was none of his business—and she'd never tell her husband about it. Yes, he knew she was no virgin. But if he'd known exactly what her past experiences entailed, she wasn't sure how he'd feel about it. And she had no reason to revisit her past. What was done was done. She'd had her fun—but now she was a mother and very much in love with her husband. These two things had changed everything, to her way of thinking, though not to her brother and sister-in-law's mindset. They were committed "swingers" who changed extramarital partners frequently. To each his or her own.

"Maggie Rae made herself available. She derived great joy in pleasuring other people. But it was more than that, really. She wanted to be humiliated, wanted to be hurt. She wanted to explore all realms of passion and that line between passion and pain," Bill said, looking directly into Annie's eyes, with a little lift of his eyebrow. Was he flirting with her?

Annie fussed in her seat as Bill leaned forward, never taking his eyes from her. "Let's change the subject, shall we? Are you still a suspect in the murder?" she asked, looking away from him momentarily, then meeting his glance with a coldness.

"Yes, I am. I could never kill anybody, you know," he told her.

"That's what they all say," she answered in a clipped tone. She didn't like this man—it was that simple. She couldn't imagine her friend Vera with him. He thought he was smarter than Annie—and had this patronizing quality to him. She recognized it.

She also recognized how he was gauging her reaction to his flirtations and the conversation about sex. She knew that some guys get off on just talking about it— they want to engage a woman.

He ignored her comment. "Yes. As far as anyone knows, I'm the last person to see her alive before she was murdered," he answered, and leaned back in his chair. "That makes me feel a little weird. I keep going over our last conversation in my mind. It was minimal. We hardly spoke to one another, ever, but that night . . . I just can't remember if she said someone else was coming there. I don't think she'd said anything to me."

"Did you happen to notice a pile of garbage on her curb?"

He shook his head no. "I always left from the other door—the basement door."

Of course, you did, asshole.

"So, Bill, how did the police find out you were there?" Annie asked.

"DNA evidence," he said. "They found it when they did the autopsy, and more of it in her place. I'd been with Maggie Rae for a while, so it was everywhere."

Lovely image. Enough to make your stomach turn.

"Did you ever stop to think what would happen if your wife found out?"

"Hmph," he said. "Vera's in her own little world. The dancing. The scrapbooking. Now it's the baby. I doubt she even gave it much thought or consideration."

"Maybe that's because she trusted you."

Bill's face fell, eyes lowered. Annie looked away.

"I wonder if we've tampered with evidence," Annie said to the scrapbookers.

"What do you mean?" Vera asked.

"I mean, I think that whoever placed the scrapbooks on the streets must be the one who killed her. I wonder if there were fingerprints? Or, I don't know, DNA?"

"Well, if there were, we've done messed it up, I'm sure," Paige said, twirling one of her long earrings.

"Not necessarily. I'll ask Detective Bryant about it on Monday. I'm supposed to be interviewing him. Mike will be home in the morning to watch the boys, so I'm heading over to Bryant's office," Annie said, taking a bite of the lemon bar.

"Have you seen Robert since that night?" Vera asked.

"No, and I don't want to. The whole thing freaked me out."

"That's why you need a gun," said Beatrice, who was just opening the basement door. A basket full of muffins slung over her arms.

"Mama! You and your guns!" Vera said.

She looked perplexed and shrugged. "If that man had been on my porch, I'd have had no problem using it."

Sheila took the muffins and set them on the table. "What do we owe the honor of your presence?"

"I wanted to bake, and then I saw all this food I made and thought I'd share. That's all," she said, sitting down next to Annie. "How are you, dear? Do you need to borrow my gun?"

Annie smiled. "No thanks. I bought a baseball bat. I'm more comfortable with that."

"A bat could do some damage," Beatrice said.

"Thanks for the book. I'm almost finished with it," Annie said.

"Take your time, dear," she answered, looking over Annie's scrapbook. "What cute boys you have."

"Thanks," she said, and held up the book. A few of Maggie Rae's photos that she hadn't placed in a book yet slipped out of her new soccer scrapbook.

"Are these Maggie Rae's pictures?"

"Yes," Annie said. "This picture right here sort of haunts me."

All of the women stopped what they were doing and gathered around Annie.

"Why?" Vera asked. "I mean, it's a picture of her when she was a child, and it's sad that she came to the ending she did, but what's disturbing about it?"

"Well, now," DeeAnn said. "That's not the same man who was at the wake and was introduced as her father."

"That's right!" Sheila said.

"Oh, now," Bea said slowly. "I remember this family."

"Oh, my God, yes," Vera said. "Her father was brutally murdered. Remember, Mama? What was that all about?"

"Um, I don't remember all of the details. But there was that crazy hiker who came down from the Appalachian Trail. That was horrible. So tragic. It left his family without much," Beatrice said. "But this picture is really odd because those girls were much younger when their father died. Or at least that's how I remember it."

All of the women stood together; each one was trying to remember any little thing.

"Well, if it was in the paper, I can find out about it," Annie said. "I do remember Tina Sue saying something about a stepfather."

"Who is this?" Beatrice asked, reaching for a picture of Tina Sue as a teenager.

"That's Maggie Rae's sister," Vera said.

"She looks a lot like her sister," DeeAnn said.

"Sure does," Beatrice added. "This old brain of mine . . . it's so frustrating sometimes. Lately, I can't keep people apart." She looked at the picture again. "Of course, a really odd thing about this picture is, who in his right mind would plant an apple tree so close to a house?"

"Now, think, Mama," Vera said. "Don't worry about that damn apple tree. Do you remember anything else about this family?"

"I'll remember later, I'm sure, at some inopportune moment," she said, reaching for a muffin. "Do you mind? Move over, Vera."

Sheila grabbed the picture. "Wait a minute," she said, holding the picture up to the light. "Hmm. Maybe this is a fake picture." She took it to her light table and placed a magnifying glass over it. "Well, I'll be. This picture has been Photoshopped. Someone placed a new head and face on this other man's body."

"Why on earth would someone do that?" Vera asked. "It's . . . I don't know . . . creepy."

Chapter 43

Beatrice never felt better—other than the regular aches and pains that came with aging. The dark presence that she came to think of as Maggie Rae seemed to be out of her life—even though Bill was not. Vera was not letting him come home, but they saw each other almost every night. And Bill couldn't find an apartment with a month-to-month lease, which he insisted he needed in case Vera let him go back to his house.

Beatrice hated to admit it, but it was nice to have a man around the house to help her out occasionally. Bill turned out to be good company. She forgot how comforting it was to have a companion. They had breakfast together every morning; sometimes he'd come home for lunch. They'd chat about the hummingbirds, the leaky faucet, or, sometimes, Vera.

Bea was torn between hating him and trying to behave in a good Christian hey-you-were-a part-of-my-family way. They'd always gotten along. What was there *not* to like about Bill, but there was really nothing *to like* about him, either. He was always sort of nondescript in Bea's mind. If the woman he cheated on hadn't been her daughter, she'd think the cheating thing was the only interesting thing about him.

Even though many people might think Vera would be miserable with her husband gone, Beatrice was sure her daughter had never been happier. Maybe it was the pregnancy. Four months along now, and really showing this beautiful bump, Vera looked better than she had in years. She wasn't dying her hair and wore little makeup—her natural beauty was really shining. Beatrice loved that. After all of these years, her daughter was gaining in confidence and, perhaps, happiness, though Beatrice didn't want to pry. She knew Vera would tell her when she was ready.

But on this Sunday morning, Vera made a special effort to join Bill and her for breakfast. She wanted to share some news with them. Beatrice was curious, as was Bill, who was happily whistling through the house, waiting for Vera.

When she arrived, she held a cardboard box of muffins and cream puffs from the bakery. "Dig in," she said.

Vera poured them decaf—Vera was no longer drinking any caffeinated beverages. They sat around the table, and Bill nonchalantly put his arm around Vera. He laid it on the back of her chair.

"So you said you had something to tell us," he said.

"Oh, yes," Vera said, sounding as if she'd forgotten. "I'm leaving tomorrow on a little trip."

"Alone?" Bill asked, setting down his muffin.

"I've talked to the doctor about it, Bill. I'll be fine to travel—it's just to New York. I'm going to take a teaching workshop, maybe look up some old friends. Hang out at some of the old places. I don't know. I thought it might be fun," Vera told them.

"Alone?" Bill said again, as if he could not believe it.

"Well, yes. I am a grown-up. I know my way around the city. I'll be fine. It's something I wanted to do for a very long time. Take a trip by myself. I saw this workshop and I thought it was a great opportunity. I'll be gone a couple of weeks," she told them, and licked cream from the top of her cream puff, leaving a fine layer of powdered sugar on her lips. She then wiped off her mouth with the napkin.

"Alone and pregnant in New York?" Bill said again.

"I think it's a fabulous idea," Bea chimed in. "You should do it now before you have the baby."

"My thoughts exactly," Vera said.

"I'm not sure I like this," Bill said after sipping his coffee. "I mean, what if something happens to you? To the baby?"

"God forbid, but I do think they have hospitals and doctors in New York City," Vera said, and smiled at him. "I wonder if you'd like to house-sit for me, Bill."

"House-sit? It's my own goddamn house," he said, his face turning red. "House-sit while you're gallivanting around New York? I'll be damned."

"What's wrong with you?" Beatrice asked calmly. "My goodness, Bill."

His eyes lowered.

"I guess I thought you'd come to a decision about us, Vera," he said after a moment. "We've been getting along so well."

"Yes, Bill, we have. I'm just not sure about sharing a life with you. I love your company, and we're having a great time together like we are. Can we just leave it alone?"

"You mean with me living with your mother and coming to see you almost every night? It seems, I don't know, silly," he said.

"It kind of does," Beatrice offered. "But if it works . . . I don't mind having you around, and Vera will make up her mind eventually. So maybe it's best to take your time."

She could see the love in Bill's eyes as he looked at her daughter. She'd sworn she'd never seen that look before on his face. Vera, on the other hand, did not return that look. She was growing into herself, and Beatrice was not sure that there would be room for Bill. She felt a twinge of excitement for Vera, going on a trip alone to New York City. She wondered if there was more to it than the workshop. But what?

"Oh, Mama, I have to tell you I really loved going through those scrapbooks you and Bill dropped off. Looking through them brought back such wonderful memories," Vera said. "Funny. At first, I didn't even want to look at them. They sat there for days. Then one morning I opened the first one and sat there all day long looking over the pictures and clippings and stuff. It was almost like discovering myself all over again."

Bill looked at Beatrice, twisted his mouth, and then looked away.

Would her daughter ever know such love and joy as she had known with Ed? Bea contemplated. Oh, she wished that more than anything. Before she died, she wanted to see her daughter happy. She wanted to see her loved.

And Bill? Before today, she wasn't sure he ever really loved Vera. Maybe that was why he had turned to Maggie Rae. Maybe he was as frustrated by their mediocrity as Vera was static.

Yes. She was static. Had been for years. Every time Beatrice asked her if she was happy, she'd smile and say something silly. "What is happiness, Mama?" Or "Of course, I am happy."

But a mother always knew. Vera held a deep sadness within her. Sometimes it pained Beatrice to look too closely into her daughter's eyes. She could see it there. She'd tried to offer advice and be there for her—but Vera was closed off and distant. It was as if she were broken in New York—for that's when this great sadness seemed to come over her daughter's appearance. Before then, her face always rested in a happy look, with a spark of fire and passion in her eyes. Beatrice stopped trying to figure it out. Hell, her daughter was forty-one years old—by now, she was responsible for her own happiness.

If it was something about her childhood, or the way Beatrice and Ed brought her up, surely she would be over it by now. No. Vera's childhood was happy, even with a mom whose passion was not necessarily mothering, a mother who understood more about mathematics and physics than she did about changing diapers and breastfeeding. But still, even with all of that, Bea loved Vera and was always there for her, wasn't she? Even when she was working on a project and Vera would come into her office, she would stop and chat with her or find out what she needed. Vera was her priority for many years. It was the same way with Ed.

No. It wasn't her childhood. Something happened to her in New York. Giving up her dance career and staying in Cumberland Creek might have been the start of it. But surely, she'd have gotten over that; and surely, she could have gone back to New York anytime when she was younger. But she insisted on staying here, her hometown, with her mother, after Ed's death. Beatrice asked her to go back to New York time and time again. Bill supported her decision and they were married quickly, even though he was just finishing law school.

"This is what I want, Mama. I want to make a difference to this community so children won't have to travel to Charlottesville for dance classes. And I want my own family here, not in New York.

Beatrice wanted to believe her, and soon she did. But perhaps she should not have. For after all of these years, that was the only thing Beatrice could think of that would affect her daughter's happiness so much.

Later, after Vera left, and Beatrice and Bill were cleaning up the kitchen, Bill said he'd have to follow Vera to New York to make sure she was okay.

"Now, listen to me, Bill. That is the worst thing you could do. You need to allow her to spread her wings a bit. Don't try to stop it—else it will come back and bite you in the ass," Beatrice said firmly, as if she were scolding a child. And, in truth, she felt like she was. A man in his forties was still a baby, at least to her, and he needed to rein in those overprotective tendencies where her daughter was concerned. Vera was a grown woman.

True, dangers existed in New York City—but for God's sake, Bea had been stabbed in Cumberland Creek, in the supermarket, in front of God and everybody—and they still had no idea who had done it. No place was safe anymore.

"We're sorry," the young officer had told her. "But the way the security cameras are positioned in that store is unhelpful. We saw you enter with no knife in your neck. We saw you leave with the knife. We never saw it happen and, of course, nobody else did, either."

She had grunted in recognition. "Well, don't that beat all."

Breaking out of her reverie, Beatrice spoke aloud.

"So, Bill, how is the murder investigation going?"

She was wiping off the kitchen counter and reached for a lavender dish towel with embroidered flowers on it. *Lavender. Flowers.*

"I really don't know much about it," he said. "The last account I heard is that they'd like to find out who placed the scrapbooks out on the curb for the garbageman."

Lavender. Flowers. At that moment, something clicked in Beatrice's brain. She was outside early on the morning she was stabbed. She had decided to go for a walk before going to the grocery store. She could remember it as if it were yesterday. She had pulled on her red sweatpants and matching jacket. She liked to wear red on foggy spring mornings. She felt safer that way.

As she walked around the corner, she had heard a box

being thrown to the ground with a thud. It had frightened her. Who would be up and outside at five in the morning?

"Oh, Bill," she suddenly said. "I think you need to take me to the police department. I know who placed those boxes on the sidewalk."

As she said that, she felt a slight breeze move through her, and a sweet scent filled her. Light. Cool. Crisp. Everything made a sudden interesting sense to her: Why Maggie Rae was angry. Why she was still earthbound. And why she came to Beatrice.

Why hadn't Bea thought of it earlier? Then she suddenly smelled her husband's tobacco, which she took as a good sign.

"Smell that?" she asked Bill.

"What?"

"Oh, never mind," she told him. "I'm going to get dressed."

But first she called Annie.

"Annie, I remember. It was the woman in the picture."

"What? Who?"

"It was Maggie Rae's sister I saw at the curb that morning."

"Her sister? Tina Sue?"

"You interviewed her, right?"

"Yes."

"What did she seem like?"

"She seemed really dedicated to her sister. Oh, I don't know, Beatrice. Her sister?"

"There's much more to the story than what we know. How about we try to get the scoop before I go to the cops?" Beatrice's heart was pounding in her chest. Damn, she was excited. Could Maggie Rae's sister be a murderer? And what would possess a woman to kill her own sister? "I'll take you out there—but you have to promise me that you'll take me with you to the police station when you tell Bryant. I want to see the look on his sexist, know-it-all face."

"I'm in," Annie said. "I'll be over to get you as soon as I can."

"Where are you going, Bea? I thought we were going to the station," Bill said, walking into the room.

"Changed my mind. Going to see Tina Sue with Annie," she said, hanging up the phone and grabbing a sweater.

"What? Why? What's going on?"

"Never mind, Bill. I'll fill you in later."

"Beatrice, I don't like this," Ed said, and stood in front of her.

"Now, Ed, don't worry about me. It's the most fun I've had in years."

"What?" Bill said.

"I was talking to Ed," she said as she walked out her front door.

Chapter 44

The hollow between Cumberland Creek and Lynchburg was an odd little community. Called Jenkins Hollow, it was known for being backward. Some families didn't have indoor plumbing, let alone a computer or the Internet. The same families lived there for generations, marrying among each other and bringing outsiders in from time to time—but residents rarely moved from the hollow.

"I really hate this place," Beatrice said. "It plays into all the clichés about my people. Sometimes there's a grain of truth to clichés, but I hate that people generalize so much."

"What exactly do you mean? What kind of clichés are you talking about?" Annie asked as she turned left onto a narrow asphalt road.

"The folks in this community are mostly uneducated. A lot of them have never been out of the area, you know. The families are all related."

"But Tina Sue is a teacher," Annie pointed out. "She must be educated."

"Yes, but I believe this is where her husband's people are from. I don't think she and Maggie Rae grew up here. But I'm not too sure about that."

As they drove farther, the road became a dirt road, and the houses along the road became decidedly smaller and less kept up. They went around a curve in a road and spotted a house that waved a huge Confederate flag in the front yard.

"Nice," Annie said.

"Hmph. That ain't nothing, Annie. Look at that."

Annie stopped herself from stepping on the brakes— someone had painted a huge swastika on the side of a garage. A swastika? Her heart leaped into her throat—a swell of anger, more than a hint of fear.

What am I doing here?

"Bea, it occurs to me that maybe we shouldn't be here. Maybe we should call Detective Bryant."

"Can't now. Your cell wouldn't work out here," Bea said matter-of-factly. "Probably some young idiots painted that. Probably nothing for us to worry about."

Still, Annie was shaken—between the drunken visit of Robert Dasher and the snarky sexism of Detective Bryant, she was already a nervous wreck.

Now, this—a swastika?

This was something she had only seen in history books and scribbled on underpasses by city teenagers. Bea was probably right. It might be that the person who painted it had no idea what it really meant. Maybe. But she couldn't help but feel a surge of fear rip through her—call it an irrational, inherited fear. But it was strong. Her stomach clenched and her heart raced. She slowed the car down and pulled over to the narrow side of the road. She breathed deeply.

"Are you okay, Annie?"

She nodded. "I'll be fine." She drank from her bottled water and noticed an odd structure standing behind a house ahead of them.

"Is that an . . . outhouse?" Annie asked.

"Oh, yes, you'll see plenty of them here. Water's a problem in this hollow."

Annie took a deep breath. Okay. There were still places on the planet that didn't have running water. She knew that, but she didn't know those places were quite so close to home. Nor did she know that people still brazenly flew the Confederate flag or, worse, painted swastikas on buildings.

As she mulled over the situation, she realized it was quite possible that Tina Sue had killed Maggie Rae. Yet, it was difficult to believe. She had fooled Annie. Tina Sue had really come off as a supportive sister. Maybe *too* supportive. Annie's instincts used to be finely honed. But not this time. She was definitely losing her edge.

The hollow was surreal—an incredibly lush place, with old trees and wildflowers scattered everywhere, beautiful old houses and barns, roads running right along the edge of steep hillsides, with breathtaking, sweeping views of the mountains. Yet, the ugliness was profound. Rusty old cars sat along a driveway. Old plastic toys scattered in a yard. Confederate flags. Swastikas.

"Did I tell you about the newspaper clippings?" Annie asked.

"No. What did you find out? Now, when you get up here, you want to bear right."

A huge deer ran across the road and Annie slammed on the brakes. "Jeez," she said.

"Yes. Take it slow. There're a lot of animals out here. We may even see a bear or two. Now, you were saying?"

"I found out that Maggie Rae's father was murdered when she was five. So you were right about that picture. Someone put his face on the other man's body. I'm thinking it was the stepfather's body. It adds up. Maggie Rae's mother remarried four years later. Then she died a few years after that."

"How sad," Beatrice said. "You have to wonder about stepfathers. Sometimes it works out okay, but other times it's not a good thing."

"She must have wished he were her biological dad, which is why she changed the picture. God, that's heart-wrenching and kind of, well, twisted. It all leads me to believe she might have been abused by her stepfather. Really, just a gut feeling."

"Or maybe she just hated him. Plenty of reasons to hate a stepfather," Beatrice said.

The sun went behind a huge white cloud, making it a little easier to see the road against the sun.

"What I don't understand is why Tina Sue would kill her. . . . I mean, what happened?"

"I know. On the one hand, it adds up. You saw her later that morning at the curb. But it doesn't add up, either. We are still missing something."

"I'm sure we'll get our answers soon."

Annie thought of her boys at home with Mike, who was able to get some time off today so she could do this—though he wasn't thrilled with any of it. Even though it was Sunday, he had planned to go to the office and catch up on paper work.

"I can't keep taking time off for you to do your work, Annie. That wasn't the deal."

"I know, Mike, and I'm sorry. But this is a major breakthrough."

"Why not let the cops handle it?"

"You know why, Mike."

"Oh, for God's sake, Annie. Your think he's a sexist creep and needs to be put in his place. You can one-up him? Is it worth risking your life?"

"I'm not risking anything, Mike. I'm just going to talk to Tina Sue. I'm taking Beatrice with me."

"Oh, like she's going to protect you. How old is she—like ninety?"

"Don't underestimate Beatrice," Annie said, reaching for the car keys. "She may be old, but she's brilliant. And I'll take brilliance over brawn any day of the week."

Mike rolled his eyes. "I give up. I know that look—it's no use arguing with you. Be careful. Do you have your cell? Camera? Recorder?"

"Yes, I have everything," she said, and kissed him quickly before heading out the door—not realizing she'd not have cell phone service in the mountains.

Annie now wished she held that kiss a little longer as she saw yet another swastika painted on a barn.

"You see that cluster of homes over there?" Beatrice pointed to a group of white clapboard homes, with a small white church in the center of them. "That's the 'Nest,' my daddy used to call it."

"What?"

"That's where we're heading. It used to be an Old Order Mennonite stronghold, but most of them moved on or died out. Some of the descendants are still around."

"Old Order Mennonites?"

"Oh, yes. There are so many different kinds of Mennonites. But those are the people you see in the horse and buggy. They don't use any modern conveniences. My daddy had several good friends that were Old Order, and he loved them fiercely—but they were a tight-knit bunch and you could only get so close to them. Now a lot of them are still in the church, but they are not Old Order. It's a tough life."

The closer Annie drove toward the community, the more frightened she became. Of course, Beatrice didn't know how freaky she found these people. And she was sort of ashamed of that. Why should she have such weird feelings about this religious sect when her own people were so persecuted?

"That's the driveway." Bea pointed.

The house was a pretty two-story white clapboard home, with the shutters painted bright blue.

"Haint blue," Bea said. "To ward off evil spirits."

Chapter 45

Vera busied herself packing. New York City! She could hardly wait. She'd built plenty of time in for herself to shop and to see at least one play. The teaching seminar should be fascinating as well.

Where did she put her red paisley shirt? Oh, it was still in the dryer. She walked down to the basement, noticing that her iPod wasn't hanging on the hook, where she usually kept it. She reached into the dryer and pulled out a ball of clothes—among the bunch was her red paisley shirt.

Now, where was her iPod? Darn, her mother had borrowed it. She glanced at the clock. Plenty of time to pop over there, and maybe have some lunch with Beatrice, too. Then she would come home and finish packing. Vera slipped on her clogs and left through the front door.

When she arrived at her mother's house, Bill was sitting on the front porch, chatting on his cell phone. He held up a finger. She waved him off and went inside the house.

"Mama?" Vera looked around downstairs. Her mother's impeccable kitchen, the dining room, not used in years, the library, the sitting room. "Mama?"

Just as she was about to go upstairs to find Bea, Bill came up behind her.

"Sorry, Vera, your mom is not home."

"Where on earth is she? She's still not supposed to be out for long periods of time."

"She's been gone . . . ," he said, and looked at his watch. "Oh, well, I hadn't realized. She's been gone about two hours."

"Two hours?"

"Yes, Annie picked her up and they were heading to Tina Sue's place."

"Tina Sue? Maggie Rae's sister?"

"Yes, she seemed excited, said something about remembering who placed those boxes out on Maggie Rae's curb. Then she took off like a bat out of hell."

The boxes? Hmm. Those boxes of pictures and scrapbooks. She remembered? Why would she call Annie? Oh, no, they wouldn't. Vera's stomach flip-flopped.

"Did she tell you she thought it was Tina Sue?" Vera finally asked Bill.

"No, but since that's where they are headed . . . ," he said, and then his eyes widened. "You don't think that old fool went out to the Nest, thinking they were going to get some kind of scoop or confession, do you?"

"Why else would they bother?"

"Why didn't they just call the police?" Bill asked. "Why would they do this?"

"Oh, for heaven's sake, Bill, get the car. I'm calling Detective Bryant," Vera said, pulling out her cell phone. She told Bryant her concerns about her mother's whereabouts.

"Let us deal with this," the detective told her. "You don't need to get in the middle of it."

"Now, just hold on one minute. My mother, who has recently been stabbed, is out there in that hollow. Don't think for one minute that I'm not going."

"Then you'll need to stay out of the way. Damn, I wish I had the use of the chopper," he said.

"Oh, Detective, I don't think you could land a chopper up there. What is the matter with you? Haven't you been to Jenkins Hollow?"

"I have. And I think Annie Chamovitz might be in more trouble than she could imagine."

"What do you mean?"

"We'll talk later. I need to get going on this," he said, and hung up.

Vera felt the hair on the back of her neck raise, prickling around her shoulders and neck. She didn't like the sound of that. Annie was visibly different from most of the population around Cumberland Creek. Surely, the people in that hollow were a good sort. At least one or two students drove from there every week to dance. All the talk of ignorance and inbreeding was just talk. The Klan was nowhere in this area anymore.

She shuddered when she remembered the last incident in her memory. She was a child when her father tended a young black man who had been beaten nearly to death by local Klansmen—most of whom lived around Jenkins Hollow, among (but not part of) the large Mennonite population.

"Did the Mennonites do this, Papa?"

"No, sugar. They are good God-fearing people. They believe in peace. I know they look different, but you can't judge people by the way they look. The people who did this are just plain evil. And the law tells me they got them, and they shouldn't bother anybody anymore."

He never mentioned the Klan after that. And Vera assumed her father was right. She'd never heard another word of it.

Bill punched the buttons on the radio as they drove along out of Cumberland Creek proper into the hills.

She glanced at the speedometer. Fifty-five. "You pick a hell of a time to go the speed limit, Bill. My mother's up there confronting a murderer."

"We don't know that, Vera. Why would Tina Sue kill her sister? It's ludicrous."

"I don't know why anybody would kill anybody, Bill. Murder never makes sense to me, unless you're protecting yourself or a child. Even then, I'd hope for a better way than to kill."

"Well," he said after a moment, "you're right. None of it makes sense. The world is a crazy, messed-up place sometimes."

They sat for a while listening to Willie Nelson crooning on the radio. Vera felt like Bill was traveling twenty instead of fifty-five. Everything was moving too slowly for her. They passed the red barn with the *Wilcom* sign on it. Hadn't they passed that already? God, she was going to jump out of her skin if she didn't see that her mother was safe. She could almost feel the mountains closing in on her.

As she mulled over the idea of Tina Sue killing her own sister, it left her with an uneasy feeling. If she could kill her sister, God knows what she was capable of doing.

"The detective was concerned about Annie," Vera said. "I wonder why."

"Well," Bill said, "maybe it's because of all the swastikas up here."

"Swastikas? In Cumberland Creek?"

"It's not exactly Cumberland Creek, Vera. One of my clients' barn was painted, and they thought they caught the young man who did it, but it turned out not to be the person. Someone is painting them all over the place. Nobody knows exactly who is doing it."

"It's not the KKK, is it?"

He sighed. "To tell you the truth, someone I know is investigating that possibility, but nobody knows."

"I thought they were long gone."

"You would have no reason to know about them, would you?"

Vera thought about that and she supposed he was right. At one point in time, when her father was the town doctor, her family knew the secrets of all of the residents. Medicine offered no judgment, her father used to say. When a person is a healer, he heals. It's that simple. She didn't know this to be true, but she supposed her father even had tended a few members of the KKK.

Vera shuddered. She thought that part of the South's history was long gone. People had evolved, hadn't they? Surely, even the folks who lived in the Hollow had heard of civil rights and freedom of religion, freedom of choice. Nobody was that secluded anymore.

Maybe it wasn't seclusion. Maybe it was a choice. An ill-formed and uneducated choice.

Chapter 46

Beatrice knocked on the door again. "Tina Sue?" she called out.

The floorboards of the porch creaked and the porch swing swayed in the gentle breeze. The place could use a coat or two of paint. But the views were breathtaking—they were on a kind of plateau, surrounded by soft, rolling hills and rocky mountains. The mountains always called out to Beatrice's ancient heart. How she loved them and couldn't imagine living her life anywhere else. Just like most of the people here.

The door opened. Tina Sue wore jeans and a Redskins T-shirt, face made up, and looked nothing like a murderer. "Well, hey, Ms. Matthews," she said. "Hello, Ms. Chamovitz. C'mon in." Tina Sue beamed. "I'm so glad you came all the way out here to see me. Must be a heck of a story you're writing if you need to talk to me again."

"Did you see the first one?" Beatrice asked.

"Oh, no, I never read the paper, unless it's the church paper. It has all the news I need to know," she said. "Please come in and sit down." She motioned them into the living room.

What a fool, Beatrice thought.

"Can I get you some iced tea?"

"Sure," Beatrice said, noting the pitcher and glasses on the sideboard.

"Oh, never mind, I'll serve myself," Beatrice said. "Annie?"

"No thanks, I'm fine," Annie said, digging through her bag and pulling out things—papers, pens, cameras, tape recorders.

Beatrice looked around at the spare room, nothing on the walls, except a cross hanging over the fireplace.

"No pictures of those pretty nieces and nephews of yours?" Beatrice asked as she sat down with her iced tea.

"Oh, no," Tina Sue said. "My husband's family is partially Old Order, and my dad was, too. Even though we are not, it's just one of those traditions that we've held on to. We don't believe in taking pictures, let alone displaying them."

"Maggie Rae had loads of pictures of her kids, and even some of herself as a child," Beatrice said.

"My mom always sneaked in some pictures," Tina Sue said. "My dad didn't like it. And well, you know, Maggie Rae had a mind of her own. She married off the mountain."

Odd turn of expression, Annie thought.

"What's the problem with pictures?" Annie asked, switching on her recorder.

"It's a belief based on the Second Commandment, Exodus 20:4: 'Thou shalt not make unto thee any graven image, or any likeness of anything that is in heaven above, or that is in the earth beneath, or that is in the water under the earth,'" Beatrice answered.

"That's right." Tina Sue smiled. "Not too many people know that."

"I've been in Cumberland Creek a long time, Tina Sue, though I was brought up on the mountain," Beatrice said; then she picked the glass up to her lips and took a long drink of the sweet iced tea. "Besides which, I know my Bible. Mmm. Good iced tea."

"Thank you," Tina Sue said, turning her attention to Annie. "Now, what can I help you with? Are you sure I can't get you some tea? Lemonade?"

"No thanks, I'm fine," Annie said.

Beatrice sank back into her chair, listening to the conversation, but taking in the scenery. Or, rather, the lack of it. There was no television, no stereo that she could see, not even a book, except for some Bibles. One large Bible was open on the buffet next to the dining-room table and another at her elbow on the coffee table.

The rugs were beautiful, woven by hand on the loom. Beatrice recognized them. Her mother had a few like it. Shades of green and blue woven in between the off-white. Twin brass candlesticks sat on either side of the large Bible on the buffet, and underneath was a red velvet cloth. Something about it reminded Beatrice of an altar.

The couch was green plaid and matching chairs sat on either side—one of which she was sitting on. The curtain swags even matched—but the curtains looked like plain muslin hanging from the rods. Streams of sunlight came in the living-room window. Even lit, the place was immaculate. No dust. No happy piles of magazines and newspapers. The oak furniture glistened.

"Must be pretty important for you to come all the way out here."

"As I explained on the phone, I didn't want to make you drive again. It's not a problem for me. Beatrice helped me find the way," Annie said, handing her the Photoshopped picture of her family.

"What do you think of this?" Annie asked.

Tina Sue took the photo with her facial expression empty.

"Tina Sue?" Annie said, with one eyebrow lifting. Curious. Beatrice had never noted that about her before. "Could you tell me what you think of the picture?"

"Well," she said, drawing it out slowly. "It's a picture of us on our front porch. But . . . oh, this is so typical of her." She rolled her eyes. "I can't believe she did this." She threw the picture on the floor. "Trash. That's what it is."

Beatrice set her glass down on the trivet that was sitting on the coffee table next to her. Was that sweat forming on Tina Sue's forehead? And her pretty little lipstick-smeared mouth suddenly seemed hard with tension. Bea glanced at Annie, who was trying to make eye contact with the shifty-eyed Tina Sue.

"What do you mean?" Annie asked.

"I don't know how she did it, but I'm sure it was Maggie Rae. That's the face of our dad, placed on our stepfather's body." Her voice cracked.

"Why would she do that?" Annie asked.

"How would I know?" Tina Sue snapped. "There was only one picture ever taken of our father. And he didn't like it. It was against his beliefs. She's made a mockery of both of them!"

In the silence that followed, Beatrice mulled over everything she'd just heard. She was mostly focused on the edge in Tina Sue's voice. Beatrice picked up her pocketbook and dug inside—yes, she had remembered her gun, and there was the tissue she needed to pretend to blow her nose.

"Hmmm," Annie said, finally breaking into the uncomfortable quiet that hung in the air as thick as the humidity on an August day. "Maybe she was just learning how to do Photoshop and was just playing with pictures."

"Playing with?" Tina Sue raised her voice. "No. My sister knew what she was doing. She—"

Just then, an alarm went off, and Annie gasped. Beatrice jumped, placing her hand back inside her pocketbook.

"Oh, it's just the pie," Tina Sue said. "I thought you ladies might like some pie this afternoon. I got a late start on it, though. Excuse me."

"Of course," Annie said, reaching down to pick up the picture from the hardwood floor.

She looked at Beatrice and shrugged. "This is not going anywhere."

"I beg to differ," Beatrice answered quietly. "The picture pushed her buttons. Keep pushing."

They could hear the squeaky oven door opening, a pie being slid onto the counter, and the door closing. Beatrice could smell it—it was some kind of berry—blackberry?

Annie crossed her legs and sat back in her chair, tapping her pencil on the tablet of paper sitting on her lap. Intent on her notes, Annie was slumped over them on her chair and leaning on the coffee table. Above her head was a framed needlepoint Bible verse—the Lord's Prayer—and next to Annie's elbow on the table was a statue of praying hands.

When Tina Sue came back in the room, Annie began speaking immediately.

"Well, now, Tina Sue. If you don't believe in pictures and such, how did you feel about Maggie Rae's scrapbooks?"

Beatrice stiffened. What was Annie doing?

"Her scrapbooks were empty," Tina Sue said, meeting Annie's eyes.

"But why? Why would she buy all that stuff, take photos, get them developed, and then not put them in the scrapbooks?"

"Maybe her conscience got the best of her?" Tina Sue said. "I mean, she was a modern thinker, whatever that means, and all that. But we were still raised with the idea that pictures were a sin. Maybe she couldn't place them in the scrapbooks for everybody to look at."

"It doesn't seem likely. The last time I checked, sleeping around was also deemed a sin. She did that frequently," Annie said.

Beatrice held her breath.

"I explained all that to you, Ms. Chamovitz. I don't know what else to tell you."

"Did she ever tell you who she slept with? Like maybe your stepfather?"

"Oh my," she mumbled as she sat back down, looking a little as if the air had been knocked out of her. "You sure do ask a lot of questions, and some of them are mighty unchristian, considering that I just lost my sister." When she said the word "unchristian," she emphasized it. Of course, she knew Annie was Jewish.

Annie sat up. "I think it's time to leave, Beatrice. I'm sorry if I have offended you, Tina Sue, so much that you have to bring my religion into it. And it's not the first time, I might add. I'm just trying to piece this together, thinking maybe we can help find Maggie Rae's murderer. But since I've offended you, and you won't answer my questions, I see no point in taking up your time, or mine, for that matter."

She began to gather her belongings and place them in her bag, and Beatrice took another long swallow of her tea, then placed it on the table. Was Annie really going to give up that easily?

Tina Sue's face reddened. "I'm sorry. I didn't mean—"

Annie turned around and looked directly at her, flinging her bag over her shoulder.

"I wish I had known Maggie Rae," Annie said. "Just from what I know of her, she seemed open-minded, and I can't imagine how she got out of this family with any sense of self. No wonder she wanted to be hurt. No wonder she couldn't be loved."

"What? Well, I never—"

"Why can't you answer the questions?" Beatrice said.

"She can't answer them because she's been forbidden to," a male voice came from around the corner.

Beatrice thanked the universe that she already had taken the safety off her gun; her hand searched for it in her purse. After finding the hard, cool gun, she left her hand there.

"You ladies best be leaving. You got no business out here," he said, looking straight at Annie. Beatrice assumed he was Tina Sue's husband, with wild blue eyes and curly hair, a blue T-shirt that was a bit too tight, revealing a magnificent, muscular body. Good Lord, a strapping mountain man with a pistol tucked in the front of his jeans. He noted Beatrice looking him over and smirked.

The audacity.

"We are on our way," Beatrice said, looking away, keeping her hand on her gun in her bag, hoping that Annie would just keep moving.

Just then, they all heard a loud *chop-chop-chop* of a helicopter.

"What the . . . ," Tina Sue said.

Annie opened the door and they all filed out. It was a Forest Service helicopter, trying to land in the front yard.

Well, now, doesn't that beat all? There seemed to be just enough space for them to land the green helicopter— and what on earth were they doing here? Suddenly Beatrice's thoughts swirled as she felt the onslaught of pain in her abdomen, then a violent uprising of sick. There was no way to be graceful about it. She crumpled over and vomited all over the front porch and Tina Sue's husband. An instant relief overcame her. Next thing she knew, she was being lifted into the loud helicopter sound and gusts of wind. *Poor Annie, she would have to ride home with that prick of a detective agent.*

Chapter 47

"The minute I sit down at the computer, one of them yells for me," Annie said to Mike in utter frustration.

"At least you have no hard deadline," he said, trying to alleviate her stress.

"No, but this is a great opportunity. I don't want to blow it. I can stay up to write, but then I'm tired and short with the boys the rest of the day And the two-half days in preschool and daycare simply aren't enough," She wanted to get her story written before all the information was officially released to the public on Monday.

Mike took a bite of his lasagna. She'd made a double batch yesterday so they could eat it for a few days—just reheat it, without having to cook. She wanted to get the next story in—before any other reporters came snooping around. She was sure that that would be any day now.

"I don't know what to tell you. Maybe you could hire a sitter to play with the boys when you're writing," he said. "Hmm. This veggie lasagna is so good."

"Yeah, but who?"

"Ask around. Maybe one of the scrapbook queens would know someone," he said.

"Scrapbook queens?" she said, and smiled. "Vera is out of town, finally. Maybe Sheila would know someone."

* * *

Vera had finally caught her plane after being assured by the doctors that Beatrice's own stomach expunged all of the poison that she drank in Tina Sue's iced tea. It didn't have a chance to seep into her bloodstream. Thank goodness, or they would have lost Beatrice. Her sensitive stomach saved her life.

Annie thought over the events of the day and wanted to get them all down before she began to lose some detail. Of course, some details, she'd rather just forget. The strange place of Jenkins Hollow filled her with dread and sadness all at once. She thought the ride to Tina Sue's was eye-opening, but the ride back into town was even more so, with the detective in the front seat and Tina Sue and her husband in the backseat. Unfortunately, the only police transport was the helicopter, and it was a tight fit, not enough room for everybody, so Annie's vehicle was commandeered.

When they passed the swastika on the garage, Tina Sue's husband mumbled something; then he said it louder. "Filthy Jews, pshaw."

A shock of anger and disbelief ripped through Annie as she gripped the steering wheel. Did people still talk like this? Think like this? It turns out her parents and aunts and uncles were right. Anti-Semitism still existed. Oh, Annie knew that on some level, but to be confronted with it in this day and age—well, it was just plain scary.

"Now, dear, we should pray for them," Tina Sue said. "We need to pray for people who have not accepted Jesus Christ as their Savior."

"Would you two shut up?" the detective said sheepishly. "I'm sorry, Mrs. Chamovitz. We're not all like that."

She glanced at him and nodded. *What should I say? Thank you, sexist bastard? Humph.* She bit her tongue and concentrated on navigating the twisty dirt roads.

* * *

"The sitter's worth a try," Mike interrupted her thoughts.

"I want milk," Ben said.

"Juice," Sam said.

"No juice," Annie said. "It's too late for juice. Milk?"

"Okay," Sam said reluctantly.

Annie leaned over and kissed him. He reached for her Star of David necklace.

"Careful," she whispered.

Such a sweet boy. She felt a fluttering in her belly. She'd been missing out on some things while she was working on this story. She'd been distracted. Why wasn't being a stay-at-home mom enough for her? Why did she feel the pull to the computer every night to write? Some days, she could be there; and other days, she found herself cleaning her kitchen floor and staring out the window.

She'd thought that being a mother would be the best thing she could do with her life, that it would be the most fulfilling and satisfying thing she could do. And it had its moments. But mostly it bored her, and she hoped that it would change. She hoped she'd somehow turn into one of those women who lived for their children, who knew everything they did and said and didn't care about things like writing, or doctoring, or quantum physics.

Some days with her boys were magical and wondrous. But most days were not like that. Most days were constant piles of laundry and toys and crayons and sticky juice messes. How could she have bought into that Hallmark version of motherhood? Was that really what she expected?

But the truth of the matter was, nobody ever knew what to expect from being a parent. Who knew what kind of a kid he or she would have? How she would react to that child? How that child would react to her?

So how did her writing fit in with this mothering thing? It was a sloppy balancing act. She'd have to let laundry go on some days so she could finish the first draft of an article. She'd give the boys more television time so she could do a little more research. So her mothering suffered a bit. She also felt like her writing did. She did not have a clear head when she approached the keyboard. Mama-voices whispered in the back of her head: *When was the last time Ben took his antibiotics? Don't forget to give him his next dose. What time is that appointment for his shots tomorrow? When is that puppet show going to happen, again?*

And then there was Mike. How to fit in what she was supposed to be to him—what she wanted to be to him—and still be a decent mom and good writer? Maybe it was all too much, she conceded. Maybe she'd have to give up the writing again. But maybe if she found a sitter, it would work.

She picked up the phone and pressed the button for Sheila's number.

"Hi, Annie," Sheila said.

"Does your daughter babysit?"

"Donna could. I'm not sure she's responsible enough to be alone with small children," Sheila said.

"What about something like a mother's helper?"

"What did you have in mind?"

"Someone to play with the boys, maybe get them snacks from time to time, but I'd be right here, writing."

"I think she could manage," Sheila said. "And it may be just what she needs. Thanks for keeping us in mind. When would you like her?"

"How about tomorrow?"

"Sounds good."

The two women exchanged good-byes and hung up.

"I've got good news, boys. Sheila's daughter Donna is coming to play with you guys tomorrow so that I can get some work done," she said.

"That's fabulous," Mike said. "I hope it works out."

It seemed like it could be the best of all possible worlds. Why did she have a sense of guilt, like she was being less of a mom by even caring about things other than her children? She would have to work through that. Other women did. It was possible to write and to be a mom—she just knew it was.

What an odd twenty-four hours. Driving out into the middle of nowhere and seeing swastikas. Tina Sue's comment about Annie being unchristian, and then her husband, Zeb, popping out of nowhere. The helicopter's arrival.

Detective Bryant had just rolled his eyes at Annie when he saw her. But he didn't have time to talk—Beatrice was in a crumpled heap at her feet. She was long gone, flown to the hospital, by the time a flustered Vera arrived on the scene. Vera had to turn around to get to the hospital, where her mother already was.

The doorbell ringing barely registered with Annie until she heard a crash and a groan.

"Mike?" She ran out of the bedroom, to find Mike on top of Robert Dasher, blood spewing from somewhere on Robert's face.

"Is this your husband?" Robert managed to say.

"Mike!"

"Yeah, I'm her husband, you sick son of a bitch. And you don't have a good reason to be here," Mike said, enraged.

Annie never saw him look like that—or sound like that. His face was red and swollen with anger. He almost didn't even look like her husband. "Mike, please get off the man before the boys hear this," she said, trying to control her voice. She walked over to him and placed her hands on his shoulder.

He held Robert by his collar and smashed his body

once more into the floor. He pointed his finger in Robert's face. "If I ever catch you around here—"

"You'll what? Kill me?" Robert said, wiping the dripping blood from his face with his shirt.

"Mike, please. Go sit down on the couch. Please. Robert," Annie said, pulling her husband off Robert by the scruff of his neck. "What are you doing here?"

"I wanted you to know. I am off the list. They found the killer. I'm not the man you think I am, Annie Chamovitz. I've been cleared. Yeah, I'm a bit messed up. I'm a drunk. I lose my temper. But I don't kill people," he said, looking over at Mike.

"Why do you care what my wife thinks of you?" Mike said, still furious.

He looked to the floor, out of breath, blood still pouring from his lip. "I don't know. Maybe because she seems . . . a lot like Maggie Rae. So smart. But so not like Maggie Rae, too. So good. So true. You know? I'm sorry I didn't mean to scare you. . . ."

Annie rolled her eyes. "Yeah, Robert, we already know you didn't kill Maggie Rae. But why wouldn't I be afraid of you? You were trying to get in here one night when you were drunk. And I'm pretty sure you followed me home one night. So if you don't want people to think you're a freak, you better start checking yourself."

Chapter 48

Vera wasn't sure she could tell any of her friends what had happened in New York City. It was the best thing that had ever happened to her—and she couldn't share it because it was also kind of embarrassing. Besides, she was just so busy getting the studio ready for the fall that she didn't have much time to chat. She'd also been avoiding Bill.

"How was the workshop?" Annie asked after sipping a glass of white wine.

"It was lovely," Vera said.

"Lovely?" Sheila mimicked. "Well, what did you do up there? Learn a new way to arabesque?"

"No, dear. We learned some different methods of teaching. I looked at different syllabi. I'm looking into something other than the Royal Academy of Dance's curriculum. Oh, and I also made some great costume contacts. Thrilling stuff, you know," Vera replied, feeling a blush creep onto her face. God, she hadn't blushed in years. She hoped nobody noticed.

"Vera, you're blushing," DeeAnn said. She just placed a pictured onto a page and looked up at her.

"Oh, I am not," Vera chided. "Mmm, love this lemon poppy seed muffin."

"I think you are," Sheila said. "Good muffin, I agree."

"Spill the beans, lady," Paige said.

"What?" Vera said, grinning.

They all stopped and looked at her. Annie's beautiful oblong face, Paige with her rosy cheeks, DeeAnn with her freckles scattered across her nose, and Sheila, hair needing combing, but lipstick carefully applied, for a change. All eyes on Vera.

"I ran into an old friend," she said.

"An old friend?" Annie asked.

"You didn't know this, but I worked as a dancer the same year I graduated from college and I know some people there." She smiled.

"A man?" Sheila prodded.

"Tony," Vera said.

"Tony!" Sheila squealed. "Now I remember something about him. Now, let's see. Is he the man from Brooklyn?"

Vera nodded.

"Uh-huh," Sheila said. "Really hot guy?"

Vera nodded again.

"I remember. It's all coming back to me now," Sheila said. Her grin was as wide as her face.

"Well, tell us," Paige said.

"Not much to tell, really," Vera began.

Sheila cleared her throat. "That's not how I remember it."

"Well, you know. We were both so young, and it was in the days, you know, so much experimenting and things."

"You slept with him?" DeeAnn asked.

"Boy, did she ever," Sheila said. "I remember."

"So?" Annie said. "Haven't all of you ever slept with other men besides your husbands?"

The room was quiet.

"Oh, Annie, good Southern girls, well, we don't usually talk about such things, if we *do* those things, you know," Sheila replied, stumbling.

"Well, that's strange," Annie said. "God, you women have known each other forever. I think it's time you compared notes."

"Surely not," Vera said.

"Let's start with what happened in New York."

Vera nodded. "No, I'm afraid not. What happened in New York stays there. Or at least for a little while longer."

What happened in New York was that she found Tony, and it was as if no time had passed at all. He reached for her when he saw her and she slid into his arms, where she stayed for a good part of five days. She didn't go to New York to look for him—he just happened to be in the same workshop, which made it very difficult for both of them to concentrate. He had an ex-wife, he told her, and a child, now eighteen. He had been divorced for several years.

"We tried," he told her. "But we both have fallen out of love, I suppose. She's had countless affairs. Me? Well, there's been one or two. Finally we decided to just give up. You know."

He was a little thicker—as was she—but the years were good to him. He loved her little baby bump and ran his hands over it with tenderness.

He had danced professionally up until a few years ago, when his knees just could not take any more, even after surgery.

It was difficult to leave him, not knowing if she'd ever see him again, if she'd ever feel this rawness, this energy, this passion—unrequited, though it was—one more time. He insisted he would come to Cumberland Creek for a visit. She said she'd love to have him, but in her mind's eye, she could not see it. He'd stick out like a sore thumb—a dark New York man, with a strong Brooklyn accent. Tongues would start to wag. And, Lord, she didn't need any more controversy in her life. The town didn't need it, either, with reporters in and out, along with TV crews and radio crews. She just wanted things to get back to normal.

She was creating a new "normal" in her life, though. Once the baby came, her attention would focus on him or her, and her reality would switch again. Maybe then, she'd be ready for Bill. But she hung on to thoughts of Tony—even though she still loved Bill. However, she wasn't sure she could trust Bill again, ever. He'd been screwing that young woman for years, and she'd never known it. He'd made a fool out of her in front of the whole town.

Yes, she knew it was her silly pride that was keeping her from taking Bill back. But it was also something more. *She* was more now.

Chapter 49

Beatrice popped another one of those painkillers that the doctor had given her. Damn neck. Her neck still hurt like hell every once in a while. It was the damnedest thing. It didn't hurt when the knife was lodged in—but now it hurt like hell. The body's a funny thing. She took a long drink of her water and felt the pill go down. She hoped the painkillers would help with her stomach pain—from all the stomach pumping—just to be on the safe side.

Her bare feet hit the floor, feeling its cool smoothness. She rose and walked down the creaky stairs to the kitchen, where the stove light shone into an otherwise dark kitchen. Oh, she'd forgotten about that slice of apple pie. She'd like to have it now, so she took the plate and fork back upstairs with her. Nothing like apple pie to start a Monday morning. She'd eat it in her own bed, too. Oh, luxury and joy.

A grandmother. Would it be a boy or a girl? she wondered as she plopped back into her bed. A girl would be sweet. A girl with a love of math and science. Oh, no, not a girl. Vera would dress her up and parade her around just like a doll. That wouldn't do.

A boy would be nice, too. They'd not had a boy in the

family. It would be a new experience for all of them. A soccer-playing boy. She grimaced at the thought of becoming one of those soccer grannies, but she supposed she would. She supposed she would—her heart leaped.

A baby.

Mmm. Damn this pie is good. A nice thick crust, just the way I like it. And is that bourbon in it? One more bite, hmm? Yes, it is. Just a hint of it.

What would Vera and Bill name a child? She wondered. They surely had some strange ways. It was hard for Bea to think old Bill actually had enough get-up-and-go to even make love to her daughter, let alone make a baby. Stranger things have happened.

Bill was gone for a few days on a business trip, so she didn't hear him moving about the house. It was so quiet. Strange. It never occurred to her that he was a noisy man—but still, even quiet roommates make life noises. The creaking of the floorboards, the opening and closing of the refrigerator or a cupboard, and the running water of the shower. Beatrice missed it. She missed Bill. Then she laughed out loud at the thought of it. Bea had not really liked him when he was still living with Vera as her husband. Something, though, about the way he turned to her during their trouble endeared him to her, she supposed.

Then there was the night of the attic incident. They'd shared something that most people would have called them crazy for. Still, they were both there, and they had held on to one another as the paper in the attic had flown around and the dark specter had released itself through the window.

"Did you smudge the attic?" Rose had wanted to know when she called her to tell her what had happened.

"No. That's the one room I didn't smudge or put holy water in. I didn't even think about it."

"Interesting."

"Well, she or it seems to be gone now."

"And it all makes sense now?"

"Oh, yes, indeed. If I'd only remembered that I saw Tina Sue that morning, I'd have known. She killed her sister and she saw me on the sidewalk that morning and she is definitely the person who stabbed me. She's on the tape. Well, her arm is. They could tell because of the purple jacket."

"What is the world coming to, Beatrice, when a sister murders her own sister? That's why I stay on my mountain."

"But the world keeps spinning, Rose, with or without you."

"We create our own reality."

"That's my line," Beatrice said, and laughed.

Bea leaned back in her rocking chair and watched the hummingbirds feed. Such tiny, beautiful little birds. Fall was coming and soon they would be gone. It was quite a summer for her birds, for her daughter, and for her town.

She looked across the street and the homes and some of the shops at the edge of Cumberland Creek proper. Even with all the new populace and new shops, she supposed Cumberland Creek was better than that damn mountain, probably better than most places—except for maybe Paris. She smiled. She and Ed had planned to go there so many times—both could speak French, and Ed had a passion for French food. But he had died, leaving her alone with all of the dreams.

"You should go," he said to her.

She looked over at him—his ghost was sitting on the wicker glider. *"Go where?"*

"Go to Paris."

"Oh, I don't know. I'm kind of old to go gallivanting around the globe, in case you hadn't noticed."

"Oh, no," he said sweetly. *"I hadn't. To me, you will*

always be that eighteen-year-old physics student, with a mind like a steel trap, the face of a goddess. . . ."

"Well, now," she said. *"Maybe I will go to Paris. If I die there, I die. Who cares? At least I'll have seen it. For both of us."*

"I'll be there, too," he said. *"I'm not going anywhere."*

"But you have. You are gone, Ed," she said, with her stomach twisting. *"You died twenty years ago."*

"But I'm still here. Here we sit, talking. We talk like this every now and then."

"I know, but why haven't you gone over, Ed?"

"You don't know?"

"No."

"I'm waiting for you, my love," he whispered.

"Well, now," she finally said. *"That's a hell of a thing to say."*

He was gone again, just like that, just like always—coming in and out of her reality at a whim, or so it seemed. The breeze chilled her as it moved across her papery, freckled skin.

Old age ain't a pretty thing.

She rose out of her chair and headed for the kitchen. She lit the stove and put the pan of beans on it. Leftovers for lunch. She could eat beans and corn bread almost every day. And sometimes she ate it twice a day.

She stirred the beans and soon they were ready. Popped the corn bread in the microwave to heat it up a bit. She took a bite of it before she even sat down. "Damn, I make some mighty fine corn bread."

Of course, it was her mother's recipe. Women didn't cook like this anymore. All the fat and sugar were no-no's. But damn, they were good. Beatrice remembered eating corn bread on the porch of her family's mountain home, looking out over the hills, at her mother's feet. Her mother was humming "Amazing Grace" and stroking Beatrice's young head.

It's funny how food brought up such vivid memories.

She placed her dishes in the sink and the skillet back in the refrigerator and walked into the library. She sat in Ed's chair. She loved this room of their house. Could always feel him here.

"I'm waiting for you, my love," he had said to her.

His words shook her. Is that why he had been in and out of her world all these years? For a woman who prided herself on her intelligence, sometimes her own stupidity amazed her. All he wanted was for her to join him.

She opened the desk copy of *Leaves of Grass* and read over one of his favorite passages:

> *"Miracles"*
> *Why! who makes much of a miracle?*
> *As to me, I know of nothing else but miracles,*
> *Whether I walk the streets of Manhattan,*
> *Or dart my sight over the roofs of houses toward*
>   *the sky,*
> *Or wade with naked feet along the beach just in*
>   *the edge of the water,*
> *Or stand under trees in the woods,*
> *Or talk by day with any one I love, or sleep in the*
>   *bed at night with any one I love. . . .*

Beatrice found herself unlocking the desk drawer and running her hands under the paper to the small pistol he had kept there for years. She pulled it out and held it in her hand.

"I'm waiting for you, my love." His words came to her again.

The cold metal of the gun felt soothing to her. He was just waiting for her. Was it time to end it, here and now? She could pull the trigger and be with the man she longed for every day and every night, knowing there was really not much else to this life. But wait, there was Vera, who still needed her—even though she was quite happy. And the baby. Yes, she was going to be a grandmother. And who would feed her hummingbirds and take care of Bill? And then there was Paris.

Well, Ed's waited this long, he can wait a little longer.

Chapter 50

Maggie Rae Dasher was nobody's fool. Still, she ended up murdered in her basement, while her children were sound asleep upstairs. They did not hear the gun because it had a silencer and was muffled even more by the pillow—the fibers were found clinging to her lifeless body. None of the neighbors in the small town of Cumberland Creek, Virginia, heard the gun, either. Nor would they have ever suspected a murder in this quiet neighborhood—or the secret life this young mother of four was living.

"I didn't know her that well," says 80-year-old Beatrice Matthews. "It turns out that nobody did—not even her husband."

Robert Dasher, her college sweetheart, who was the number one "person of interest" in the murder investigation, is a tall and almost painstakingly thin man. A long-distance runner turned accountant shortly after college graduation, and a quick marriage to Maggie Rae, he thought he knew her, too. They'd dated all through college—she enjoyed a good football game, came from a good Southern family, and was a brilliant writer, given scholarships and awards for her writing, but she always wanted a large family of her own. She grew up with just one sibling—a sister—and she'd always wanted more, so they started on the family early on, even though Robert had misgivings.

"She was always sort of fragile," he said.

Which would be in line with the suicide verdict handed down shortly after her death. But things didn't add up, according to Detective Adam Bryant. The placement of the gun in her hand—very few guns would stay in the hand like that after shooting oneself. And the angle at which the bullet entered Maggie Rae's heart made it nearly impossible for it to be a self-inflicted wound. Besides, Maggie Rae was left-handed and the gun was in her right hand.

According to the National Coalition Against Domestic Violence statistics, nearly one-third of female homicide victims that are reported in police records are killed by an intimate partner. In 70 to 80 percent of intimate-partner homicides, no matter which partner was killed, the man physically abused the woman before the murder. Had Maggie Rae been abused?

Maggie Rae's papers, which included cards from her husband, apologizing for abusive behavior, would suggest that is the case. Robert Dasher denies these allegations and maintains his innocence, even when the papers are in front of him.

"These cards are personal," he said. "Hurting doesn't mean beating."

If Robert Dasher was abusing his wife, he wasn't the only one. Maggie Rae had a legacy of abuse in her family. She had never known another way.

Maggie Rae was labeled a "bad girl" from early on—even by her mother, then her stepmother, who saw her flirtations with her new husband (Maggie Rae's stepfather) as a competition and could not wait for her to go off to college, and didn't pay much attention when she was away from home for days doing God knows what. Her fears were well founded. Because Maggie Rae was abused by her stepfather, and she could not end it—even as an adult. If she thought moving to Cumberland Creek would prevent it, she was wrong.

Maggie Rae's sister always suspected her sister and stepfather were involved. Once she asked her sister about it, and Maggie Rae said she hated every minute of it, but yes, she confirmed it. Tina Sue was shocked, frightened, and felt perplexed. He'd never so much as kissed her inappropriately. What was it about Maggie Rae that invited men to help themselves to her?

Though Tina Sue loved her sister, she could not imagine why she'd slept with their mother's husband, even up until the week before she died. "I was more than a little agitated with her when I found out. Why would she let it continue? Why didn't she stick up for herself? I'll never understand it."

Then, of course, the agitation became fury when she found out that her sister had also been bedding her own husband off and on for years. "I've never judged her for her ways. I've always supported her. Stuck up for her. Then to find out. . ."

The confrontation between the sisters came during early-morning hours, after Bill Ledford had left the premises.

"What are you doing here?" Maggie Rae asked her sister. "It's three in the morning."

"I'm here to ask you if you've been sleeping with Zeb."

"Now, Tina Sue, let's go downstairs and chat. I don't want to wake up the kids."

The sisters tiptoed into the basement, where Maggie Rae's writing office was, as well as her own bed, where she'd entertain her lovers. The next room over was her children's play room.

"Now, Tina Sue, you and I have talked about the way I feel about sex."

"Now, that's true. But how about the way I feel about sex, Maggie Rae? How about the way I feel that it's only good between married partners who love one another? A couple that is true to one another," Tina Sue said, her voice shaking. "It's a sacred bond."

"It can be," Maggie Rae said. "But it can also be a lot of fun without those bonds."

"Fun? You are changing the subject on me. Did you sleep with my husband?"

"Yes, sweetie, I did."

And that, says Tina Sue, is really the last thing she remembered before scrubbing blood off herself.

"I may have piled the scrapbooks and boxes on the corner. I can't say for certain, but Beatrice Matthews says I did, I guess I did. It makes sense. I wouldn't want anybody to know what kind of life she was living. Not only was she sleeping around with strange men, but also our stepfather and my husband. That would bring shame to the family."

But then again, so would a murder—especially committed by your only sister.

—Annie Chamovitz

"Damn, I really like that ending," Sheila said as she slid the photo cutter across a picture.

"Me too," Vera agreed as she took another bite of the lemon poppy seed muffin. "Ironic."

"Thanks," Annie said.

"Great article," Paige said, placing her scrapbook on the pile of scrapbooks they would be delivering to the Dasher family later.

"Poor Tina Sue," DeeAnn said, changing the subject

while cutting a pink velvet ribbon. "I mean, I know she killed her sister, but who knows how any one of us would react to that situation?"

DeeAnn wrapped the bow around her fingers and created loops—to be formed into a great big bow to be placed on the package of scrapbooks.

"It wasn't just that situation," Annie said. "It was a lifetime of humiliation and embarrassment brought on by her sister. She claimed she was okay with her lifestyle, but Tina Sue was boiling with resentment for many years."

"So when she find out about her husband . . . it was inevitable," DeeAnn said.

"She still claims she doesn't remember a thing, until after she did it. But she figured it out pretty quickly," Annie said.

"But she does remember my mother that morning," Vera said.

"Yes."

"And she remembers stabbing her?" Sheila asked.

Annie nodded, then flipped Ben's scrapbook page over to a blank one. Which picture or event to focus on next? His birthday? Hanukkah?

"And she's the one who placed the doll on your mother's porch."

Vera rolled her eyes. "My mom told me nothing about that. And how creepy is that? Why would a grown woman do something like that?"

"It's freaky," DeeAnn said. "She probably wanted to scare Bea."

"Shows she never knew Bea," Sheila said, and laughed.

"That family picture still freaks me out. Why would Maggie Rae change that picture?" Vera said, holding out a stack of paper like a deck of cards. Shades of purple and pink.

"Just a sign of how disturbed Maggie Rae was," Annie said.

"Now we know why she never filled those scrapbooks," Sheila concluded.

"We do?" DeeAnn asked as she wrapped a ribbon around the stack of scrapbooks. Six scrapbooks were stacked neatly on the table—books chronicling the lives of Maggie Rae's children, her own, and her family's. All wrapped up neatly for them to flip through and remember.

Annie hoped it brought them all some measure of comfort—even Robert, whom she had almost forgiven for his odd behavior. Besides, he was working with a caseworker, who was helping him along with the children, and she'd heard that he'd started going to Alcoholics Anonymous. She gave the man credit for trying to turn his life around.

"I know why, at least. There's something permanent and celebratory about scrapbooks. She came from a family that didn't really believe in taking pictures. She could go as far as taking pictures, but not placing them . . . in the book for everybody to view," said Sheila.

"That, and I thought maybe she was, in her own strange way, honoring her biological father," Annie said. "After all, it was his death that brought chaos to that family—and her stepfather, I gather, tried to erase any memory of her dad. They weren't even allowed to mention him."

"Maybe she remembers her real father in an idealized way. But that's not how I remember him," Paige said, placing her zigzag scissors down. "He was a harsh man as well."

"So you knew him?" Annie asked.

"Yes," she said, picking up the scrapbooks as all of the women filed in around her. It was time to visit the Dasher family. "I grew up right outside of Jenkins Hollow. I remember him quite vividly."

The mention of Jenkins Hollow made Annie's stomach churn. She didn't care to ever go back. She sighed, thanking the universe she would probably never have another reason to venture into that hollow again.

Harsh fathers led women to harsh husbands, and gave them children caught between. Annie said a prayer to herself that she and Mike could continue being decent parents. Tempers flared and children internalized it. She was eager to get a glimpse of Maggie Rae's children today, hoping for some clue, some psychic knowledge that they would be okay.

The women walked silently down the sidewalk of their Cumberland Creek neighborhood. Maybe they were all thinking similar thoughts with their arms full of colorful scrapbooks tied with ribbons—Maggie Rae's life was pieced and bound in each of them.

Glossary of Basic Scrapbooking Terms

Acid-Free: Acid is a chemical found in paper that will disintegrate the paper over time. It will ruin photos. It's very important that all papers, pens, etc., say acid-free, or eventually it can ruin cherished photos and layouts.

Adhesive: Any kind of glue or tape can be considered adhesive. In scrapbooking, there are several kinds of adhesives: tape runners, glue sticks, and glue dots.

Brad: This is similar to a typical split pin, but it is found in many different sizes, shapes, and colors. It is very commonly used for an embellishment.

Challenge: Within the scrapbooking community, "challenges" are issued in groups as a way of motivation.

Crop: Technically, "to crop" means the cutting down of a photo. However, a "crop" is also when a circle of scrapbookers gets together and scrapbooks. A crop can be anything from a group of friends getting together, or a more official gathering, where there are scrapbook materials for sale and there are games and challenges and so on. Online crops are a good alternative for people who don't have a local scrapbook community.

Die-Cut: This is a shape or letter cut from paper or cardstock—usually by machine or by using a template.

Embellishment: Embellishment is the enhancing of a scrapbook page with trinkets other than words and photos. Typical embellishments are ribbons, fabric, and stickers.

Eyelet: These small metal circles, like what's used on a shoe to thread laces, are used in a scrapbook context as a decoration and can hold elements on a page.

Journaling: This is the term for writing on scrapbook pages. It includes everything from titles to full pages on thoughts, feelings, and memories about the photos on a page.

Matting: Photos in scrapbooks are sometimes framed. Scrapbookers mat with coordinating papers on layouts, often using colors found in the photos.

Page Protector: These are clear, acid-free covers that are used to protect finished pages.

Permanent: Adhesives that will stay are deemed permanent.

Photo Corners: A photo is held to a page by slipping the corners of the photo into photo corners. They usually stick on one side.

Post Bound Album: This term refers to an album that uses metal posts to hold the binding together. These albums can be extended with more posts to make thicker. Usually page protectors are already included on the album pages.

Punch: This is the tool used to "punch" decorative shapes from paper or cardstock.

Punchies: The paper shapes that result from using a paper punch tool are known as punchies. These can be used on a page for a decorative effect.

Repositionable Adhesive: Magically, these adhesives do not create a permanent bond until dry, so you can move the element around on the page until you find just the perfect spot.

Scraplift: When a scrapbooker copies someone's page layout or design, she has scraplifted.

Scrapper's Block: This is a creativity block.

Strap Hinge Album: An album can utilize straps to allow pages to lie completely flat when the album opens. To add pages to the book, the straps are unhinged.

Template: A template is a guide to cutting shapes, drawing, or writing on a page. They are usually made of plastic or cardboard.

Trimmer: A trimmer is the tool used for straight-cutting photos.

Vellum: Vellum is a thicker, semitransparent paper with a smooth finish.

Scrapbook Essentials
for the Beginner

When you first start to scrapbook, the amount of products and choices can be overwhelming. It's best to keep it simple until you develop your own style and see exactly what you need. Basically, this hobby can be as complicated or as simple as you want. Here is all you really need:

1. Photos
2. Archival scrapbooks and acid-free paper
3. Adhesive
4. Scissors
5. Page protectors

Advice on Cropping

Basically, two kinds of crops exist. An "official" crop is when a scrapbook seller is involved. The participants sample and purchase products, along with taking part in contests and giveaways. The second kind of crop is an informal gathering of friends on a somewhat regular basis in order to share, scrapbook, eat, and gossip. (Just like the Cumberland Creek Croppers.)

1. In both cases, food and drinks are usually served. Finger food is most appropriate. The usual drinks are nonalcoholic—but sometimes wine is served. But there should be plenty of space around the scrapbooking area—if something spills, you don't want your cherished photos to get ruined.
2. If you have an official crop, it's imperative that your scrapbook seller won't come on too strong. Scrapbook materials sell themselves. Scrapbookers know what they want and need.
3. Be prepared to share. If you have a die-cut machine, for example, bring it along, show others how to use it, and so on. Crops are about generosity of the spirit. A shared offering can be as small as some paper that you purchased and decided not to use. Someone will find a use for it.
4. Make sure there's a lot of surface space—long tables where scrapbookers can spread out. (Some even use the floor.)
5. Be open to giving scrapbooking advice and receiving it, which you can always ignore if it's bad.

Ideas for Making Your Own Gift Scrapbooks

When many people think of scrapbooking, they think of a linear chronicle of their children's lives—or some other person or event. But when it comes to making gifts, you can really get out of the scrapbooking box with some creative options. Along with making scrapbooks for the Dashers, Vera makes ballet books, and Annie is starting a soccer book. You don't have to fill a huge book for a gift book—mini scrapbooks are great for this.

1. *An advice scrapbook.* When a child goes off to college, for example, make a Top Ten list of advice, pull in photos of them—you can make it funny or inspirational. They can take it off to school with them to help with the freshman homesick blues.
2. *A recipe scrapbook.* Pull in recipes from your grandmothers or aunts. If you have photos of them, place them alongside the recipes. If you have memories of the person or the dish, journal them. Make it so delicious that future generations will fight over it.
3. *A themed scrapbook.* Some of my favorites center around particular activities, like ballet and soccer. It can be holidays, weddings, or baby showers. But I've seen clever ones, like "Ten Things I Love About You," "A Play Day at the Park," and "Gardens I Love."

4. *A book about yourself to give to a loved one.*
   Think about it. How cool would it have been if
   your grandparents—or great-grandparents—
   left a scrapbook about themselves. Remember
   not to embellish . . . too much.
5. *An answer-question scrapbook.* This is a lot of
   fun to do with little kids. Ask questions like,
   "What do you want to be when you grow up?"
   or "Who are your best friends?" You will have
   those answers and photos preserved. Also,
   think about an answer-question scrapbook
   with some of the older members of your family.

Frugal Scrapbooking Tips

1. Spend your money where it counts. The scrapbook, itself, is the carrier of all your memories and creativity. Splurge there.

2. You can find perfectly fine scrapbooking paper in discount dollar stores, along with stickers, pens, and sometimes glue. If it's labeled "archival," it's safe.

3. You can cut your own paper and make matting, borders, journal boxes, and so on. You don't need fancy templates—though they make it easier.

4. Check on online auction sites for scrapbooking materials and tools.

5. Reuse and recycle as much as you can. Keep a box of paper scraps, for example, that you might be able to use for a border, mat, or journal box. Commit not to buy anything else, until what you've already purchased is used.

Turn the page for a special preview of the next book
in Mollie Cox Bryan's Cumberland Creek mystery series,

SCRAPBOOK OF SHADOWS!

A Kensington mass-market coming soon!

Chapter 1

Spending Sunday afternoon watching the police drag a body from a river was not what Annie had planned for the day. She was kicking a soccer ball around in the backyard with her boys when she was called away.

She took a deep breath as she walked through the crowd and over the yellow tape, which roped off the section to the river where the police and paramedics gathered. Flashbulbs popped. Ducks swam in the river. A comforting arm slid around a woman standing in the crowd. A group of Mennonites stood from the bench they were sitting on and lowered their heads. What were the Mennonites doing at the park on a Sunday? Odd.

Across the river, where the park was more populated, Annie saw children playing on the swings and bars on the playground. Also, a rowdy game of basketball was taking place in another corner of the blacktopped surface. In the grassy area, a Frisbee was being thrown between three friends. Groups of mothers gathered on the benches, trying not to alert their children or to watch too closely what was happening across the rushing Cumberland Creek River.

A hush came over the crowd on this side of the river as the nude body of a small, red-haired woman emerged from the water in a torn sack, her hair dangling over the side, along with a foot. The body, mostly shrouded by the shredded sack, was placed back on the ground. Cameras flashed—again.

Every time Annie viewed a dead person, she silently thanked one of her old journalism professors who insisted that all of his students witness autopsies. "If you're going to get sick, it's better here than in front of a cop. He'll lose all respect for you."

"Hello, Annie." It was Jesse, one of the uniformed police officers she came to know over the past year of reporting about Maggie Rae and her family. Now, Annie found herself under contract with a publisher to write a book about the case, which she was just finishing up. But she was still freelancing for the *Washington Tribune* from time to time, and was called in that morning to check this out. Was this incident another murder in the small town of Cumberland Creek?

"Hi, Jesse, where's your boss?"

"Behind you," came Detective Bryant's voice. Then he walked by her to look over the body more closely. His eyebrows knitted and he leaned in even closer, sliding gloves on his hands. "What the hell is this?"

"Scratches?" Jesse said, looking closer.

Annie was hoping to avoid looking closely at the actual body. Although she'd seen way too many dead bodies during her tenure as a reporter, it was never any easier. And she thought she'd left this behind her when she left Washington. She'd somehow been sucked back into reporting during the Maggie Rae case. She was just beginning to get some breathing space—her book sent off to the publisher, nothing much else to report on in Cumberland Creek—and now this. She hoped it was an accident and not a murder.

"No," Detective Bryant said. "Look closer. They are little markings of some kind. I can't quite make them out. Where's the coroner?"

Annie forced herself to look at the gray-blue arm the detective was holding gingerly in his hand. *Okay, it's just an arm*, she told herself. But she could see the markings.

"It looks like Hebrew," she blurted.

"Really?" Jesse said.

"Look again, that's not Hebrew," Detective Bryant said.

Annie leaned in closer. She had to admit—now that she looked closer at it, it didn't look like Hebrew at all. The detective dropped the arm as the coroner came up to the group. "I want close-up photos of these markings. Photos from all angles."

"Must be a recent drowning," he said. "If that's the cause of death."

"What makes you say that?" Annie asked.

"You can still recognize the body as a person. If it goes too long, it's difficult."

Annie's stomach twisted.

As Detective Bryant dropped the arm, she viewed the face of the victim between the clusters of shoulders of the police as they backed away. Young. Blue eyes staring blankly. Tangled red hair. Her face showed no sign of struggle—like a grimace or a look of anger or regret. The woman looked like a gray-blue rubber doll. Of course, what expression would a dead person have but none?

"Who found her?" Annie asked.

"It was a runner this morning—a Josh Brandt," Detective Bryant answered. "He's home now. I'd appreciate it if you gave him some time before you zoom in for the kill," he said and grinned, his blue eyes sparked.

Annie refused to engage with his taunting. She watched as he brushed away a strand of red hair from the girl's face. It was the gentlest gesture she'd ever seen him make.

"So what do you think the markings are?" Annie asked the detective.

"I really have no idea," he said. "But I'm going to find

out. I have a friend that specializes in symbols—if that is what these markings are."

"Will you let me know?"

"Sure. I've got nothing better to do," he said and smirked.

"Any idea who she is?"

"None," he said. "Check back with us tomorrow."

"Thanks," she said and walked away.

It was a beautiful fall day—so much color—gold, red, crimson, orange, yellow. The fall in Cumberland Creek looked like it had been taken right out of a painting. Annie looked off into the distance at the mountains. Bryant would probably not let her know about those symbols, Annie decided. She would have to research them herself. She was sure of it. She stood on the dirt path and quickly sketched some of the symbols—if that is indeed what they were and not some strange scratches from a struggle with rocks or the limb of a tree that sort of had a symbolic look to them. If they were simply scratches, though, the markings were weirdly smooth. Her stomach twisted, again. Another murder. They just needed to confirm the cause of death and call it one— but Annie felt that it was a murder. That the body was in a sack made her more certain, and she had to wonder if it had been weighted before the river's rocks and current slashed it to pieces.

She walked along the riverside path toward Cumberland Creek proper, where she lived. She walked right passed Vera's dancing school, closed, as were all of the town businesses, because today was Sunday. It wouldn't do anybody any good to open on Sunday. There would be no customers. Most of the population in Cumberland Creek spent Sundays in church and at home—except for Annie, Vera, and their friends, who were usually nursing mild hangovers from a Saturday night crop, when they gathered to scrapbook in Sheila's basement.

Annie reached the sidewalk which veered toward

Vera's house. When she talked with Vera that morning, Vera said Cookie was coming over and was planning to watch Vera's daughter, Elizabeth, and make her special pumpkin soup, while Vera went to the grocery store. Annie's mouth began to water. The woman could cook.

She could also do some yoga, twisting her body into all sorts of poses as if it were nothing at all. Annie loved Cookie's Friday evening yoga class. Because of her class, Annie was keeping a yoga journal. Cookie explained to them one evening how she kept a yoga journal as a beginner and how it helped for her to see how much she'd progressed. Now, Annie was working on an actual yoga scrapbook or dream book of sorts—very mundane, with ordinary beginning scrapbook techniques interspersed with writing about a pose or thought. She was using self-portraits—this was a different kind of scrapbooking than what Annie first learned from the Cumberland Creek Crop—it was more like art journaling.

Annie took yoga classes when she lived in the DC area, but none were like this. Cookie created a safe environment in which you could explore and reach out for new poses—but she was not a teacher who pushed you to do anything painful.

Annie thought about stopping by for a few minutes before heading home—but she really should be getting home to Mike and the boys. But it would be nice to see her friends after witnessing the disturbing events at the park. Of course, she'd have to fill them all in.

"Oh God, there you are!" Sheila came around the corner, nearly knocking Annie over. Her hair need brushing, her glasses looked crooked, and her t-shirt was a wrinkled mess.

"What's going on?" Annie said, steadying herself. Why was she so tired today?

"Did you hear? They found a dead body in the river," Sheila said, panting.

"Man, this place is amazing," Annie said. "News travels so fast."

"What?" Sheila said.

"I was just there," Annie said.

"Well, for heaven's sake," Sheila said, taking her by the other arm. "Are you heading to Vera's place?"

Annie nodded. Okay, so she wouldn't stay long.

When Vera opened the door, smiling, the smell of pumpkin, cinnamon, and cumin met Annie with its promise of warmth—the image of young drowned woman fresh on her mind.

Chapter 2

"Well, if it isn't the scrapbook queen, looking like hell on a Sunday afternoon," Beatrice said to Sheila as she walked in the kitchen, where they were all gathered.

Sheila waved her off and walked by her. Vera just shook her head. Sheila and Vera were best friends from childhood and Beatrice loved to pick on Sheila, just for the fun of it.

"Nice to see you, Bea," Annie said.

"At least someone around here has some manners," Bea said.

"What are you doing here?" Annie asked.

"I came to see my grandbaby and was just on my way out. The child is sound asleep."

"I went to the store, came back, Mom was here, and Cookie had things under control," Vera said.

Cookie poked her head in from around the corner. "Yes, Elizabeth went straight down after you left. I made soup and tried to get your mother to stay."

"I will now," Beatrice said. "If everybody else is going to eat the vegetarian organic stuff she calls food, I guess it can't but be so bad."

Beatrice hated to admit it, but the pumpkin soup did smell heavenly. All of this vegetarian, back-to-the-earth nonsense. She had enough of that to last a lifetime. She suspected if any of these young, flighty types really had to survive from the earth, they wouldn't know the first thing about it. But, she couldn't help but like this Cookie—even though she had many of the characteristics Beatrice would have despised in anybody else.

First, she was too damned thin—even thinner than Annie. The woman looked like she needed a big, thick, bloody steak. She was pale and wispy, with long black hair that she sometimes pulled off her face with a thick, colorful headband. Strange, eastern-looking silver jewelry always dangled from her. Her eyes were almost unnaturally green and she carefully applied a bit too much eye makeup. Meanwhile, Vera, her own daughter, changed hair color more frequently than anybody she ever knew. Beatrice always preferred the natural look.

Cookie was a yoga teacher and began teaching classes in Vera's dance studio. Yoga was a good thing, Beatrice knew, but this woman took herself a bit too seriously with all the "namaste's" and "peace be with you's." Who did she think she was—a divine messenger?

Ah well, she chalked it up to youth. Basically, Cookie was a good sort—very good with Elizabeth, Bea's one and only granddaughter. She sat down at the kitchen table with the other women. God knows what they were chattering about. She wasn't paying a bit of attention. She was suddenly thinking of going upstairs and waking up Elizabeth just so she could hold her, play with her. Of course, she'd never do that—well, not in front of Vera, anyway.

"Did you hear me?" Vera was suddenly sitting next to her. "A drowned person washed up in the park today."

"What? In Cumberland Creek?" Beatrice said, clutching her chest. Cumberland Creek, population 12,000, going on 20,000, or something. When Beatrice was a girl, there was a fuss about the population reaching 750. It was 2,000 for twenty years or so. She lost count a few years back with all the new housing developments on the west side of town. McMansions.

"Yes, in the river at the park," Vera said. "Scary."

"I imagine. Who was it?" She asked Annie, who was sitting down at the table next to Vera.

"I have no idea. Detective Bryant said they might know her name by tomorrow."

"Her?"

"Well, it was sort of hard to tell, but there was a lot of long red hair," Annie said, twisting her own wavy black hair behind her ear.

"Hmmm. I don't know of many redheads around here. Do you? Of course, sometimes I feel like I don't know half the people here anymore."

"Could be from somewhere else," Annie said, just as bowls of steaming pumpkin soup were being passed around the table.

The scent of the spiced pumpkin reached out and grabbed Beatrice. The scent of pumpkin, spiced with cinnamon and cumin, filled the room. Suddenly she was nearly salivating in anticipation. She reached for the crusty whole wheat bread and spread butter on it—still warm from the oven. Goodness, Cookie had gone to a lot of trouble—she had even baked bread.

"Great soup, Cookie," Vera said and sighed. "You really didn't have to do this. I wasn't expecting you to bake bread, just watch Lizzie while I went out for a bit of exercise."

"Now, don't worry about it," Cookie said. "Since she went right to sleep, I had some time on my hands. I just wanted to help out. I know how hard it can be. I was raised by a single mom."

Beatrice grimaced at the phrase "single mom," which was not what she wanted for her daughter, who had not been able to get over her husband's cheating on her and wouldn't let him move back in. Thank the universe he moved out of Bea's house and into his own apartment,

finally. Bea hoped that she could forgive him—for the
baby's sake—but Vera couldn't. Beatrice couldn't really
blame her for that. Also, Vera was seeing a man in New
York. They rarely saw each other and Vera had yet to
bring him home to Cumberland Creek. Though she stole
away to New York when she could. Beatrice doubted that
it was serious. Bill, however, was seething. Served him
right. Any man who cheated on his wife for years with a
woman almost half his age who was also married, well,
what could you say about that?

So there was another strange death in the small, but
growing, town of Cumberland Creek. It seemed to
Beatrice that things had just calmed down from the
Maggie Rae case. Just what the town needed: more
media attention, more outsiders, as if the new McMan-
sion dwellers on the outskirts of town weren't enough for
her and the other locals to manage. Beatrice hated to
generalize about folks—but they all thought they were
mighty important.

"So, does the death look suspicious?" Bea asked.

"I hate to say it," Annie said, dipping her bread into
the orange creamy soup. "But it does to me. It looks like
she was placed in a sack—I'm not sure she could have
put herself in it. And there were these weird markings on
her arm."

"Markings?" Vera said. "Like scratches?"

"Sort of," Annie said. "It might not mean anything,"
She turned back to her soup. "Man, this is good Cookie."

A smile spread across Cookie's face. "Thanks."

Cookie didn't smile like that often, Beatrice mused, not
that she was gloomy. She always had a look of bemused
happiness. But it was in her eyes and the way she spoke.

Red hair. Drowning. Gray blue body. A sack. Weird
scratches on her upper arm. Beatrice tuned out the
chitchatting. Until they knew it was a murder, what was
the point in speculating? She didn't want to believe there
was another murder in this community.

Damn, the soup and bread were just what she needed today. She hadn't realized how hungry she was.

Just then, there was a knock at the door. It was Detective Bryant, who walked into the kitchen. "I heard you were at the park this morning," he said to Sheila. "Did you see anything suspicious?"

He looked happy, like a man with a mission, energetic. Bea looked at Annie, who was enjoying her soup and not looking at him at all. Annie looked tired, run down. Poor thing. Those boys of hers kept her busy while trying to manage a freelance career. It couldn't be easy.

Sheila thought for a moment. "No. It was pretty quiet. But if I remember anything, I'll let you know."

"Oh my God it smells heavenly in here," he said, stretching his arms, then turned around to see Beatrice. "But look what the devil brought in."

Beatrice swallowed her soup. "Bite me, Bryant."

He chortled.

The detective sure could hold a grudge. But then again, so could Beatrice.